ALSO BY CHARLAINE HARRIS

Gunnie Rose series

An Easy Death
A Longer Fall

A Novel of Midnight, Texas series

Midnight Crossroad
Day Shift
Night Shift

A Sookie Stackhouse Novel series

Dead Until Dark
Living Dead in Dallas
Club Dead
Dead to the World
Dead as a Doornail
Definitely Dead
All Together Dead
From Dead to Worse
Dead and Gone

Dead in the Family
Dead Reckoning
Deadlocked
Dead Ever After
The Complete Sookie Stackhouse Stories
The Sookie Stackhouse Companion

An Aurora Teagarden Mystery series

Real Murders
A Bone to Pick
Three Bedrooms, One Corpse
The Julius House
Dead Over Heels
A Fool and His Honey
Last Scene Alive
Poppy Done to Death
All the Little Liars
Sleep Like a Baby

Gunnie Rose:

BOOK 3

THE RUSSIAN CAGE

CHARLAINE HARRIS

SAGA PRESS

LONDON SYDNEY **NEW YORK** TORONTO NEW DELHI

SAGA PRESS

AN IMPRINT OF SIMON & SCHUSTER, INC.

1230 AVENUE OF THE AMERICAS, NEW YORK, NEW YORK 10020

First Saga Press hardcover edition February 2021

SAGA PRESS and colophon are trademarks of Simon & Schuster, Inc.

For information about special discounts for bulk purchases, please contact Simon & Schuster Special Sales at 1-866-506-1949 or business@simonandschuster.com.

The Simon & Schuster Speakers Bureau can bring authors to your live event. For more information or to book an event, contact the Simon & Schuster Speakers Bureau at 1-866-248-3049 or visit our website at www.simonspeakers.com.

Manufactured in the United States of America

1   3   5   7   9   10   8   6   4   2

Library of Congress Cataloging-in-Publication Data has been applied for.

ISBN 978-1-4814-9499-1
ISBN 978-1-4814-9501-1 (ebook)

My heartfelt thanks to friends who helped me get through 2020—Paula, Dana, Toni, Treva, and my fellow church members. Couldn't have made it without you.

ACKNOWLEDGMENTS

My friend and assistant, Paula Woldan, who helped me with the research necessary for this book. My agent, Joshua Bilmes, whose belief in my work has never faltered. My editor, Joe Monti, whose enthusiasm gave me courage. My husband, Hal, whose reassurance gives me strength.

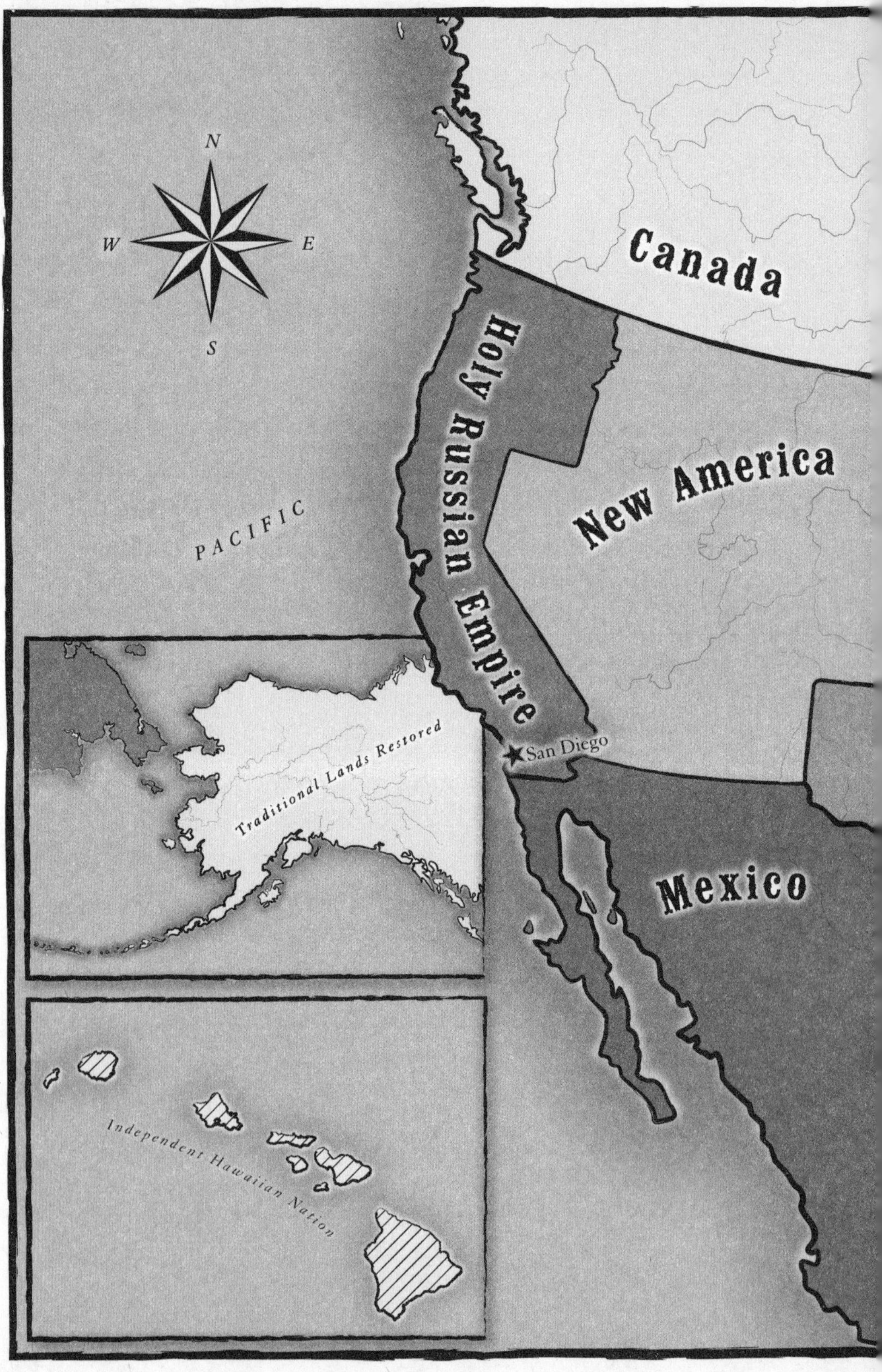
N
W
E
S
Canada
Holy Russian Empire
New America
PACIFIC
Traditional Lands Restored
San Diego
Mexico
Independent Hawaiian Nation

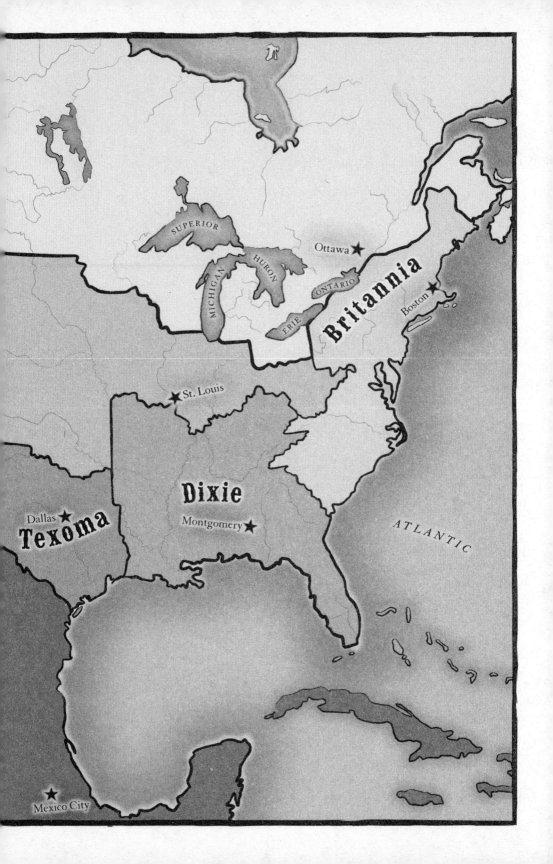

CHAPTER ONE

I sat at the table in my cabin, my sister's letter in my hand, and read it for the third time. After that, it was hard to sit still. Part of my head was making a list of the things I had to do *now*. The other part still couldn't believe Felicia's message. I'd gotten a letter from her right after Christmas, a thank-you note for the deerskin jacket I'd sent her. Getting another letter this soon after the first one had been a surprise. As I'd walked out of the Segundo Mexia post office, I'd stuffed it in my pocket, figuring it was full of chatter about what the students had done for the rest of the holiday. Holy Russian stuff.

I hadn't felt any need to hurry back up the hill to my cabin, and I'd put away my groceries before I'd opened Felicia's letter.

Dear Sister, Felicia began. *Thanks so much for the warm jacket. It is eligant!*

Right away a bell had started ringing.

From eleven-year-old Felicia's very first letter to me, every word had been spelled correctly (her handwriting had steadily improved, too). Her whole class had to write letters home at least once a month—at least, those who had homes—and they had to keep a dictionary beside them while they wrote.

Felicia had underlined the misspelled word. Just in case I didn't notice.

Too bad I can't use it now. It was lovely and warm. I know you spent a lot of time with it. It's stored away in a box until you can repair it.

With it. Not *working on it.* She'd had to put away her deerskin jacket? Why? I knew winters weren't really cold in San Diego, but surely a jacket . . . ?

I wish you were closer, so we could talk face-to-face. Maybe you could visit. Let me know! I remember when I met you in Mexico, and you sent me here to the HRE. That was a great day with good companions.

I hope you're well and you feel like traveling again soon. Your sister Felicia

I hadn't spent much time with my sister—hardly any, in fact. But I knew some things about her. Not only was she smart, she was devious.

Felicia expected me to figure this out.

All right, working backward. The "good companions" we'd had on the train platform in Ciudad Juárez were Klementina and Eli, both wizards from the Holy Russian Empire. Eli had been on a mission to find descendants of Grigori Rasputin, since Rasputin had died. The wizard's blood had been keeping Tsar Alexei alive. Felicia was Rasputin's granddaughter by one of his bastards. Klementina, ancient and powerful, had come to check on Eli's progress. She wasn't the only one.

A group of grigoris who wanted to topple the tsar had shown up to stop Felicia from reaching him.

The aged Klementina and I had held them off while Eli and Felicia boarded the train to the Holy Russian Empire. Klementina had been killed. I had survived. Eli and Felicia had reached the HRE.

So that left Eli. *Eligant.* Felicia was telling me that she couldn't see Eli any longer. That now he was in a box. She couldn't mean a coffin; I could "repair" it.

I stared at the letter for at least three minutes before I understood.

Eli was in prison.

Felicia hoped I could get Eli out. She wanted me to come bust him out of a cell. My mind raced ahead, much as I told myself to slow down.

I'd have to take a train, probably several trains. I needed to go to my mom's house and fish my money out of the hidden hole in the wall in my old room. I hoped I'd have enough. I actually rocked on my feet, torn between running back to town to visit my mother and Jackson and packing my stuff here and telling my nearest neighbor, Chrissie, I'd be gone for a while.

In the back of my head, I knew the smartest thing to do was to sit tight. Eli was resourceful; he could get out of this dilemma by himself.

But I knew I wouldn't do that.

CHAPTER TWO

My stepfather, Jackson Skidder, took me to the train station in Sweetwater the next day. I'd worked out my route on the railway timetables Jackson kept at his hotel. I had to travel light. I had two changes of clothes, some extra ammunition, my savings in New American dollars, and fifty dollars in HRE money courtesy of Jackson.

Jackson had always been good to me. This was the best. And he didn't get all upset like my mother had. She was a calm and beautiful woman, but she hadn't been calm when she'd found out what I was planning. Jackson, who understood me better, knew I had to go.

On the drive to Sweetwater, Jackson said, "Pretty dangerous in San Diego, from the papers. Lots of men out there who were let go when the armed services collapsed."

I knew exactly what desperate men were like. I nodded.

"Bring Eli back here, when you got him."

I'd get Eli out or die trying. I hoped I'd see Jackson again. He'd always been good to my mother and me. "I will," I said.

As I got on the train with my leather bag slung over my shoulder, Jackson said, "Easy death, Lizbeth."

My backbone felt straighter when he said the good-bye reserved for gunnies. I nodded.

And in ten minutes I was on my way.

I was scared shitless.

CHAPTER THREE

It took me four days and three nights to reach San Diego. We passed out of Texoma (used to be Texas and Oklahoma) and into New America pretty quick. The flat land and broad plains, the empty towns everyone had left to find a way to survive, poured past my window in a steady stream of sameness. Every now and then we saw buffalo, or a pack of wild dogs, or some little settlement clinging to life.

I ate the food I'd brought with me. There wasn't such a thing as a dining car on most of these trains. Every so often, I got off at a stop and bought whatever I could find available—mostly tamales, at little stands run by children. I can't say I was too hungry. The constant sound, the constant movement, and switching from one train to another as my route required shook me up.

At least the trains weren't crowded until we got closer to the Holy Russian Empire, which used to be California and Oregon, my mother had told me.

I wore my guns the whole time, so only people who saw no other vacant place sat by me. They didn't know what a risk they were taking. I was short on patience and long on aggravation. One man thought I might be posing as a gunnie, and he had a broken finger to add to his problems after he touched me while I slept.

After so many hours I'd lost count, I was on the final train, the one that would cross the border between New America and the Holy Russian Empire. A billboard announced it as HOME OF THE MOVIE INDUSTRY, ORANGE GROVES, AND THE TSAR AND TSARINA.

And right after I'd read the sign and gotten all excited, the train stopped. We were at the border. I'd expected this stop from hearing the other passengers chatter.

I didn't expect two guards to board the car. The two men wore gray and red uniforms and black gloves. One had probably wandered for years with the tsar's flotilla when he escaped from the godless Russians. I figured that because he had a gray mustache, and he just looked different. The other man? Probably born in the state of California, as it had been.

Both of the border guards looked bored until they saw my guns. They were checking passports, recording the name of everyone going into the HRE.

Lucky I'd had the time (while I was getting over my last gunshot wound) to get a passport, just in case.

I handed the tan and green booklet to the born Russian. While his buddy looked at my sidearms real careful, the older man opened the passport to look from my picture to me.

The American-born one said, "You'll have to put your guns in the safe at your hotel. You can't carry 'em openly in the HRE."

I nodded. The two passed on, the Russian having handed my passport back to me.

Welcome to the Holy Russian Empire.

CHAPTER FOUR

By the time the train pulled into San Diego, I was hardly able to put two words together. It was evening when I stepped out of the station on Kettner Street. Lucky all I had to do was find a hotel.

The first place I stopped was too expensive. I plodded on. About six in the evening I found a place I could afford two blocks east. It was called the Balboa Palace. It was not anyone's palace. But the place looked clean, and I could pay for it without crying.

"Can't carry guns on the street," the clerk told me, nodding at my Colts. I nodded back, to show I'd heard him, and he handed me my key. My hand was shaking. I took the stairs to the third floor. The clerk called, "We have an elevator!"

I nodded to show I'd heard him, but at the moment I wasn't up to anything new. Stairs were good enough. I locked my room door behind me. I stripped off my nasty clothes and dropped them to the floor. Then I was in a real bed, and it did not move, and I slept for twelve hours straight.

When I woke up the sun was shining in the window, and the sounds of a city were cranking up outside. I lay there thinking for a bit but then couldn't stand myself anymore. I had a bathroom of my own, not the norm at Texoma or New America hotels. There was a showerhead over the tub. By the time the water got the right temperature, I was excited about stepping in.

I washed myself twice. Then I washed the clothes I'd worn since I stepped on the train in Texoma. I hung them up around the room. With the windows open to the cool air, I figured they'd dry pretty quick.

I put my guns in the wardrobe and hung out the DO NOT DISTURB sign as I went in search of food.

I hadn't even registered that there was a dining room the night before. It was right off the lobby and two steps down, and it had windows onto the street and its own door.

I was glad to sit at one of the tables to watch people pass by. It was like watching a circus. I drank good coffee and ate good pan-cakes and eggs. I saw Chinese people and old-fashioned Russians and quite a few I could not even identify.

There weren't any women wearing jeans and boots like me. Oh, some women wore pants, but they were loose in the leg and tight in the waist and matched their blouses. Their shoes had heels, which I was not going to do. I'd worn 'em in Dixie. I wouldn't do that again.

The clerk—not the man from the night before—was standing behind the reception counter, going through a stack of white cards. He was in his fifties, I reckoned. Not as weatherworn as people got in Texoma, but he didn't look soft. "What can I do for you this morning, miss?" he asked, real polite.

"Rose. Lizbeth Rose." I shook his hand, which surprised him.

"Paul McElvaney."

"Do you have a map of the city?" I didn't know if this was a ridiculous question or not, but if I didn't start asking, I'd never get answers.

"Right here." McElvaney pointed at a rack to the left of the high counter. "They're free."

That was luck. I took one and said, "If you got a minute, can I ask some more questions, Mr. McElvaney?" There wasn't anyone else within earshot.

McElvaney nodded. "Call me Paul."

"Is it really against the law to carry guns on the street?"

"Yes. The police don't take kindly to open carrying. It would be a big risk on your part, not one you should take."

"Then do you have a safe? That guests can put things in?"

"We do. You can put in anything you want."

"I'll bring my guns down, then. How would I look up someone's address?"

"Phone book. There's one in the phone booth on each floor, next to the elevator."

I had wondered what that was. "Thanks. I heard about trolley cars. How do you get on one? How do you buy a ticket?" San Diego was too big for me to walk everywhere.

Paul told me what I had to do. He hesitated for a second. There was something else he wanted to say.

I made a *come on* gesture.

"I should warn you," Paul said. "When California broke off, there were a lot of USA army and navy men here. Quite a few of them didn't go home. Some of them got jobs in the guards, the police force, for builders. A lot of them didn't. There are gangs in San Diego that make the streets—well, you have to be careful."

"I thought the HRE was hard on lawbreakers." Tracked them down and killed them, was what I'd heard.

"If robbers or killers are on their own, the grigoris and the police take care of them pretty quick. But the gangs have more strings to pull. And there are some Russians mixed in."

"Thanks for telling me," I said. I offered him some of my Russian money.

"No," Paul said. "I was warning you like I would my own daughter. She's your age."

"Good to know," I said. "Thanks, Paul."

"I can tell you're a young lady who's used to taking care of herself," the clerk said. "This is a lovely city, and I don't want anything bad to happen to you here."

I nodded, and went to the elevator. Getting the free map and the good advice had made me bold. I watched other people for a minute until I understood the procedure. I pressed the button to call the elevator. It came down, the doors opened, and there was a woman sitting on a little stool.

I stepped inside.

"What floor, please?" the woman asked.

"Three," I said, and she closed the open grille and then the elevator doors and pulled her handle. Up we went. I had a little whoopsy feeling in my stomach, that was all. The elevator came to a decided stop. I didn't know what to do next, but the woman opened the doors, first the grille set and then the solid set, and there was my floor. I'd already had my first adventure of the day.

I found a pad of paper and a pen handy in the desk in my room, both printed with BALBOA PALACE. I carried both back to the phone booth, marveled at the folding door on it, opened and shut it a few times just to avoid the next step in my search for information.

No one interrupted me while I looked up a lot of places I needed to visit and wrote down the addresses. Then I read all the directions on the pay telephone, so if I had to use one, I was ready.

While I did all this, the maid had been cleaning my room. I sat at the desk with my maps, both the street map and the trolley map. My head was tired by the time I had it all worked out.

The Grigori Rasputin School was on the mainland side of the bay, not far from the palace and many government buildings located on North Island, which wasn't really an island.

After I figured out my route to the school, I estimated it would take me forty minutes to walk there. I thought of calling the number I'd written down just to forewarn them I was coming to see my sister. But that seemed . . . not as good as showing up, somehow. Also, phone calls cost money. So step one was decided.

Next, I looked for "Savarov." Prince Vladimir Savarov had been Eli's dad. The prince still had a listing on Hickory Street, which was close to a big park. There were two other Savarovs listed, separate addresses on a street a few blocks away from Hickory. I was fairly sure those were Eli's older half brothers.

I refolded the map and the trolley schedule. I got my guns. I went down the stairs to the lobby and gave the guns to Paul. I watched as he put them in the safe. He gave me a receipt.

Then I clenched my teeth and stepped out of the hotel into the city, by myself. It was different from looking out the window.

There were cars *everywhere*. No horses. Lots of people on foot or riding bicycles.

By the time I'd walked three blocks, I'd gotten a few second looks, but there were so many different kinds of people around I didn't think I stuck out too bad.

I took a deep breath and went on.

I walked for a good mile, maybe farther. I saw a trolley car and stopped to watch it pass. They ran on electricity, Eli had told me. At its next stop, I got on and put a coin in the slot, one Paul had given me in change. He'd told me that was the right one to pay for my fare. I was nearly sure I was going in the right direction.

Not often I felt this uncertain. And I'd been in cities before. I figured out why by the time we'd gone a block.

San Diego, at least in this part, had tall buildings, many of them five or six stories. There weren't many clear lines of sight, and those were all at intersections. There were so many people. Even in these hard times, many of them looked prosperous.

It was almost a relief to see a beggar sitting on the sidewalk, his hat in front of him.

I thought I was at the corner where I should get off, and I inched my way to the door. But the trolley took off again before I could push past the people who'd just gotten on.

At the next stop I made my way off with some energy.

I was so relieved to be on the sidewalk with space around me. I leaned against a storefront. I didn't care if this looked strange or not. I wished like hell I could get out of this place, go back to where I knew the rules.

But then I might never see Eli again.

I told myself Felicia had written me because she thought I could do something about his being in prison. The confidence of an eleven-year-old girl was not much to lean on, but it was all I had. I straightened up, oriented myself with the map, and walked some more.

Then I could see the water. San Diego Bay. I could see the "island" where the tsar lived surrounded by as many houses of his courtiers as could squeeze into the space, and a large contingent of armed guards.

You could tell even from a distance that there was a lot of construction going on. A ferry was halfway from the mainland to North Island. The sun was making the water sparkle.

I let myself look for a good long time. I had never seen so much water. It was worth the trip. I promised myself I would find a spot where there was no island to block the view. I tore myself away and returned to my task.

Across the street from me was a low wall topped with an iron fence. It said, *You can see us—so we are open. But you can't come in— so we are closed*. There was a short sidewalk to double front doors that would have looked fine on a church. The building itself was shaped not unlike a church, not too wide but deep. A covered walk-way led from the middle of that building to another one, smaller and plainer. Between the covered walkway and the fence, the whole yard was planted with grass and flowers and bushes. In the middle of this was a tomb, very fancy, white marble on a gray base. I guessed the gray stone was granite. There was carving in the marble. The side I could see read GRIGORI RASPUTIN. Some withered bunches of flowers were wedged in the iron fence, I noticed.

I'd found my way to Felicia's school. I felt as proud as though I'd won a contest.

I peered through the barred gate that lined up with the big doors into the churchlike building. I figured the covered walkway led to the student dormitory. That was where Felicia and about half the stu-dents lived, she'd told me in her letters. The other kids lived at home.

I didn't want to bang on the gate until I understood it. I looked real close at the latch, then realized all I had to do was lift the U-shaped bar and pull the gate open. Could not understand the point of having a gate anyone could simply walk through. It wasn't like they were keeping goats in. There should be a lock, to protect my sister.

Maybe the gate was spelled? But I didn't feel any magic on it. I pushed the latch back down and turned to face the building. I straightened my back, walked up to the big wooden door, and opened it. It was a public building. I figured I didn't have to knock.

The reception room was decorated with a big rug in shades of blue and rose over a tiled floor, a group of dark upholstered chairs, and a desk. Of course. For the gatekeeper.

The person behind the desk was a man. I could tell he was a grigori, so I knew why they hadn't felt the need to lock the gate. Grigoris start getting tattooed the minute they qualify. As they gain in talent and experience, the tattoos extend from beneath their shirts. This man's had crawled up his cheeks, even.

This particular grigori had been reading, and he didn't like being interrupted. His scowl made that clear.

"Good morning," I said, in the most pleasant voice I could summon.

"How can I help you?" the grigori said, in a voice gauged to make sure I knew he didn't want to help me one bit. He was a blond with big brown eyes and broad shoulders. Those should have added up to a good-looking man, but he was too scary to appeal to anyone with sense. One hand was in a pocket of his grigori vest. Yep, he was ready to defend the school.

"My half sister, Felicia Karkarov, is a student here," I said. "I've come to town on business. I didn't have time to let her know I'd be here. I'd like to see her."

"Your name?" He looked a fraction less hostile.

"Lizbeth Rose." I had not been able to figure out why I should lie about any of this. Which was a relief. In a town full of grigoris, it was a good idea to tell the truth anytime you could.

Without introducing himself, the blond grigori opened a desk drawer, pulled out a worn book, and opened it to consult a chart. Then he glanced at a clock on the wall. "Miss Rose, Felicia is in class right now. You can't see her for an hour."

I think he hoped I'd say, *Oh, gosh, I can't possibly wait that long*. But I didn't.

I sat down in the one of the upholstered chairs (after the train seats, it was heaven to my rear) and prepared to be patient. I'm pretty good at that. Being a gunnie is not nonstop excitement. It's lots of boring hours of being watchful with (every now and then) some shooting thrown in. I read a brochure about the school while I waited, and I read all the signs in the waiting room. NO VISITORS AFTER 5 PM, read one. NO SMOKING OR ALCOHOL ON SCHOOL GROUNDS, read another.

After that, I looked over at the gatekeeper, who had returned to his book. I wondered if he was reading a novel or a textbook.

I wondered if he knew Eli. If I asked, he might tell me he had put Eli in jail, and then I'd have to kill him.

I wondered how long I could afford my hotel. It was the same as $2.50 New American. Thanks to my stepfather, I had a huge cushion. But I had to eat, and I might have to bribe someone.

I sure missed my Winchester. It had been my grandfather's. It was a fine rifle. I felt like it was part of me. But I couldn't figure any advantage to lugging it all the way to San Diego. In a city a rifle wouldn't have been as much use as my two handguns, and they were locked away. I was carrying knives, of course. I didn't know of a law against that, and I wasn't asking. Wasn't going anywhere unarmed.

The hour passed. I heard a bell ring from deeper in the school. The grigori, roused from his book, touched a machine on the desk in front of him and said, "Felicia Karkarov to Reception, please." Then he looked at me and nodded, like he'd fulfilled a promise. I wondered where he was from. He was no Russian emigrant, and no English one, either. English wizards were flocking to the HRE because they wanted to openly practice their talent, forbidden at home.

In a minute or two, I heard footsteps in the hall that led back to (I assumed) the classrooms, and I stood.

I didn't know her for a moment, though it had only been a few months. I'd last seen her on the train platform in Ciudad Juárez. Felicia had been grubby, and her hair had been a coarse black tangle. She had been skinny, like a bunch of slats tied together. She'd looked younger than her age.

Now she'd filled out and grown and groomed herself.

When Felicia saw me, her face blossomed with all kinds of emotions: she was relieved, she was glad, and she was angry.

My sister shrieked and hurled herself at me. I caught her. It was like we'd grown up together, rather than having known each other for two terrible days in the slums of Ciudad Juárez.

For the first time, I realized how hard it must have been for Felicia, hauled away from everything she'd ever known to a place where she knew nothing and no one. Because that was the way I felt now.

"I'm so glad to see you," Felicia said. Her voice was all clogged up. She was on the edge of crying. She was crafty, but I didn't think this was feigned.

"No tears, now, sister," I said. "I know it's a surprise, but here I am, ready to spend time with you. Can I take you out to lunch?"

"I have to go tell Miss Drinkwater." Felicia raced away back down the hall into the depths of the school. I marveled again at how her body had filled out. Regular eating will do wonders for a half-starved girl.

The grigori had put down his book. "Felicia has the blood of our holy Father Grigori," he said.

I nodded.

"But not you?"

"Half sister," I reminded him.

I absolutely did have the right blood. We had the same father, a bastard son of Rasputin. I'd found that out only a bit more than a year ago. But not only did I not give a flip about the tsar, I figured he'd got one of us—he didn't need both. Besides, I already had a job.

If the grigoris knew we shared a father instead of a mother, I'd never leave this place. Only Eli knew.

Then Felicia was back, and we were walking out of the big doors and through the gate. It was like getting out of prison, which reminded me of Eli. I wanted to fire questions at Felicia, but this was not the time or place. I had no idea where we would go to eat, and I had to ask her for ideas.

"I don't get outside the school much," my sister said. She kept glancing at me sideways, like I'd vanish.

We'd see a restaurant or soda fountain somewhere along the street, I figured. There were so many office buildings on the surrounding blocks, it stood to reason there'd be places for all these workers to get lunch. So we walked, and I looked at her, and she looked at me. Felicia had cheeks now, and they were rosy brown. Her black hair looked glossy. It lay down her back in a neat braid. She even made the school uniform, navy blue and yellow, look good.

"You look real pretty," I said. "You've done some growing."

"You look good, too. Your hair's grown out a lot." Felicia grinned at me, reached over to touch a curl.

"Last time I saw you was three weeks after I'd shaved my head," I said.

"No wonder you . . ."

"Looked so awful?" I smiled.

"No!" Felicia said quickly. "So . . . different."

I cast around for something else to say. "What about this place?" We went into the shop, a bakery. It smelled wonderful, like butter and sugar and baked meat. After looking at the chalkboard, I ordered a chicken potpie, and Felicia asked for a grilled cheese sandwich and some soup. The food came pretty quick, and we tucked in. It was good. Seasoned different from what I was used to.

Other customers were jammed in close to us. We still couldn't have the conversation I craved.

"Tell me about school," I said. Probably a safe topic.

Felicia didn't seem to know where to start, so I primed the pump by asking her what kind of room she slept in, how having a roommate was, what classes she was taking. She'd touched on all this in her letters, but I wanted to know more. Once she opened her mouth, all I had to do was sit back and listen.

Felicia shared a room with Anna, a girl from one of the families that had fled godless Russia with the tsar. Anna Feodorovna already knew she was an air wizard, and she had long blond hair. They each had a bed. Anna didn't snore unless she had a cold. When Anna was thirteen or fourteen, she'd go to the middle school to begin her serious grigori training. Now she was getting her background in all the same things Felicia was taking: English, penmanship, arithmetic, the history of (what used to be) California, Russian history, and the basics of magic.

Anna's parents lived north of here, around Redding, so Anna only went home on the long holidays.

Felicia didn't have a home to go to. I felt worse and worse, angry at myself.

"Does Anna already try out her magic?" I asked. I'd been watching Felicia's expressions.

My sister's eyes opened wide, all innocence. So Anna had been doing exactly that—Felicia, too, most likely. I was sure that was forbidden.

"No, of course not, that would be dangerous," Felicia said with a great air of virtue.

"Do you . . . ?" I hoped she'd understand without me finishing the sentence. Our father (I never thought of him as "Father," but that was who he was) had been a confidence man with some magic, just enough to make a living off other people. Maybe Felicia had inherited more of that ability than I had.

Felicia looked at me with wide eyes. "Of course not," she said.

"Um-hum. We're going to talk about that later," I said.

Felicia did her best to look astonished.

She went back to telling me about the food at school, and how all the girls thought Miss Drinkwater was sweet on the mathematics teacher. We finished our lunch. Left to find a less public place, or at least a public place less thick with people.

I suggested the courtyard at her school, but Felicia said, "You can never know who's listening there. Some of them can hear without being in sight."

"I would not like that at all," I said. Didn't even have to think a moment.

"I wouldn't, either."

There it was again, the undertone of anger.

Finally, we crossed the wide street, dodging cars, to sit on a bench outside the Ministry of Finance, whatever that was.

"We got to talk about Eli," I said. "But first, I got to explain to you. I'm real sorry. I didn't expect to live."

She looked down at her feet and didn't say a word. She wasn't going to make this easy. But why should she?

I took a deep breath. "When I put you on the train with Eli, I thought I was giving you a life. I thought of it as providing for you, since I didn't expect to be around. Giving you a way to get an education, make a living. Until I saw you today—really, until I found out how scared I was to be in a city so far from home—I never imagined another way to look at it."

"You mean, like the way you were getting rid of me? Sending me far away with a man I didn't know?"

"Hey! You didn't know me, either!"

Felicia opened her mouth to give me an angry answer, but then she smiled just a little. "I didn't," she admitted. "I was scared of you. You told my uncle you were my sister. Is *that* true?"

I hadn't known she still wondered about our exact relationship. I hadn't really thought about all this at all. I'd taken care of her by finding her a place to live and a means to better herself, and I'd only felt pretty proud of that. I had been an idiot.

"Yeah, it's true. I'm your half sister. Your dad was my dad. Oleg."

"So what happened to him? Uncle Sergei never explained it. They went up to Texoma to earn some money. Only Uncle Sergei came back alone. Dad's dead, right? Or was Sergei lying about that? He never hurt me, but he didn't always tell me the truth."

"Our father is dead. I do not want to talk about that now." I didn't want to talk to her about it, *ever*.

Felicia looked like she meant to ask me another question. But she didn't ask the one I expected. "Is your mother alive?"

I nodded. "Yes. Her name is Candle. She's a schoolteacher. Lives in Segundo Mexia, like me. She's married to a man named Jackson Skidder. He's been good to me."

We looked at each other for a long moment. "You remember your mother?" I asked.

My sister shrugged. "A little. Her name was Marina Domín-guez. She was half-Russian, and her mom was a witch. Her Mexican part was from a middle-class family in Ciudad Juárez. I don't know how she met Dad." Felicia paused, trying to think of what more to say, I guess. "Her family disowned her, Dad said. She died of a fever. Dad didn't want to take her to the hospital. I was five. I saw my grandparents at the funeral, and some cousins. They blamed my dad. I never saw them again."

People were failing Felicia right, left, and sideways.

"I want to listen to whatever you got to say. But I'm guessing they expect you back at the school before long. Please tell me about Eli." It was all I could do to keep my voice level.

"I see Peter at least once a week. He has a class next to my class-room. He's nice to me."

"I've met him." Because of Peter, I'd had to spend months recov-ering from a gunshot. But I thought the better of an eighteen-year-old who would pay attention to a kid Felicia's age.

"I know," Felicia said, as dryly as an eleven-year-old can. "He talks about it. A lot."

"Why? He doesn't really know me."

"About as well as I do."

"Ouch," I said. "I note that. Get on with it."

"Instead of Peter, Eli came to see me. The Friday after he got back from his last trip. To Dixie, right?"

I nodded.

"He told me you'd had to wear dresses in Dixie. He thought it was funny, but he said you looked real pretty."

"Eli's idea," I said, looking the other way.

"I figured." She smiled. "And I was glad to see him. Even if he talks to me like a child."

She was eleven. Would Felicia ever get to the point?

"Eli didn't want to come back here. He didn't want to leave you," Felicia said.

I sucked in my breath hard. Why had he not written me?

"Tsar Alexei ordered Eli to come to court. Everyone at school's been talking about the plot against the tsar. For a while, no one wanted to be friends with Peter because of his dad being involved. Then Vladimir got killed somewhere in Texoma. Was that you?"

"Yes. But I got shot by his bodyguards." Thanks to Peter's unwanted intervention. "Took me a while to get well. You better get a move on with the story. I don't think they'll be happy if I keep you out all afternoon."

"Why'd you shoot Eli and Peter's dad?"

"Eli made me promise to kill him if I ever saw him again."

Felicia laughed, as if she couldn't believe that, but it was true.

"Thanks to Peter, I almost died," I said. "I'm not holding it against him, because he didn't know. I'm just saying you better be sure you understand a situation before you act."

Felicia looked at me for a long spell. Maybe she was thinking about me dying. Then she'd have no family at all. Or maybe she was thinking about what a rube I was.

Felicia started her story again. "When Eli told me the tsar had called him in, and gave me the mushy message for you, he said that the tsar didn't know the truth about anything, and that he—Eli—felt like no matter what he'd done, he hadn't cleared his half of the family name." Like me, Eli's father had another family, from a wife who had come before Eli's mom, Veronika. Bogdan and Dagmar Savarov, Prince Vladimir's older sons, had joined with their father in plotting with Grand Duke Alexander, who wanted to seize the throne.

"Eli told me to explain to you that he didn't know what was going to happen to him, but he was afraid that someone was trying to put the whammy on him and Peter and his sisters and mom."

"What does that mean?"

"That someone wants to do them in. Discredit them."

"I don't know why anyone would do that."

"Eli thinks it's his older brothers." She clenched her teeth before she could call me an idiot.

I gaped at my little sister. "This is the kind of thing you talk about at school?" When I'd been at school, we'd talked about who was sweet on whom, and the price cattle were fetching, and how long it would be before the whole town got electricity. My life was a lot simpler.

"At our school, anyway." Felicia looked hard and cold. "Politics. We'll all serve the tsar in some way. Me and the other bastards keep him alive. The grigoris will keep him safe. Some of us can do both."

I didn't think I'd known the word "politics" when I was eleven. "Wait," I said, reviewing her words. "Wait. You have magic ability?" Made sense, now that I knew she was three-quarters grigori.

"You know someone's been watching us?" Felicia said.

"Yep, that grigori from the school. The receptionist."

"Tom O'Day. He's from Texoma. You know him?"

"No." As far as I knew, grigoris always came from Russian families who'd emigrated with the tsar, or from England, Scotland, or Ireland. "I never knew there was such a thing as a homegrown grigori," I told Felicia, making myself smile. "Does some grown-up from the school always watch you when you leave the grounds?"

Felicia nodded, also smiling. "And it's called the campus. When we go out, we're usually with a staff grigori. They're afraid we'll try something magical when we're out. And in this instance, they don't know you."

I knew we weren't sticking to the subject—our watcher—but I couldn't help but ask, "Are there others besides you? Not full grigori?"

"A boy older than me. He's another Rasputin grandkid. A couple of babies, the same."

I looked at my sister, thinking a lot of things at the same time. First, my sister was going to be a great grigori. She would be a valuable asset to the tsar. Not only did Felicia have the blood that would keep Tsar Alexei's illness at bay, but she had magic, too, like Rasputin, our grandfather. Second, Felicia knew this already. Third, I didn't believe my sister was eleven. She was older.

Had Felicia ever actually told me she was eleven?

Tom O'Day had slipped off, I guess to return to the *campus*. He'd been replaced by a really young grigori gal, probably hadn't even gotten half her chest tattooed yet. It had taken me a few minutes to notice O'Day, but this replacement was either really poor at tracking or she didn't care at all that we saw her.

"We better get up and start walking," I said. I didn't want to. I still didn't know anything. We had to keep on track in our conversation.

"I guess so." Felicia stood, looking down at me with an expression I couldn't read.

"I got knives," I said, feeling naked without my guns. "Do you think she can hear what we're saying?"

"Her name is Andrea. She fucks anything that has a cock, and I bet she has diseases," Felicia said.

My mouth dropped open.

"Ha! She can't hear us. She didn't even twitch." Felicia grinned.

Oh, that had been a test for Andrea. Not me. "Tell me, quick as you can, what happened to Eli. We're running out of time."

Finally, Felicia got down to business. She switched to Spanish. I could understand it better than I spoke it. "Eli told me he might not be back for a while. That if I needed help, I should go to Peter. Eli suspected he was about to be arrested. Eli, not Peter."

"Did he say why that was going to happen?"

"Some grigori had brought charges against him about something in Dixie. Some killings."

Actually, it was true that killing had taken place, though it wasn't Eli who'd done *all* the killing.

"Why would he kill other grigoris, unless they attacked him?" I pointed out. Same went for me. I didn't go around shooting people just to see if I could hit the target.

Felicia shrugged. "I don't know what the case against him is. The next day, Peter sent me a note to tell me Eli'd been arrested and taken to the main jail. They have special cells for grigoris. Eli had told Peter to be sure I got the news to you."

"Where is the jail?"

"On Folsom, he said."

"Does Eli have regular jailers? Or are they grigoris, too?"

"I don't know."

"If there are visiting hours, I could see him." I closed my eyes for a second.

"If you just show up at the jail and ask to see Eli, you'll be marked as an enemy. You won't be able to do anything else in San Diego. The police or the grigoris will ask you to leave town. And 'ask' doesn't tell the whole story. Not with grigoris. Peter went to see him, but he's already in their black book." Felicia didn't look anything like a child when she told me this.

"I need to talk to Eli's mom, in case she knows anything I don't know. And I need to talk to Peter. He can tell me how the jail's laid out."

"You gonna bust Eli out?" My sister's new coat of polish had disappeared. She sounded like the Mexican street kid I'd met.

"I am." I just didn't know how yet.

"You'll get killed," Felicia said, and she sounded . . . resigned.

"I might." I couldn't lie about that. "But I gotta try."

"You love him."

I glanced away. "Yeah," I said finally. I tried to look casual.

Felicia shook her head. "You are *so* bad at that," she said.

A church nearby chimed one o'clock. The school was in sight, but we dawdled.

"You have to come back, promise?" Felicia said. "You have to come see me again."

"I'll see you as much as I can while I'm in San Diego. Ah . . . did Eli ask you to tell me to come here?"

"No. He wouldn't. He'd be afraid you'd be killed trying to help him. But he wanted me to tell you why he wouldn't be writing. I knew you'd get the clues. Coming or not coming was up to you."

O'Day was back at the reception desk, looking as though he'd never left to follow us. He nodded when we came in.

I hugged Felicia good-bye under his gaze.

Young Andrea walked past us and into the back of the building as if she hadn't ever seen us before. She tossed O'Day a long look. I had a gander at her. Andrea was dressed to draw attention, not a great idea if you were following someone and didn't want to be noticed.

Maybe Andrea hadn't cared if we saw her.

Or maybe she hadn't thought we were smart enough to notice.

I smiled down at Felicia, and she smiled back. It was the same kind of smile.

"I'll see you in the next couple of days?" Felicia said, sounding even younger than eleven. How did she do that?

"You're why I came to San Diego. Mom wanted me to see how you were doing." I wanted O'Day to think we shared a mother instead of a Rasputin-related father.

"Tell Mom I'm well," Felicia said bravely. "They are nice to me here, and I get to eat, and I have new clothes."

"I'm proud of you," I said honestly, and I hugged her again. "I'll see you soon. I'm going to do some sightseeing."

I patted her shoulder and walked away. I looked back to see her start back down the long dark hall, her shoulders square.

I wondered how well she'd be able to shoot when I got to teach her.

CHAPTER FIVE

This was my day for talking and walking. The walking was just fine, with the sun and the mild temperature and the big blue sky, what I could see of it between the buildings. The talking—well, I'd see.

The walk to the Savarov neighborhood was uphill, like so many things in San Diego.

All I had to occupy my mind was going over what Felicia had told me.

I'd never met Bogdan and Dagmar, but I hated them already. They were willing to throw their half brothers to the wolves, and their stepmother and stepsisters, too. The two men, who Eli had told me were in their late thirties, had been in on Grand Duke Alexander's plot with their father. When it had failed, they'd had to grovel their way out of disgrace.

Also, I didn't know how much Peter had told his family about that day in Segundo Mexia, when Vladimir had come to kill me and I'd killed him instead.

When I'd had my fill of worrying about that, it was time to face what I'd done to Felicia. I knew now I'd done her wrong, even if I'd had good and solid reasons to do so. I was sure my sister had been concealing a lot of herself from me.

When I reached Hickory Street, I was glad I could stop thinking about our rambling conversation. There was a grocery store on the corner, and it was doing a brisk walk-in business. After that, the street was all homes.

I'd thought the Savarovs would have some kind of mansion, but Hickory Street was lined with large houses. They'd be ranked mansions in Segundo Mexia but not here. The yards weren't huge, but everything was very carefully tended and fenced in—not with any chicken wire, of course, but wrought iron or brick or stucco walls topped with spikes. No outhouses in the back. All these places had inside bathrooms, I was sure. There were telephone wires and electric wires strung all over. One house had a fountain in the front.

Water was so precious in Segundo Mexia that a fountain as yard decoration was the most extravagant thing I could imagine.

The Savarov house was three stories tall, white-painted wood with dark red shutters. There was a brick driveway running under the double gate, and it widened into a parking area at the front door. A narrower extension went straight behind the house, where I caught a glimpse of a garage in the corner of the backyard. I bet there was a back entrance in the fence there, too.

But all this study was just to dodge the moment. I couldn't do that anymore.

My boots sounded loud on the brick driveway. Of course there were steps, and of course there was a roofed porch. Big urns full of plants surrounded the door. San Diego was sure a flowery place.

I'd gone past a big car parked in the driveway. Looked like the Savarovs already had company. I rang the doorbell before I could talk myself out of it.

A woman answered. She was wearing a black dress under a

white apron, and her graying brown hair was all gathered up in a thing that looked like a little fishing net. "Can I help you?" she asked. She had a heavy Russian accent. Eli's was not nearly so strong.

A chandelier hung over the center of the entrance hall, which was tiled in black and white. I could see a big stairway to the left side of the hall.

"I'm Lizbeth Rose. I'd like to speak to Eli's mother, please."

I'd shocked her. I could tell by the way she stared at me.

"You are a friend of Prince Savarov's?" she said, as if she could scarcely believe my words.

"I am." When she didn't move, I looked at her real steady.

After a long pause, the woman said, "She has other guests at the moment. If you will wait here." She stood aside to let me in, and she pointed to a chair against the wall. "Here," she said, and it was more of an order. And she vanished, but not far enough. She was standing by the doorway on the other side of the hall, and she was listening to the conversation taking place in the room.

I was real surprised. This was bad behavior, for sure. I found I could hear the voices, too. One was a mature woman's. I figured she had to be Eli's mom . . . since the other two voices were men's, also sounded adult, and also sounded unhappy.

"We have made you a cordial offer," one of the men said. "Magda and I would be happy to have you in our home."

"What do you propose we do with this house?" the woman said. I could tell she was hanging on to her manners by a thread.

"We could sell it. Or we could all live in it," said the original voice.

So he was trying to tell her that she could be a roomer in her own home. What a tempting offer.

"No, thank you," said the woman. "I think we would be too crowded. Peter and the girls and I are quite happy here."

"It's a large, expensive house."

"Luckily, your father left me enough money to make that possible."

Good for her, I thought, and liked her already.

"We could provide protection for you," said another man.

"Dagmar, the only protection I need is from your treason," Eli's mom said.

"If you cling to Alexei, you will go under," said Dagmar.

"If you think our father, your husband, was wrong in his allegiance to Alexander . . ." said the other man. This was clearly meant to be a threat.

"I think I have made it clear I do think he was wrong, and he may have cost my children their livelihood and their reputations," Eli's mom said.

I have to admit, this was more than I expected from a first visit to Eli's home. I had only hoped to make it into the house.

While Eli's half brothers argued with his mother, I looked around me. I could see a piano through the double doorway, though the people talking were out of my sight. There was a dark red rug with a golden pattern. A bookcase. The end of a sofa. To the left of my chair was the doorway to a smaller room, which seemed to be an office or a library, judging by the shiny desk and the bookcases.

I heard voices upstairs, though I couldn't make out the words. I turned my hat in my hands and studied my feet, wishing I were anywhere else in the world.

I heard some shifting-around sounds. The voices got louder. The three in the parlor had gotten up, and the visitors were heading to the front door. The maid vanished in the blink of an eye, leaving me sitting in the entrance hall all by myself.

The men were clearly brothers; they were both in their late thirties, with dark hair and stocky builds. One was taller than the other, his eyes were colder, and his jaw was more aggressive. I was willing to bet this was Bogdan, who had appeased the tsar with a valuable gift upon the death of Vladimir. Bogdan had also written the tsar a letter renouncing all his father's doings.

So Bogdan was a big liar, as was his younger brother Dagmar. They were both looking at me with great displeasure. They were not impressed with what they saw.

Eli's mother stood in the doorway of the parlor, looking a bit younger than her stepsons. Veronika had light brown hair like Eli. And greenish eyes. She was slim as a reed, and had a very straight back. At the moment, she was surprised to see anyone in her home, and she was as little pleased as her stepsons.

"I'm sorry, I didn't know I had another guest," she told me. And she said it politely enough. "Bogdan, Dagmar, good-bye. Say hello to your wives from me."

The two made grunty noises, and left.

The maid appeared again. "This is Miss Rose, Mrs. Savarov. She is an acquaintance of Mr. Eli. She says."

"You know my son, Miss Rose?"

I stood to face her. "I do."

"Then you know he is not here."

"I know."

"Are you going to tell me you are with child? Ask for money?"

"No, ma'am. I'll excuse you for saying that because I know you must be worried about Eli."

She blinked, took a deep breath. "I'll start over. My name is Veronika Savarov."

"I'm Lizbeth Rose. I'm from Texoma, a little town called Segundo Mexia."

"And you've come on the long journey here . . . why?"

"Because I want to find out what's happened to Eli and see if I can get him out of trouble. Or at least out of jail."

Veronika Savarov kind of gasped. "You know where he is?"

She was horrified that an outsider knew the family secret, at least that was the way I read it. "I got a letter from my sister. She's at the Rasputin School. She knows Peter and Eli," I explained.

"And you came all this way from Texoma?"

"Fast as I could."

Veronika Savarov seemed to stand a little straighter. "Then I expect we need to sit down and have something to drink."

So that was what we did.

Eli's mom gestured me into the parlor, and she rang a bell. The maid returned, casting dark little looks at me every other second, and Veronika sent her to get Eli's sisters and me some tea. The sisters crept into the room like they were haunting their own home.

The sisters didn't look as much like him as I'd expected. One looked to be about seventeen and told me her name was Lada ("but here I am called Lucy"). The other girl, Alyona, was maybe fifteen and told me she was called Alice. They seemed young for their ages—or maybe I was old for mine.

Lucy had had her hair bobbed, but Alice still wore hers down her back. They were both taller than me, and their hair was a darker brown than their mom's. Lucy had a heavy jaw and wide cheekbones, but she had a steady, sensible way about her. Alice looked kind of skittish.

"How do you know Eli?" Veronika was trying to act like this was a regular social visit. She was pouring me tea and sitting in a social way, her knees together and angled toward the side, her back straight.

I knew Eli every way a woman could know a man, but I said, "We've worked together. I've been his protection on a couple of jobs."

"Protection?" Veronika looked puzzled.

"I'm a gunnie."

The three women glanced at one another in a puzzled way.

"I'm a hired gun," I explained. "I usually work with a crew. We guard cargo of all kinds until it gets where it's going."

Lucy's face lit up, Alice looked scared, and Mrs. Savarov looked shocked. But then she smiled. "Eli's spoken of you," she said. "You went with him to Dixie. And Mexico?"

"Yes, ma'am."

"Please, call me Veronika."

"Lizbeth."

"As you already know, Eli was arrested two weeks ago," Veronika said.

"What charges?"

"The arresting officers, grigoris, didn't tell us."

"Isn't that against the law?" Even in Texoma, you had to tell someone why they were being hauled off.

Veronika shrugged. "Not here."

Well. Russians. "What led up to the arrest?"

"When my son returned from Dixie, he reported to the palace.

Then he came here. He'd been wounded. I suppose you knew that?"

"I killed the man who done it. Did it."

The Savarov women didn't seem to know what to do with that information. But Lucy smiled a little, looking down at her hands.

Veronika pulled herself together enough to say, "Eli told us another wizard, Felix, had helped to heal him, and you and Felix had gotten him out of the hospital so you could leave Dixie fast."

I nodded. "Did Eli recover fully from the wound?"

"Mostly. He slept and ate a lot. But he seemed very unhappy."

I had been, too.

"Eli told me he had been . . . double-crossed." Veronika looked a little proud of knowing that phrase. "He didn't want us to worry, so he didn't tell us all of it."

And see how well that worked out?

"Other grigoris tried to kill us in Dixie. And before that in Mexico," I told Eli's family.

Alice and Lucy looked stricken. They said something to their mother, words overlapping, in Russian.

"English, please," Veronika said. She told me, pride in her voice, "We speak English when we are out, but I wanted all my children to learn their mother tongue."

I didn't care.

"Why would other grigoris try to kill you?" Lucy asked, speaking to me directly.

"I figure it had something to do with the movement to replace the tsar with his uncle," I said. "If there was another reason, I don't know what it would be. Do you?"

There was a long silence.

"My husband has done harm to this family, and he is still doing it, even now that he is buried," Veronika said, anger clear and strong. "He made us outcasts, and he's made Eli's and Peter's lives hell. I wish he had died sooner."

The girls did not look surprised at hearing this. Maybe they all said this before every meal, like a prayer.

Veronika broke the silence. "Were you there? He died in Texoma in a bar. You live there. I'm just now adding it up. Did you see Peter there? My younger son's story of that day is . . . changeable."

"I was there," I said. I thought about my next words. This felt pretty strange, talking to the family of a man I'd blown up. "Prince Savarov was killed by a spell." I stopped there. Hoped they wouldn't ask more.

"Peter's? Eli's?"

But they did. At least, Lucy did.

"Ah . . . Eli's. He had given me a rock with a spell cast on it."

"He wasn't there. You threw the rock." Not a question, exactly.

"Yeah. I did it. Peter was there and intended to kill him, but that's not what happened."

"Good." Veronika was relieved. I could tell that Peter, in the irritating way of very young men, had been mysterious about the whole episode.

"Eli," I prompted.

"Yes." Veronika left the happy subject of her husband's death and got back to the grim present. "After Eli had been home from Dixie for a few weeks, and he was healthy again, and working again, the grigoris arrived, six of them. The leader of them, a woman, told Eli they had come to arrest him. She said she hoped that out of courtesy to his family and their health, he would not put up a fight."

"He should have," Lucy muttered. Alice nodded so hard I thought her head would fall off. That was surprising.

"He went quietly with them," Veronika said. I saw a big tear land on her lap. "And we three have not seen him since."

"But Peter has." I was feeling restless. I had already talked more today than I did in a week at home. I had to finish this conversation. I needed the information.

"Peter was the only one given permission to visit. You will want to talk to him," Veronika said. She was right. "Peter is living at the Rasputin School. It's his next-to-last year."

"Did he say Eli looked as if he'd been beaten?"

Veronika flinched, but she said, "Peter says Eli didn't look mistreated. But he hadn't heard anything about a trial or a hearing, and no grigori lawyer had visited him."

So as far as Eli knew, he was there forever. And I didn't know what "grigori lawyer" meant. But I needed to get out of this quiet house where I could practically hear the dust settle. I didn't like the way the maid was lingering around the doorway, though the Savarov women did not seem to notice.

"What is your best guess about why all this happened?" If Veronika knew anything more, I needed to find out now.

"My best guess . . . is that the tsar's uncle, Alexander, who should have been executed, has bribed or persuaded Gilbert, head of the grigoris, to back him in his struggle for the throne. Since my son has always been loyal to Alexei, getting Eli out of the way will deprive Alexei of a good ally, one who has kept him alive."

"But surely the tsar knows where Eli is?" He'd told Felicia he had to report to the palace.

Veronika shook her head. "Sometimes he is as blind as his father.

Alexei believes since he's had a son, his throne is secure. But the baby could have the bleeding disease like Alexei. What will happen when he is a bigger child and wants to run and play? Will we be dictated to by another Rasputin?"

She'd gotten angrier and angrier as she spoke. Wasn't the time to let her know that Rasputin was my grandfather.

"If Alexei knew what had happened to Eli, do you think the tsar could do something about it?" What was the point of being tsar if you couldn't get a friend out of jail?

"The tsar is a good man," Lucy said. (All of a sudden, she was on fire.) "Of course he would. Eli helped keep him alive."

I was sensing a division of opinion in the Savarov household. Not too surprising.

"Then why haven't you told him?" I said.

There was a long moment of silence while they all looked at me like I was an armadillo—something totally out of place in their parlor, and strange-looking to boot.

"It's not that easy to talk to the tsar," Veronika said. "If I sent him a letter, his secretary would read it first. His secretary is sure our whole family is full of traitors. If I showed up in person, I might never get to see him."

"Have you tried?"

"No," she said, very short and huffy.

"If you don't ask, you don't get," I said, sounding exactly like my grandmother. I was really put out. I was fed up with Eli's mother. The Savarov women needed to get their butts out of the house and go to the palace, or whatever it was called. I stood up.

They all seemed surprised.

"You are going so soon?" Lucy said.

It had seemed like hours. "I don't think I'm doing Eli any good here." I left it at that.

"What are you going to do?" she asked, as if she couldn't imagine me, a woman, doing anything that would get her brother out of jail.

"I'm working on a plan," I said. "I'll be in touch." I nodded to each of them, and then I walked out. I was sure there was some big good-bye ritual we were supposed to go through, but I'd had it.

I shut the gate behind me with deep relief. I would have to call the school, or return to it, if I wanted to talk to Peter. I didn't know if there was enough time today. It was getting late in the afternoon, and the school wouldn't take visitors after five. I strode along the sidewalk in the direction of my faraway hotel.

When I'd unwound enough to notice, I heard footsteps behind me. I had company. I whirled around, my hand coming up with a knife.

A short black-haired man was hurrying to catch up with me. He stopped when he saw the blade. "Felix," I said, about as excited as if I'd stepped in a mud puddle.

Felix looked better than the last time I'd seen him, somewhere on the road between Dixie and Texoma. He'd died then. Eli had brought him back.

"I'm not surprised to see you," Felix said in that snippy way of his.

"My sister wrote me," I said, by way of explaining.

"Felicia," Felix said, in a sort of considering voice. "She's a tricky one."

"Raised tough." I wondered how and why a full-fledged grigori like Felix had any contact with a young student like Felicia. The list of things I didn't know was getting longer by the minute.

We started walking. We were about the same height, and our steps matched.

"How was the widow Savarov?" Felix said.

I glanced over at him. He'd changed a bit. Though Felix's dark hair was still a tousled mess, and his beard was still cut short, there were lines on his face that hadn't been there a few months ago. There were a few more gray hairs in his beard, too.

"Sitting on her butt in her pretty house," I said. "I thought I was going to smother from the dead air."

"She tried to visit Eli when Peter went," Felix said, not really defending her but pointing out the fact. "They wouldn't let her in."

Veronika hadn't told me that. I would have thought better of her if she had. "But when she says she doesn't think the tsar even knows Eli's in jail, yet she won't go sit on his doorstep until he sees her, I got to think she's scared or selfish."

Felix considered this. "You're partly right," he said, after we'd gone another block.

I about fell over in my tracks.

"But in Veronika's defense," he continued, "she's trying to think about her girls. If Veronika got arrested, too, what would happen to Lucy and Alice? Their half brothers don't give a damn about them. They'd broker the girls to their friends or marry them to their low-born conspiracy accomplices, thugs who want some noble blood in their family to brag about."

Felix had actually told me something substantial.

"Those girls are both old enough to be out working and making their own lives," I said. "Sitting in that house doing nothing when they're grown!" I threw out my hands.

Felix stopped in his tracks. "How old were you when you began your . . . career?" he said.

"I was sixteen," I said, embarrassed. My mother had been protective. "Later than most, I know."

Felix had some big brown eyes, and he was giving me the full force of 'em. It was like he was seeing me for the first time. "All right," he said slowly. "I can understand how the Savarovs seem useless, to you. But in our culture, the one we brought with us, families that can afford to keep their girls at home do so. Until the girls receive an offer of marriage."

He was just stating a fact. Not bragging about it or saying that was the only right way to do things.

"That's no favor to the girls," I said. "Women have to learn to earn their living, and it's better if it's not earned on their backs."

Felix looked real shocked. After a moment, he said, "You're saying such a marriage is like being a prostitute?"

"'Course it is. But worse. 'Cause most women who are professional prostitutes, they didn't have much choice in the matter. Have to earn some kind of living, no other skills. 'Course, some of them are just lazy. But mostly they just see it as the only trade they can ply. The men, too."

"You've talked to a lot of prostitutes?" Felix looked unsettled.

"A few. I travel."

And that kept him quiet for about one heavenly minute.

"What will you do next?" Felix said.

"I want to see Eli," I said, before I knew those words would come out of my mouth.

Felix nodded. "But then?"

"I have to figure out a way to get him out," I said. "Then we'll leave. He can go to New Britannia, or up to Canada, and make his living there."

"What about you?"

"I'll go back to Segundo Mexia, find another crew to sign on with." As long as Eli was out and free. That was all I wanted. I wasn't telling myself any fairy tales. "I may not be real popular," I confessed. "My last two crews have gotten killed."

This time the silence lasted longer. I kind of hoped Felix would peel off and go in another direction. At the same time, I knew Felix was resourceful and quick to act, and I knew for sure he was ruthless. If he had a plan, I wanted to hear it.

CHAPTER SIX

Did your mother have two daughters?" Out of the corner of my eye, I saw Felix raise one dark eyebrow.

So Felix was going to make me pay for his help.

Since Felicia was known to be the daughter of Oleg Karkarov, the bastard son of Grigori Rasputin, and I was Felicia's half sister . . .

"What do you think?" I said.

"I think you are one of the people who should be living in the dormitory of the palace, waiting to serve the tsar by giving him a transfusion." Only Rasputin's blood had kept Alexei from bleeding to death as a child. Even before Rasputin died, a search had begun to find any heirs of his. He had had legitimate children and many bastards, so for now the tsar was in luck. "Or maybe," he said even more slowly, "you should be living in the dormitory with Felicia."

"And yet I live in Texoma. And I have no plans to move here."

"You could be provided for for life, like your sister."

"I already have a job," I told Felix. "If you try to tell the tsar's caregivers that I'm available, I'll kill you."

Felix heaved a deep sigh. "I am not threatening you," he said. "Though that would be really satisfying."

He meant *that*.

"I know you've inherited some ability from your father. That's why Eli had enough juice to start my heart again."

"Eli's pretty powerful," I said. "All by his lonesome."

"But he's not a reanimator, like me," Felix said flatly. "He could not have revived me without a boost from someone. It's a mark of how strongly you two are bonded that you would let him use you to do that."

"You got the knowledge of my father on me. I saved your life. Even."

"I value my life highly," Felix said, in a voice as dry as toast. "So I think you still have the advantage."

I heard running footsteps behind me and wheeled, reaching for the gun I didn't have. *This damn city and its rules!* But my knife slipped back into my hand.

The young man dashing up to me came to a halt and took a few deep gulps of air, staring at my knife.

"Peter," I said.

"Lizbeth, it's you." Eli's younger brother was red-faced from his sprint to catch up with us. "My mother told me you had been at the house." Peter suddenly realized someone was with me. He was mighty put out about it. "Felix! What are you doing here?"

"I am talking to Lizbeth about how we can get Eli out of prison," Felix said. He was not disturbed at all by Peter's sourness.

"I didn't know you knew Lizbeth," Peter said, scowling.

This was a day of too many words, but I had to say something. "Peter," I said. "I haven't seen you since last year in Segundo Mexia."

"What were you doing in Segundo Mexia?" It was Felix's turn to be unhappy.

"We don't need to talk about that," I said. Peter had opened his mouth. We'd never get back on track if the two kept this up. "Peter, your mom said you'd been to see your brother in jail."

"I have." Peter looked proud.

"Describe his cell."

That wasn't what Peter had expected. I had no idea (and cared less) what he'd thought we'd talk about. All our precious moments together?

"For you," Peter said, with a painful sincerity.

Eli and Felicia had both hinted that Peter had a crush on me, but I hadn't taken it seriously. I bit back a sigh.

A car slowed down as it passed us, and the driver, an older man in a fancy jacket, gave us a good long look. We stood out in this neighborhood like warts on a movie star.

"Let's go to my place," Felix said, and we began walking.

I didn't know how Peter had pictured our meeting, but I could tell this wasn't whatever he'd had in mind. I didn't know what to say to the boy. He hadn't meant to get me shot, and I didn't hold it against him . . . much. But I'd learned Peter was impulsive and didn't notice what was going on around him. Maybe that was what young men were like here. At home, those traits would make you dead.

At least we didn't talk much on the walk to Felix's.

I was wondering how I was going to effect Eli's release.

Felix looked so serious I was sure he was plotting.

Peter looked forlorn. Maybe he was wondering how to win my heart.

It was lucky for all three of us that we only had to walk thirty more minutes southwest.

Felix's neighborhood consisted of small houses, every now and then a block of shops: a news agent's, a grocery, a laundry, a hardware store. I felt more comfortable than I had at the Savarovs' place on Hickory Street, for sure.

Felix's little house was shoehorned between two others the same size. There were only a few people out and about in this neighborhood; Felix said they were all at work at jobs on the waterfront or at the big park or at the zoo . . . or in the military. I tried to imagine working at a zoo. I couldn't.

I'd supposed the inside of the little house would be dark and messy, like Felix, but the living room was orderly. The sun poured through the windows. The old furniture looked comfortable.

Felix checked his mailbox and brought in his newspaper, started a teakettle, and generally bustled around doing little things. Peter threw himself onto the couch. I wandered around a little.

The tiny kitchen looked onto the backyard, where a car was parked. It took up almost all the space behind the house. It wasn't that the car was that big, it was that the yard was so small.

Felix owned a car. That would make him a rich man in Segundo Mexia.

The teakettle whistled, and Felix said, "Want tea, Lizbeth? Peter?" Peter accepted, but I'd had enough of tea at the Savarov home. The rich man asked me if I wanted a Coca-Cola instead. Felix also owned a Penguin refrigerator, a Canadian import, and the drink would be cold, so I said yes.

Though the day was moderate, the cold sweet liquid felt good in my throat.

When we were all beveraged up, we sat in the living room, Peter and I on the couch and Felix in the armchair.

"So, Eli's jail cell," I said to Peter. I wanted to get the conversation moving so it would be over with sooner.

"The grigori cells are below the regular jail. The cells are spelled to keep magic suppressed. There are special jailers, people who have no magic at all and aren't affected by it. They call them nulls. There are harsh punishments for prisoners observed trying to use magic."

"How many cells?"

Peter counted mentally. "Just six, three on each side. One person to a cell."

"Which one is Eli's?"

"He's in the third cell on the left when you enter the cellblock."

"Can he see anyone who asks to see him?" Felix said. "Or is there a list of approved visitors?"

"They wouldn't let Mother in, but I don't know if she was on a list or not. She didn't say. They didn't explain. When I went, I didn't see the jailer consult any list. I just said I was his brother. They searched me and handcuffed me and let me sit on a bench outside his cell so we could talk."

"Handcuffed?" I said.

"So he couldn't use his hands to cast spells," Felix told me, in a way that said I'd missed something remarkable. "Peter was wearing his grigori vest, I'm sure." Felix looked right into my eyes and tilted his head toward Peter.

I looked at the boy and saw what I should have commented on right away.

Peter had earned his vest. That was a big landmark in a grigori's education, a coming-of-age marker. Peter was looking down at it, doing everything but patting it. The fabric still looked stiff and new.

I complimented Peter on his achievement, and I even managed an apology for not saying anything earlier. Peter had clearly been waiting for me to remark on it.

When I'd said as much as I could summon to satisfy his pride, I returned to the important thing: the facts about Eli's jail.

"Was there a time limit for your visit?" I wanted to know everything I could before I tried to see Eli.

"Fifteen minutes," Peter said.

"How many are in the cells now?" Felix leaned forward in his chair. It was a dark crimson velvety thing someone's mom had tired of. Peter and I were on the couch, which was similarly dark and cushioned but blue.

"Let's see." Peter stared at his hands. "Okay, there were two women."

"Aren't women in a separate jail from men? Or a separate wing?" That had always been my experience in any town of more than five thousand.

Felix said, "Magic users are all together. There aren't enough grigoris in jail to keep two separate cell areas."

"Jane Parvin," Peter said. "And Svetlana Ustinova."

Felix looked worried, an expression I'd never seen on his face. These women must be grigoris of some reputation. "Jane's in for killing one of the new grigoris in a test combat. Svetlana, I don't know. Who else?" he asked.

"A man I didn't know. At least twenty years older than me." Peter was just barely eighteen, I thought.

"What did he look like?" Maybe Felix could identify the other prisoner from a description.

"Very tall, big head, reddish beard," Peter said. "He's next to Eli. The women are across the corridor."

"That's John Brightwood," Felix said. "He's a killer."

"I haven't met a grigori who wasn't," I said.

Peter looked from one of us to the other, his mouth open. He'd seen me kill his father and his father's hired hands, but I was no grigori. Maybe Peter hadn't ever seen what Eli could do, what Eli's deceased partner Paulina had been capable of doing, by way of destroying another person.

From Peter's look of dismay, for the first time I wondered if all grigoris weren't death dealers. "Are there grigoris who don't . . . ?"

"Kill others? Yes, there are." Felix grinned. "You didn't know."

"How could I? The only other grigoris I've ever seen were trying to kill me."

Peter was still recovering. "Truly, Lizbeth?"

"Truly," I said.

"How did you survive?"

"I killed 'em first." How else?

"You . . . shot them?"

"I did."

"Eli knows this?" he said.

"Eli was with me."

"Does *Eli* . . . ?"

I felt a little bad for Peter, who was shocked, like his world had been turned upside down. I reminded myself that Peter had been prepared to kill his own father. "Peter, Eli was given a job to do. Some other grigoris didn't want him to be successful. They did their best to kill us. I don't enjoy killing, but I'd always rather it be them instead of me."

I didn't know what world Peter had been living in, but it wasn't the same one as mine.

Felix was smiling, but when I looked at him, the grin vanished. He said, gently for him, "Peter, we have to do whatever is necessary to get your brother out of jail. Otherwise, he'll be dead before he sees the outside of that cell."

"But why? What has he done?"

I shrugged. "I don't know. I don't care. We'll get him out. Felix, you're in?"

"Yes," Felix said.

"Why are you helping?" Peter asked. "Felix, you've always impressed me as, excuse me . . . selfish."

I was curious to hear the answer, because I'd thought the same thing. Why *was* Felix willing to risk his life and career for the sake of Eli?

Both Peter and I were astonished when Felix answered, "I want to marry your sister, Peter."

"Which one?" Peter was definitely out at sea now, and I was right along with him.

"Lada. Lucy."

I was glad it was Lucy, since she was older. But that only meant she was seventeen. I was sure Felix was thirty. At least Lucy seemed braver and smarter than her sister or mom.

"Does Lucy return your feeling?" Peter was suddenly the head of the family, at least in Eli's absence.

"She doesn't hate me," Felix said mildly.

But there was a lot Lucy didn't know about Felix, I was willing to bet good money. I'd never pegged Felix as the marrying kind.

I did enjoy the moment, because it was the first time I'd ever heard Felix sound anything but confident.

"We need to finish talking about Eli. Peter, are you in?" I said.

"Eli is my brother," Peter said with dignity. "Yes."

So I had another crew. I didn't wholly trust or like Felix, and

Peter hadn't been tested yet. But I didn't have to crack Eli out of jail by myself.

We talked a little more, but it was late afternoon by that time, and I needed time to think by myself.

Peter returned to Hickory Street, which was where he'd been headed when he'd spotted me and Felix. He was staying at his home about half the time now, because the atmosphere in the school dormitory was hostile, he told us.

Felix, who had also been on his way to visit the Savarovs when he'd seen me, offered to drive me back to my hotel. I was glad to accept. The traffic was heavy, so I kept quiet as Felix drove. I was thinking it would have been a busy afternoon for the Savarov women if Peter and Felix had not followed me.

As I got out of the car in front of the Balboa Palace, Felix said, "Let's meet tomorrow. I have to be on duty for six hours, but after that we can work on a plan."

"When and where?"

"I'll come by here at four o'clock."

"See you then." I went into the hotel, got my key from Paul McElvaney, and went to my room to ponder. In no particular order, I thought about these things: (1) Felix and Lucy as a couple felt funny and odd. (2) Peter was sure green for a man his age. (3) Maybe some of the grigoris in the cellblock with Eli would be released before we made our attempt to free him, or more would be under arrest. Random factors.

(4) I wondered if there was any way I could carry a concealed gun. I felt very uneasy without one. I could be attacked at any moment. I'd been keeping my eyes open as I walked today, and I'd seen a few clusters of men I deemed dangerous. And I had enemies

here; now the older brothers, Dagmar and Bogdan, knew what I looked like. I was real sure they slipped that maid money to find out what happened in the Savarov household.

Maybe bloodshed could be avoided if I could make my way in to speak to the tsar. Though if a genuine aristocrat like Eli's mom was convinced she couldn't get in to see Alexei, I didn't stand much of a chance . . . if I tried to get in the normal way.

When I'd reached that point in all my wondering, my room felt too small, so I went to get some dinner. Afterward, I could have gone to a movie (something I'd only done once before), but I wasn't in the mood to have fun. So me and my big ball of worry went back to my room to play catch some more.

CHAPTER SEVEN

I found the jail on Folsom Street early the next morning. It was designed in Spanish style and looked almost like a hotel . . . at least from the outside. There was a sort of plaza, and then you walked through an archway. I stood across the street from that plaza and archway for a long time.

Eli was just in there. Only yards away. I touched the little pouch that hung around my neck.

In a sheer crazy moment, I decided I'd go back to the hotel. I'd get my guns from the safe. I'd return to this spot and walk through that archway and shoot everyone I saw. Take the keys from the corpse of the jailer. Free Eli from his cell. We would leave, leave this city.

I struggled against this impulse with all the strength I could muster.

"Keep off the sidewalk if you ain't walking," a stumpy man growled at me as he shoved me aside.

I nearly drew my knife. That proved to me that I wasn't thinking clear. The man didn't deserve to die for shoving me. Probably.

I lingered for five more minutes. I wished with all my heart that Eli could know I was close.

Then I made myself leave before someone in a police uniform noticed me.

I went by Felicia's school, but the woman on duty in the reception room said Felicia was in class and couldn't be disturbed. I asked the grigori to tell Felicia I'd been there, and she said she would. I believed her. She was nicer than that Tom O'Day.

At loose ends, fighting the urge to return to Folsom Street and yearn across the pavement some more, I walked through the botanical gardens. I didn't have anything else to do. It was pretty, if you liked plants. The climate of San Diego was so moderate that flowers were showing now, in January.

My mother would have enjoyed it a lot more than I did.

I was standing outside my hotel at four when Felix pulled up to the curb.

"You look like death warmed over," he said as I climbed in. He pulled right back out into traffic, which was heavy. And noisy.

"Yeah?" I said. I realized I hadn't eaten lunch. I thought I'd eaten breakfast? Maybe. And I hadn't slept well, despite all the walking I'd done the previous day. I'd been thinking of Eli in a cell.

"This has to end soon," I said.

Felix gave me a quick sour look. "You haven't twitched when people died in front of you. But Eli's arrest has wiped you out?"

"Yes."

"You're so strange. Pull your socks up, gunnie."

"Pot's calling the kettle black." I could hear my grandmother's voice in my head as I repeated her favorite saying.

"Fair." Felix nodded.

"Do you really want to marry Lucy?" I said. This was not an unrelated thought.

Felix gave it some thought. "I respect her," he said at last. "She's young, and she's been brought up an aristocrat, but she's strong. Lucy would be career suicide for most men, after her father was branded a traitor. For me, it won't make a difference. And that would leave only one sister's future for Eli to worry about."

I figured it was possible Veronika Savarov wanted a future, too. She couldn't be much more than forty. Maybe Felix thought Veronika had had her chance.

There were some words I hadn't heard that I'd hoped to hear. "Love" and "affection," mainly. Even knowing what I knew of Felix, those were possible. "So you've decided to marry Lucy to help out Eli," I said. It sounded unbelievable even as I said it.

"No one cares what grigoris do." Felix shrugged.

"Somebody sure seems to care what Eli does."

"Oh, of course, maybe princes like Eli. But I'm nobody, in a social sense," Felix said. He didn't sound particularly bitter. "I have no pedigree to live up to. Lucy will be lowering herself if she accepts my proposal. But I think marriage to me is preferable to staying home with her mother and sister for the rest of her life."

"Romantic," I said. "That'll sweep her off her feet."

Felix shrugged again. "It's the truth. And it's also the truth that I think we would suit each other. Lucy's young, yes, ten years younger than me. But I don't care. Maybe she won't."

I understood Felix's reasons for marrying Lucy, and they were all practical. I wondered if such a marriage would live up to Lucy's expectations. Only if she were very unworldly or very . . . hell, who cared about my opinion, anyway?

"Do you think Peter can carry out a plan?" I said, changing course. "He doesn't think before he acts."

"Peter almost got you killed, Eli told me."

"Hadn't been for Peter's interference, I wouldn't have gotten shot. Or at least, not shot so bad." I had worked out my plan so carefully. Peter's sudden appearance had set off the chain of events that had put me in the hospital.

"I think if he has clear directions and we drum it in that he has to stick to them, Peter will be fine. He loves Eli, and he's talented. He may be as good as Eli, someday, if he lives that long."

"Also, no one else is going to volunteer to help," I said.

"That is absolutely the truth." Felix looked grim.

"I have a plan," I said.

"You too? All right, we'll hear yours first. Now, we're going to go to my house, and I'm going to watch you eat something and drink a lot of water or lemonade. Then we'll plot."

So that was what we did.

"Plot" sounded like we were doing something wrong, and getting Eli out of jail was absolutely right, so I preferred to call it "plan."

Felix fried sausages and potatoes at his house.

I watched him moving around the little kitchen. Maybe I didn't dislike Felix as much as I had. He was not friendly, and he was a killer, and he loved secrets, but he'd done a few decent things.

I couldn't sit idle while he worked, so I began to straighten the living room. Felix didn't seem to mind. It wasn't like I mopped. It was a matter of refolding newspapers, stacking magazines, dumping the wastebasket. I found what might be a dustrag and used it to wipe surfaces.

"How long have you known the Savarov family? Did you come over on the boat with them?" I called, so he'd hear over the pop of the grease and the scrape of the pans.

The fleet following the ship on which Nicholas Romanov and his family had fled had been ragtag and varied, all sizes of boats crowded with all sorts of people. The refugees were united by one thing: the fact that they would have been killed if they had stayed in Russia.

A bullet had actually whizzed past Nicholas's head as he'd boarded. He'd insisted on being the last to get on the ship, so he would be the last to leave Russian soil. Romantic. Dumb.

Felix stood still, spatula in hand, and looked down at the potatoes like they were a crystal ball. "My sister and I were on one of the smaller vessels, hardly better than a fishing boat," he said finally. One corner of his mouth turned down. "Our father *just* qualified to be on the boat, since he was one of the tsar's favorite attendants. Our mother was dead by then. The quarters were crowded. That's putting it mildly. But that didn't last long."

I waited, because I was sure he was going to tell me more. I was right.

"We didn't have enough food or water. We were as hungry as we'd been in Russia. My sister died on the boat. We had to push her body into the ocean." Felix turned the sausages over again, but he was doing it without thought.

I was sorry I'd asked, but now I felt obliged to hear the rest of his story.

"We wandered for years, waiting for someone to give us asylum. When William Hearst offered a temporary refuge to the tsar and his family, the rest of us disembarked as well. A few of us went to the Hearst ranch with the royal family, but he hardly wanted all of us to camp around it. At least the tsar found a barracks for us to stay in, down where the palace is now. Many of the sailors had died—were dying—from the influenza. We scrubbed out a building and lived in it. We didn't exactly have American permission, but no one told us we couldn't." Felix smiled to himself, though nothing about the story was funny. "Then America cracked apart, and California needed its own government, and behold! There was a true hereditary ruler on California soil, and the Romanovs had become the favorites of the rich and of the movie industry. Finally, someone offered Alexei a job he was qualified to do."

That was debatable, considering the state of his realm now. But I would not open that can of worms.

"Did you know the Savarovs?" I said.

As Felix put the food on plates, he nodded. "I knew Eli a little. We were both magic users. His mother and father were invited to San Simeon; the children weren't. Prince Savarov wasn't going to miss the opportunity to bond himself to the old tsar and Alexei, who was thirty by then. So he left Eli and the girls in the barracks with us. Veronika had a connection, Maria Orlova, an aristocratic old lady with a lot of dignity. She hired Maria Orlova to keep an eye on her children, and she hired my mother to help Madame Orlova. My father was busy helping to clean out the barracks, and we needed the money." Felix shook his head. "I don't know how Madame Orlova managed with the two oldest, Eli's half brothers. I think she more or less washed her hands of them. They were thugs. But Eli, Peter, Lucy, and Alice were good children, or as good as children ever are. I helped my mother keep track of them, keep them busy. I would take Eli with me when I tried to earn a little extra money, so we could eat. Even before the tsar was asked to rule here, Rasputin founded the school, though he didn't have a building at first. When the starets founded the school, it saved my life. And by then, I knew Eli had the power and saw the possibility in Peter."

Felix had had enough. I opened my mouth to ask one more question, but he shook his head.

"You've learned enough about me and the Savarovs," he said, finishing his food to point out that his mouth was busy doing something else.

"Where's your carpet sweeper?"

Felix pointed to a closet. I got his carpet sweeper out and ran it over the rug and the wooden floors. It looked better by the time I was ready to put the sweeper away.

Felix had been right when he told me I needed to eat. I washed the dishes to show I was grateful.

He didn't protest.

"So, what's your plan?" I asked, sitting down opposite him.

"I must explain a few things," Felix said. "First off, the tsar has secret police, the same way his father did in Russia. Their job is to look for plots. Anything that goes against the government is an affront to the tsar. It's not as dreadful as it was in Russia, but there are penalties."

I nodded.

"Alexei may very well be ignorant of the fact that Eli is in jail. But if we break Eli out of his cell, we'll be disrupting the law, and we may face very unpleasant consequences."

"Even though Alexei has every reason to like Eli and trust him."

"Alexei does like Eli. He's used to Eli sitting by him when he's sick, Eli arranging for the transfusion. And the blood comes from donors Eli tracked down."

"So why hasn't the tsar asked where Eli is?"

"Eli's father was a traitor. Even though Prince Savarov's plot was foiled, even though his older sons made amends and vows and gave gifts, even though Prince Savarov died mysteriously far from home . . ." Felix arched an eyebrow at me.

I looked out the window.

"Alexei's favorite minister urged Alexei to remove Eli at least temporarily, to show he wasn't soft. That even favorites would be punished if they were connected to treason. Bogdan and Dagmar were likewise banished from court for a time, even for all their gestures of atonement and protestations that they were not involved in their father's plot."

"I bet that's a lie."

"I know it is. Bogdan and Dagmar are much more like their father than his second family. Veronika is a better woman than the prince's first wife, though she isn't of as high a birth. Vladimir's first wife, Evdokia, was a real Lady Macbeth, for sure. More to the point, Evdokia was the niece of Grand Duke Alexander's second wife."

I didn't know who Lady Macbeth was, but I could figure she'd been a bad woman in some book. Seemed like she was from Shakespeare. Mother had made us read *Romeo and Juliet* in school, and I think one other one.

"Evdokia was too mean to live, I have been told. But she died a natural death, in childbirth, with a baby who also died," Felix said.

Eli's family history made my own seem simple. "It still doesn't make sense, if the tsar likes Eli, and the tsar believes Eli didn't have anything to do with the plot, and Eli helps to keep Alexei alive, that the tsar doesn't know where Eli is. Is he even looking for him?"

"No, it doesn't make sense." Felix sat back, his small bony hands clasped behind his head. "Sometimes I think that the backers of the grand duke have a point. Alexander would never be ignorant of one of his followers being jailed." He was looking up at the ceiling. I followed his gaze. He needed to get him a broom and go after those cobwebs.

"But Alexei *is* the rightful tsar," I said, testing the waters. I didn't care who was tsar. I cared about Eli's safety and freedom. Under Grand Duke Alexander, Eli would be doomed.

"If only Alexei were more forceful and his wife more popular," Felix muttered.

"What's wrong with his wife?" I'd been told this before, that she wasn't a hit here in America. She was a far cry from his first wife, a very wealthy girl from Dixie who had died without giving him a child. Caroline was royalty (one of the Scandinavian countries), and she'd had a son by Alexei. Her position should be solid.

"Caroline." Felix kept his head tilted back, but his eyes were on me. "She's not a bad sort, and if she was in Russia, back when things were the way they were, she'd be fine. But Caroline has no clue that she actually needs to be popular. I also know that she thinks her family sold her off to get rid of her since she was soiled goods. But rather than being grateful that she's managed a good marriage to an emperor from a pure line, Caroline apparently feels she deserves a better country than the Holy Russian Empire."

Sounded like Caroline deserved a swift kick in the pants.

"In fact," Felix said, and he straightened and focused to make sure I was listening. "In fact, Caroline is taking a walk tomorrow in the botanical gardens, her grigori guard tells me. And you should, too."

I must have looked blank.

"Just go," Felix said, clearly irritated with my stupidity. "You'll know what to do when you see it happen."

"And that's your plan? I show up in the gardens and wait to see what happens?"

He nodded, looking smug.

"I have a plan a lot better than that." I was really disappointed. "I thought you would be telling me some wonderful plot. Instead . . . walking in the gardens."

"Oh? Please do tell me this wonderful idea."

When Felix sounded this sarcastic, I wanted to never speak to him again. He made me feel stupid and obvious. "Felix, I don't understand you. You say you want to get Eli out, and he's your future brother-in-law. But you don't want to go directly into a plan to get him out. Instead, you want me to approach something I can't predict, from the side, not even head-on. Why can't you just explain things as we go along?"

"You've probably been direct all your life," Felix said, after a moment of silence. He didn't sound like that was a good thing.

"Yes, and why not?"

"But I notice you have secrets you don't talk about."

"Because they're none of your damn business."

"Well . . ." Felix looked frustrated for a moment. "This *is* your damn business, but there are things I can't tell you about. I just ask that you go armed when you go to the gardens. You always are, so I wasn't going to bring that up. And understand that something may go wrong, and nothing may happen at all. Or you may be hurt."

"Oh, Felix. What else is new?"

CHAPTER EIGHT

If Felix was expecting Peter to show up for our little consultation—I'd assumed Peter was coming, myself—he was disappointed.

Instead, I got Felix's broom and got the cobwebs down because they irritated me, and after that, Felix gave me a ride back to my hotel, taking a detour through the gardens so that I could see the route the empress's party would be likely to choose for their outing. Felix said Caroline often took her walk between eleven and twelve o'clock but stayed on the palace grounds. Tomorrow she was going to venture out where the public could see her so they would be charmed. (In theory.) When we got close to the hotel, Felix glanced at the sidewalk, started, and drove right past the door.

"What?" I hated not having my guns.

"I saw a couple of people I know. They may be here by coincidence. But maybe they know exactly who you are, and your connection with Eli, and they want to kill you."

"Which people were they?"

"The short woman with brown hair and big hips and the stout man with the homburg. He was wearing a red vest."

I had them in my mind now. I wouldn't forget. "Names?"

"Katharine Demisova and Derek Smythe."

"How come you don't know which side they're on?"

"How do you define the sides?" Felix said. Smiling. Again.

"Anyone not for Eli is on one side. Anyone for Eli is on the other." Simple.

"I'd have to say they are in the middle. I don't think they care about Eli one way or another. I don't think they know him particularly well. They're in the Water Guild, they're older than Eli, and they'll do whatever they're told."

"Told by who?"

"By their guild superior."

"Who is?"

"Ivan Godunov. Calls himself Ike Goodyear now."

"Should I kill him?" I really needed something to do.

"I can't see the point of that," Felix said, but only after he'd considered it. "Eli is air, you know. I am, too. Though I have some rare talents for an air."

I tried not to shiver. Felix was a reanimator. He could make the dead move and speak. It was a terrible drain on his life force, but he had made some bones into a real man and then turned it into a statue. (For all I knew, the statue was still standing in a small town in Dixie.) How that tied into air, I wasn't sure. I also figured that Felix didn't have a lot of friends because this "rare talent" was seriously frightening. Not that all wizards couldn't do frightening things.

"Felix," I said, and then stopped. I had an idea that what I was about to propose wasn't going to go over well.

"Yes?" He turned his dark eyes on me, mockingly.

"I want to see Eli. Is there any reason I can't go to the jail and ask to visit him?"

Felix gave me a long, long look. Finally, he said, "Lizbeth, you're my secret weapon. It wouldn't be wise to draw you to their attention, and you would surely do that by showing up at the jail and asking to see Eli."

It was like my soul was itching inside me, and the only way I could scratch it was by seeing Eli.

Felix was still looking at me, but he wasn't seeing me. He was thinking. He said, "I can't stop you if you decide you are going to see him, no matter what. But I advise against it right now."

I nodded, trying to contain my disappointment.

Well . . . it was more like misery.

CHAPTER NINE

I had to sneak into my hotel by the back door to dodge Demisova and Smythe. I have no notion why they didn't separate so they'd be covering both doors. Maybe they figured I wouldn't recognize them, not counting on Felix's being with me. I sped up the stairs and spent a while taking a bath and trying to decide if Felix intended me to get my guns out of the safe for tomorrow.

After I decided I'd carry my knives, because as far as I knew, there wasn't any prohibition on that, I fell asleep. I dreamed about cobwebs.

The next morning, I had knives up my sleeves and in my boots as I got to the botanical gardens. I was simmering. What was I doing here? Why did I give a damn about the tsarina and her stroll through the garden? Felix hadn't given me any more direction than to tell me to be sure to be there.

Before I'd met Felix, I'd thought Eli's partner Paulina was the most irritating person I'd ever met. But I knew better now. Since Paulina was dead (at least, she'd been that way the last time I'd seen her), Felix was top of the list.

At least the Japanese Friendship Garden was a pretty place to be bored. I hadn't seen that area before, and I liked it a lot. Everything was planted and tended and green, trimmed, and neat. Maybe it really did look like Japan. There weren't too many people in the area, so it was peaceful. I can always use a little peace.

There was a restaurant, but I didn't enter. Didn't know what Japanese people ate for breakfast.

I found a bench I could sit on to look into the pond close to the restaurant. It was full of big fish, really big fish. Probably not to eat, just to look at—and probably guarded somehow or other. Otherwise, people would have tried to poach them out of sheer desperation.

I got less jangled every minute I watched them gliding through the clear water. Nice. I pulled my old jacket closer around me. It was a cool morning.

After an hour, I saw a flutter of activity over by the road. At last, something was happening. Sure enough, the tsarina had arrived. Four cars parked on the margin of the road. A group of colorful people emerged. It was easy to make out which one was the tsarina. She was in the center.

A flock of ladies surrounded Caroline. Six men, bodyguards of one sort or another, were in a loose circle around the women.

All the women were wearing slim-fitting dresses with sweaters or light coats. Though all the men wore suits, the two groups didn't match. The men were hired help: two vested grigoris, four gunmen carrying sidearms.

I was envious of the gunmen.

Like everyone else within eyeshot (a scattering of men and a woman pushing a baby carriage), I watched the royal party. The park was not busy—weekday, working hours. Most of the men in sight were gardeners, in fact.

The group formed up and began to stroll. The men looked outward, as they ought. The women were looking at the pretty bushes and flowers, exchanging comments, pointing.

Caroline was wearing a green suit with black trim, a black hat, and black leather shoes—heeled but not too high, right for walking in a park. She wore a very lightweight black coat. No purse. A tsarina wouldn't need an identification card or cash. As you would expect of a princess, she was tall and blond and blue-eyed. Almost pretty. Her jaw was a bit too pointed, and her eyes were too close together. I figured you could overlook little things like that in a real princess.

One of the women stood out because she was old. She walked well, though she carried a cane. Her pure white hair was put up in an elaborate circlet of braids, and she was hatless. Though I was sure she wouldn't appreciate the comparison, she reminded me of my grandmother. If you looked up "dignity" in the dictionary, this lady's picture would be right beside it. And she was vigilant.

A gust of laughter came from the group. It was like hearing a flock of doves coo all at the same time. The tsarina must have said something real funny. Even the guards were laughing. But not the white-haired woman. Her smile was faint and remote.

I guessed this public stroll was an attempt to make Caroline more popular. Here she was, the tsarina! Walking and talking like a common person! (If a common person could afford those clothes, good food every day, and regular baths.)

All of a sudden, my arm hairs stood up. Something was about to happen. I scanned the vicinity for something amiss. I was closer to the pond than anyone else. There were a few random people scattered in the garden, some between the tsarina's party and me.

Mom and baby in stroller. Two men in suits talking about

something serious. A few unemployed men who'd been sleeping rough. A Japanese man, concentrating on weeding a flower bed.

And the wrong one, the pale, jerky man in a filthy corduroy jacket. Messy brown hair, stubbled face. He was between me and the tsarina's party.

He was the one.

He reached inside his jacket. I began to run, ignoring the exclamations of alarm and surprise from the other people in the park. I saw the bodyguards had not yet drawn, could not understand how they could be so slow. Corduroy was pulling out his gun. His eyes were fixed on the tsarina. He never saw me coming.

I leaped the last few feet to land on his back. I bore him to the ground. He grunted as the air was knocked out of him. The smell was foul. I grabbed his gun hand and beat it against the gravel of the path, over and over. With both hands busy, I couldn't get my knife.

Corduroy wouldn't let loose.

He fought like a madman. I couldn't manage to knock the gun from his hand. It was a struggle to keep his arm pinned. If he shot me from this close, I would not live. If he shot the tsarina, I would have wasted all this effort.

There wasn't enough of me to hold the man down. He heaved me off of him and onto my back. As if I was out of the picture, Corduroy pushed himself to his feet with one hand, and the gun was going up in his other when a bullet went through his head.

Well, about damn time.

Like that, it was over. Corduroy collapsed in a bloody heap, one arm flung over me. I shoved him away, rolled, and stood, ready, knife in hand. There might be another attacker.

No one else seemed to be offering to kill the tsarina. Everyone in sight was shrieking or milling around like chickens with their heads cut off or gaping at me. (That was what Tsarina Caroline was doing.)

Even the bodyguard who'd actually shot Corduroy was looking at me as if I'd done it.

My face was wet. I'd gotten his blood spattered on my cheeks and chest. At least I had avoided the stuff blown out the back of Corduroy's head. That's hard to get off clothes . . . and out of hair.

Before I could say "Jack Robinson," two bodyguards pounced on me. *Now* they were going to try to look efficient. They were trying to throw me to the ground again, when a voice full of command said, "Leave that woman alone." Such was the force of the white-haired lady that the men instantly let go of my arms and jumped back. I nodded at her with some respect.

"Caroline," the woman said, very quietly.

The tsarina came over to me. When she got close, I could tell she was shaking. I was, too, just a bit, and I'm used to action.

"May I know who I'm thanking?" the empress of the Holy Russian Empire asked me.

"Yes, ma'am," I said haltingly, not sure how to address her. "I'm Lizbeth Rose, from Texoma. I'm glad I was able to help you."

"How did you come to be here today?"

"I'm visiting San Diego because . . ." I stopped, because this was a moment to tell the truth—or not.

Caroline raised her neat eyebrows.

"Because my friend, Prince Eli Savarov, is in jail here."

It was like I had asked the tsarina to smell my feet. She looked horrified. I couldn't tell if it was because I claimed to be friend to a prince or because she hadn't known Eli had been arrested.

"I am astonished," Caroline said, which she'd already made clear. "You say Eli, the grigori, is in jail?"

"Yes, ma'am."

"On what charge?"

"I don't know. Neither does his family."

The white-haired lady had been right behind Caroline during our conversation. She patted the tsarina on her shoulder and said, "My dear, this is not a conversation to have right here, right now." She used a different voice to say, "Young lady, can you come to visit Caroline this afternoon? We'd all like to thank you for your service."

"Yes, ma'am. When and where?"

"At the palace at three o'clock," the white-haired lady said. "I'm Grand Duchess Xenia Alexandrovna."

"I'll be there," I said. Then the bodyguards hustled Caroline away with some hostile looks thrown my way. I'd shown them up. They weren't going to forget it. *Think of how bad you'd look if Caroline had gotten shot*, I thought, and hoped that occurred to them as well.

Xenia Alexandrovna lingered for a moment to say, "Appropriate clothes, please." Then she followed Caroline and all the other ladies. I was left standing by myself, blood-spattered and bruised, in the middle of the Japanese garden. My shirt, face, and hair had gotten the worst of it. My jacket, unbuttoned, had flown back as I dived for the gunman, so it was spared the worst.

The Japanese gardener approached me in a doubtful kind of way, but he was nice enough to tell me where a faucet was. I knelt in the grass and pulled off my jacket. Putting it carefully out of reach of water flow, I cupped my hands and splashed my face and hair with the cold water. I slipped my jacket on again.

I felt much better, though as I walked out of the gardens, I knew I was still a sight. There was nothing I could do about it. I would be even more remarkable if I took off my shirt. Buttoning my jacket to hide as much of the mess as possible was the only solution to hand.

I wasn't totally surprised to see Felix's car at the curb.

The grigori was asleep in the driver's seat, his head tilted back. He looked like hell, pale and haggard. Though his turning up confirmed my worst suspicions, at the same time I was relieved I wouldn't have to walk through the city streets with bloodstains (and worse) all over my shirt.

I got in without speaking. Felix woke up with a gasp. He winced after he took in my appearance.

"That looks too close for comfort," Felix said. I would have smacked him if he'd smiled, so it was lucky he didn't.

"Would have served you right if I'd let him shoot her," I said. The first thing I'd thought after I'd tackled the guy? That it was too much of a coincidence that the morning Felix sent me to observe the tsarina was the morning she was attacked.

"You wouldn't do that," Felix said with unearned confidence. "Did the tsarina ask you to the palace?"

"Xenia Alexandrovna"—I fumbled a little on the last name— "told me to wear the right clothes when I go to the palace," I said, sounding as grumpy as I felt. "How much money do you have?"

Felix looked shocked. "She is Alexei's aunt! You spoke to her?" Then he got back more into "Felix" normal. "You didn't bring money with you?"

"I have a little emergency money, and I'm holding on to it." I was damned if I was going to spend Jackson's money on clothes, especially an outfit I'd wear once.

"I haven't got any idea what you should wear to the palace in the afternoon," Felix confessed. It was rare that he was at a loss.

"It would be different from what they were wearing in the park? There's different clothes for different times of day?" It was amazing that people could make their lives so complicated.

"The court has had to change a lot in its new home. Now they must speak English, now some of the servants were born American, now they can't all have palaces or mansions. But some things haven't changed."

I felt even grumpier. "We'll have to find out."

"I'll take you to Veronika," Felix said, smiling. "I can visit with Lucy while she kits you out."

"Veronika's been to court but not Lucy?"

"Lucy's just at the right age to have been introduced at the palace this past year if . . ."

"If her dad hadn't been a traitor."

"Just so." Felix looked all dark and brooding for a moment. Then he shrugged. "Veronika will help you."

"Do you think so? I got the feeling I wasn't her favorite person."

"You can hardly wonder," Felix said.

I scowled at him. "What does that mean?"

"Do you think Peter and Eli have not talked about you when they were at home? Do you think she hasn't heard about the black-haired shooter who saved Eli's life? Who saved Peter's? The princess must be terrified you are involved in their lives forever."

"She acted like she'd never heard my name. She asked me if I was pregnant."

"You turned up on her doorstep out of the blue, Lizbeth. She's proud, and she feels helpless. How do you expect her to feel?"

"Grateful."

Felix beamed at me. I could almost see he could be attractive when he smiled . . . but he so seldom did. "In your world, she ought to be. But her world is all upside down, and she doesn't know how to cope."

"Then she can begin coping by loaning me something to wear," I said. "Let's go, Felix." I felt all kinds of ways, and I wanted to sit and be quiet for a spell.

I was still jangly from the incident in the park.

I was still wrought up that I hadn't had a gun when I'd needed one most.

I was angry because the way I looked wasn't good enough for the tsarina's court, when I'd saved her life. I didn't want to be dressed up like a doll. I'd had enough of that in Dixie.

The drive to the Savarovs' was silent. I had no idea what Felix was brooding about, but I had so much stuck in my craw I didn't imagine I'd ever get it digested. I would have offered to drive, but traffic was heavy.

"He was already dead, wasn't he?" I had to ask.

"The gunman? Yes. He died this morning on a bench down by the water. Seconds before I found him! How's that for luck?"

I really couldn't think of words to answer.

"I raised him up, gave him a gun, took him to the park, and let him out. I parked where I couldn't be seen and gave him his commands. I take it he performed well?"

"He tried to kill her, sure enough, if you call that performing well. I barely got there in time, and when I brought him down, he fought like crazy."

"It wouldn't have been convincing if he hadn't," Felix said in a wounded way, as though I was criticizing his workmanship. I could tell Felix thought he deserved praise. Too bad.

"I guess you slept the whole time till I came out of the park," I said. Felix had a hard time recovering from reanimation.

Felix nodded.

Once we got onto the residential streets, the traffic was not so bad, and we got to the Savarov house pretty quickly. Felix pulled the car around to the back of the house. I hoped that was okay. Eli's mom seemed to like her formalities.

Felix strolled up to the back door. He knocked. The same older woman answered it who had come to the front door the day before. Was she the only servant? I wondered how many they'd had in Russia.

The woman was in yet another starched uniform, and she wore yet another grim expression as she stood back from the door and invited us in without the least bit of enthusiasm. "Mr. Felix, Miss Rose," she said. "I will see if the ladies are at home." She cast a horrified look at my shirt and jacket.

Even I understood that the housekeeper for sure knew whether or not "the ladies" were in the house. "I don't know your name," I said. "You got the advantage of me."

"I'm Natalya," she said. I didn't deserve any more of her name than that. She made that clear.

We passed through a narrow hall and into the front of the house, where Natalya bade us sit in the same room I'd seen on my first call. I noticed Felix wasn't as "at home" as he'd pretended to be. He fidgeted, jumped up to look at the pictures on the wall, sat down to pick up a magazine.

At last, we heard footsteps coming down the stairs. I'd decided Natalya was going to tell us no one was at home and we should leave. But Eli's mom came into the room with a chill around her like a refrigerator.

"Miss Rose, Felix," Veronika said. About as far from cordial as it was possible to be.

"My dear Veronika," Felix said. He sounded sober and confident, like a lawyer. "You'll be glad to know that Lizbeth has an invitation to the court this afternoon. She's to visit the tsarina."

Veronika flicked a look at me that was out-and-out incredulous.

"Doesn't seem likely, does it?" I agreed. "I met her at the Japanese garden today. I did her a favor. She asked me why I was in San Diego, and I told her about Eli being in jail. So she asked me to come see her this afternoon. In three hours. And Xenia Alexandrovna told me to be dressed properly. I'm betting you know what I should wear. And we're about the same size."

Veronika was giving me narrow eyes by the time I finished. "Is this true?" she asked Felix. "Has she gotten in to see the tsarina so easily?"

"It wasn't easy. I had to kill someone to do it." I tapped one of the bloodstains. She noticed them for the first time.

Veronika turned almost as pale as the dead assassin.

I thought it would lessen the effect if I told her the man had already been dead, so I didn't bring that up. I wanted Veronika beholden so she'd help me. Also, I hadn't fired the shot that had taken him out for the second time.

If I'd had a gun, I would have.

"So your intention is to ask the tsarina if she can find out why Ilya is in jail, and you hope she'll make sure the tsar knows about it and will get him out." Veronika was making sure.

I nodded.

"What is your interest in this?" Veronika asked me, all of a sudden.

It was lucky I had braced myself for this. "As I told the tsarina, Eli and I are friends," I said carefully.

"Told her," Veronika said.

I nodded.

"And is that the truth?"

"We're . . ." I struggled to find words. Every time I saw Eli, I was surprised to see him again. Every time he left, it took me longer to recover. "You'll have to ask him," I said. I held her eyes with mine, and I would not let her look away. I wanted Veronika to know how serious I was.

After a long moment, Veronika nodded. "Then let's get you ready for court," she said. "I'm sure we can find something that fits you passably. Felix, can Natalya bring you some sandwiches and coffee or juice?"

"That would be most welcome," Felix said gravely. "May I ask if Lucy is here?"

Veronika said, "She may be upstairs."

"I would very much enjoy her company, if she is at home—and of course, that of Alice also."

Well done, Felix, I thought.

"I will see if they are home," Veronika said.

Having an upstairs was a good out, I thought. The girls could be there, or they could not be there. Felix was supposed to be too polite to actually search the rooms up there to find out.

I wouldn't bet on that, myself.

"Please come with me," Veronika said, and I got up to follow her. She didn't sound warm, and she didn't sound excited, and she didn't sound angry. She sounded like she was mashing all her feelings down as hard as she could.

There was a lot of that going on in the house on Hickory.

Upstairs, Veronika took me to a large bedroom overlooking the backyard and the garage. "I'll be back in just a moment," she said, and glided out of the room. I could hear a door open somewhere nearby and the sound of the girls' voices asking their mother who was in the house. The voices were cut off as Veronika closed the door. The doors were thick.

Veronika must have agreed to Lucy and Alice's keeping Felix company, because I heard them chattering together as they went down the stairs. Veronika returned and shut the bedroom door behind her. Without a word, she went to the closet on the far wall and folded the doors open to reveal many, many dresses.

"How old are you, Lizbeth?" Veronika was flipping through a section of dresses. Seemed she had them divided by occasion.

"Just turned twenty."

"Barely older than Lucy." Veronika's hand froze on a hanger for a second.

"Yes." Couldn't deny it. But a decade older, experience-wise.

"You're a shooter for hire, you said."

"Yes."

"So you must be quite good."

"I'm still walking around," I said. "That means I'm better than average, I guess."

"You'll need something like this." Veronika turned, holding up a dress on its hanger. The ladies this morning had been wearing suits, mostly. They had been finer than anything I'd ever worn (or seen) but not extravagant. This dress, fitted slim until it flared from thigh to hemline, was a step finer. Looked like it would fall a bit below the knee. A rusty color was the background for a pattern of leaves in gold and brown. The fancy trim was gold. The belt was brown.

"I'll try it on," I said. "Thank you."

"I'll look for something else in case you don't care for that one." Veronika turned her back—thank you, Veronika—while I took off my clothes and figured out how to get the dress on. There was a smear of blood on my shoulder I hadn't gotten off, and I was glad Veronika hadn't seen it. The dress slithered down once I worked out the armholes. I buttoned up the front. I turned to look in the mirror. I shrugged. "This is how it's supposed to look?" I asked Eli's mom, and she turned to survey me.

"Yes, it fits very well, and it's appropriate. Or do you like this better?" She had another dress, this one a navy blue with red piping.

"This one's fine," I said, touching the skirt of the dress I had on. I didn't want to be any more trouble than I had to be.

"Then I have a suggestion," Veronika said, a little hesitantly. She wasn't sure how I was going to receive it.

I waited.

"Why don't you bathe and wash your hair? I'll get you into all the clothes and make you up. And we'll arrange your hair."

"My hair needs arranging?" The bath, yes, I needed that.

"Yes." No discussion about the hair. "I have combs that will keep it under control. You'll need hose and shoes, too."

"That's a lot of your time. I'd be using a lot of your stuff," I said, pointing out the obvious.

"You're trying to get my son out of jail," Veronika said. "That's worth *time* and *stuff*, I'd say." For the first time, she smiled, and I saw Eli in her.

An hour and a half later, I was clean, I had makeup on, and my hair had been combed into a style and pinned. I'd been as quiet and accommodating as I could. Veronika had been as patient and even-tempered as she could.

While Veronika had been working on my hair, I'd asked her if Natalya had been working for the family for a long time.

"For the past two years," Veronika had said absently, placing the hair combs yet again. They were a beautiful matched set, black with a gold inlay. Getting them lodged correctly to hold back my black curly hair was not a pleasant process. "Natalya didn't come with us from Russia. But she was on another boat. Bogdan recommended her when our Ludmilla passed away."

Veronika and her household were being spied on by Natalya, I was certain. Veronika seemed real unsuspicious for someone who'd spent a lot of her marriage sailing from one spot to another on a crowded boat.

I searched around for something to ask Eli's mother, something that wouldn't offend her. "How was it, having stepchildren?" I said at last. I looked at myself in the mirror, turning my head from side to side. I was a different woman, for sure. I looked smoother.

"When I married Vladimir, his sons were thirteen and eleven," Veronika said. "They were not . . . enthusiastic about the marriage, but my husband insisted that they be courteous and respectful." Veronika's mouth pinched up.

Figured she was remembering times they hadn't been. "When Eli and Peter and the girls came along, they seemed glad to have other siblings."

Sure they were, I thought.

"Vladimir told Bogdan and Dagmar they must keep watch on

their little brothers and sisters when our babies were small." Veronika seemed to be searching for something nice to say. Since I'd overheard them quarreling, that was kind of hard. "Even now that Vladimir is gone, my stepsons stay in touch. But they live in a different neighborhood, and they have their own families." Veronika tried moving the combs again. My scalp was getting sore.

"So you had Eli, Peter, Lucy, then Alice?" I figured this abundance of children had a lot to do with ship life being boring. All the ragtag fleet had done for years was sail from one port to another, looking for someone willing to take the Russian royal family in. Since the tsar's own cousin and look-alike, the king of England, had not welcomed the flotilla to English shores, no one else had rushed forward.

Veronika said, "Yes. All born in Russia or on board the ship. I swear I will never get on a boat again."

That had almost been a joke, so I almost laughed. "I think I'm as good as I'm going to get," I told Veronika. I had reached the end of my tolerance for having the hair combs rearranged.

"You look very nice," Veronika said.

"Thanks for the clothes and advice." Eli's mom had been giving me a little lecture on court etiquette as she stabbed me with the combs.

As I went down the stairs, I called Felix. It was time to get moving.

Felix came out of the parlor, the girls trailing behind him. Felix gave me a sharp look, nodded. Giving me his approval, I guess. Lucy and Alice smiled up at me and chattered to each other in Russian.

"Girls, English," Veronika called.

"I'm sorry," Lucy said. "You look lovely. That was what we were saying."

Alice nodded with a lot of force. "Yes!" she said.

"Thanks." Who doesn't enjoy hearing that? We were at the bottom of the stairs. I turned to Veronika. "I appreciate all the work you put in, and the clothes. I'll let you know what happens."

"Please," Veronika said, and for a moment she looked as afraid as I felt. She pulled something from her pocket and hurried after us to press a card into my hand. I glanced down. Her name, telephone number, and address—I guess in case I forgot where I'd been and whom I'd borrowed clothes from.

"Good, thanks," I said, and we were out the door and into Felix's old car.

I wanted to ask Felix for advice as we drove to the palace, but two things stopped me. First, I thought Felix himself had never been to court. Second, maybe it would be better if I made no bones about being an outsider. I might as well be traveling to the moon, this was so far from anything I'd heard of or read about. I was only sure this was my best chance at getting Eli out of jail.

"There are three ways to get on the imperial island," Felix said, maybe because I looked nervous. He glanced over at me to make sure I was listening. "It's not really an island but an isthmus."

I'd never heard that word, and I guess I looked it.

"It's attached to the mainland by a thin strip of land," Felix explained. "South of here. But that's heavily guarded, and only official vehicles involved in the building and maintenance of the palace and the homes being built are allowed to use it. Cars—aristocrat cars—going to the palace use the bridge. I figure we should use that one, since you're visiting the tsarina. So that's where we're going." Felix looked pretty grim about it, but then, Felix almost always looked pretty grim.

"Okay. What about the servants and the building workers and so on?"

Felix smiled. That had been a good question. Give me a peppermint. "There is the ferry. It crosses several times during the day and at shift changes. The guards check the identification cards against the faces of the workers before you are allowed on the ferry. Same happens when you return. If you try to swim, you are shot."

"I'm not the best swimmer anyway," I said. "I guess I won't get in the water."

We had to pull up before we reached a big guardhouse on the San Diego side of the bridge. The bit I could see of the bridge itself was new and pretty and arched over the water like . . . I don't know, it was a nice curve. As Felix talked to the guards, I watched the people coming off the ferry docked at the pier. Looked like off-duty soldiers and servants, all happy to be going somewhere more interesting.

The guard talking to Felix bent over to have a good look at me. I didn't know how I was supposed to respond, so I just looked back. After a talk with his fellow guards, all male, we got a jerk of the rifle in the direction of the island, so we were good to go. Felix didn't say anything, but he had an air of relief.

Felix drove across the bridge and stopped at the next gatehouse, on the island end. Armed soldiers came to both car windows. Were we supposed to have been replaced by hostiles on our way over?

"Hello," I said to the man who'd gestured that I should lower my window. "My name is Lizbeth Rose. The tsarina invited me to visit her this afternoon."

He had a thick brown beard and wore a pecan-colored uniform, like all the other access guards. He had never heard of smiling. He looked at a clipboard he was carrying, and he spoke (in Russian) to his buddy, who was standing at Felix's window. They had a long back-and-forth.

The Russians seemed to be hell on maintaining checkpoints and on requiring uniforms that advertised the wearer's job.

While they had their discussion, I peered out at what was going on. At least there was plenty to see.

North Island, now Imperial Island, was an anthill of activity. While Veronika had been grooming me, she'd told me a version of the same story Felix had related. When the Russian royal family decided to stay in California, the former USA military base, now almost empty after the flu, had been allocated for (or abandoned to) all the Russian emigrants. It was surrounded by water, so there was room for all the ships and boats and whatnot, and there was housing, though not exactly Russian royal standard. On the other hand, if you'd been on the water in cramped quarters for years, US naval housing looked pretty good. This had been where Felix and Eli and their siblings had lived after the tsar had been invited to San Simeon.

When the island had been chosen for the new royal family's base of operations, naturally, the higher-ranking court members had wanted to live nearby. They were building houses all along the road that led in from the mainland. In the meantime, the palace was under construction. Also more barracks for the soldiers who guarded the tsar.

Since there was no US government any longer, everything on the base was ripe for the picking, too . . . especially for a government in exile, not exactly rolling in spare money. Veronika had said the lots on the road in had gone for astronomical sums. The tsar had been the seller.

I'd never seen so much big equipment in one place. There were workmen swarming all over. At least construction workers didn't have to wear uniforms.

Seeing all the activity, I couldn't believe there were so many unemployed men in the city. With so much shoreline and so many people coming over from the mainland every day, how did the guards maintain security?

By forbidding strange grigoris to come in, I found.

"You may enter, but this man must stay outside," the guard by my window told me. I saw Felix had expected this. The tsarina's invitation had not included him.

"I will be in this parking area when you return," Felix said. "I have a book to read while I wait."

"Good-bye, then," I said, trying not to sound as jangled as I felt. I got out of the car before I could worry any longer. While one guard was making sure Felix knew all the rules for sitting in a car, the guard on my side raised his hand.

That turned out to be a signal for another car. In a few seconds, one pulled up, polished and gleaming despite all the dust on the site. Naturally, the driver wore a uniform. The guard held open the door to the back seat, and I climbed in, trying to mind my skirts. The second the door shut, off we took down the road, a clear alley between scenes of brisk activity.

We passed another car returning to the parking lot as we were approaching the royal residence. I tried to imagine driving back and forth between two fixed points all day. I shuddered.

I don't know what the palace had been in its previous life—

maybe an officers' club or the commander's home? Or both? What I knew about navies and military bases would not float a boat.

With a showy swerve, my driver turned to present my side of the car to another guard post. The man who opened my door was also in a pecan uniform, but waiting by the steps was a woman (in a blue suit, didn't know if it was an actual uniform or not) who escorted me into the building.

I wondered what the palaces they'd had in the old country had looked like, because they'd done a slap-up job with the new place. There were huge vases in many colors and patterns, benches every now and then, curtains, and so on. I'd never seen anything like it. There was no point trying to act like this was something I took for granted.

I got handed off from one blue-suited woman to the next. They always murmured to each other, as though I was a parcel destined for one person. I was supposed to pretend I didn't hear this. Wasn't any point paying attention to the words; what was interesting was the language. All the inside servants spoke Russian. I was sure some of them had been wandering around with the tsar and his court until Nicholas had received the invitation from William Randolph Hearst.

My stepfather had read me pieces in the newspapers about Hearst's land in California and the place he was building on it. During their extended stay at the Hearst Ranch in the largest guest-house, the tsar and his family were enchanted by the opulence, if not by the isolation. It was like things used to be, on some level, for the royalty, who'd been close to starving at points in their long journey.

And when Hollywood had discovered how excited people got by newsreels of the Russian royals, how the two remaining unwed grand duchesses and the young tsar-to-be were fascinating to all Americans, it had seemed almost natural when California had broken off from the US to ask its resident royals in exile to step in and be royals in residence once more.

The death of Nicholas and his state funeral had been the subject of every newsreel and on the front page of every newspaper for days. Rasputin had been alive then. In every picture of the new tsar, the magician had been a few steps behind, his beard streaked with white and his steps a little uncertain.

I had plenty of time to remember all this. Felt like I could have walked home to Texoma in the time it had taken my guide to lead me to the room where the tsarina was.

I'd assumed Caroline would be by herself. Not only was the tsarina surrounded by the same ladies who had been with her this morning (now all wearing different clothes, sure enough), but there were even more. They were all seated in chairs dotted around a salon-type room. They were all admiring the performance of a children's choir.

The first person I saw standing in the front row of singers was my little sister, trilling away in a clear soprano.

I was startled on a lot of fronts. I hadn't known the Rasputin School had a choir. I hadn't known my sister could sing. And I sure hadn't known the choir would be here today. It seemed like a massive coincidence. I hardly ever believe in coincidences, massive or tiny.

I was ushered to the back of the group of women, where a few men had been shunted, too. My guide murmured, "When the children have sung, I will let Her Imperial Highness know you have arrived."

I nodded and gave my attention to the children. Felicia spotted me after another minute, and her whole face lit up. The people seated in front of me turned a little to discover whom the smile was aimed at, and I beamed back at Felicia so they'd know. I was proud of my little sister.

CHAPTER TEN

When the singing was over, Felicia came over to me as quickly as she could, considering that everyone rose and started milling around at the same moment. She had to stop every foot or two to accept compliments and to curtsy, which was something I would never in my life have believed Felicia would learn to do. When she threw her arms around my waist, she said, "Where'd you get the dress? Why are you here?"

"Saved the tsarina," I said, as low as I could and still be heard. "She got attacked this morning." It was a bad time to explain the attack had been a setup by Felix to maneuver me into the presence of the tsarina, who was now obliged to me.

"That was you?" Felicia looked up at me, her face alight with so many things. Triumph, pride, and the other shoe dropping, primarily.

I nodded. "I got to go present myself," I said, and took her hand. We went to the knot of women surrounding Caroline, who was wearing a real pretty blue dress that matched her eyes and some diamonds that sparkled like water. Of course, her blue dress was in no way the same blue as the women attendants.

The ladies parted like the Red Sea as I approached. Caroline was looking straight at me and Felicia, and she was mighty curious.

I had no idea how to do this, but I bowed as low as I could, and Felicia curtsied, and I said, "If I'm not greeting you correctly, I apologize, Your Imperial Highness." Felix had told me that was the right way to talk to her.

"Quite all right," Caroline said.

Felicia stood straight. "Your Imperial Highness," my sister said, "this is my half sister, Lizbeth Rose."

"We met this morning," Caroline said, and the ladies managed to produce a little gust of laughter all at the same time. "Miss Rose, it's good to see you again under less terrifying conditions."

I had no idea how I was supposed to act or what I was supposed to say. "Yes, ma'am," I said. *Let Eli loose, let him out of jail.*

Felicia seemed to have mastered court etiquette in a very short stretch of months, but I'd always known there were depths to my little half sister that I might never plumb. Now she tugged on my hand to make sure I was paying attention.

"My sister came all the way from Texoma to see me," Felicia told the tsarina, and the ladies cooed because Felicia was so sweet and lovely. (They sure didn't know her.) But I had to agree with them: Felicia looked real pretty. You would never have known her hair used to look like a dusty black bush.

I smiled down at my sister. "I'm glad I did, but I also came on an errand," I said, figuring that was what Felicia was aiming for.

"Please explain. I'm so interested," Caroline said clearly, and I understood, more or less, that she wanted me to speak with the same volume and clarity. Caroline wanted me to explain my goal, for whatever reason, all over again.

"My friend Eli Savarov is in jail here. His mom has no idea why. I'd sure like to visit him. I'd like to get him out even more," I said. I'm sure that everyone in a ten-foot radius heard me.

"I had no idea that was the case," Caroline said, still at a good volume. "I'm appalled to hear it. What charges are against him?"

"Ma'am, I was hoping you could tell me." I bent my head, waiting for her next move. Caroline was aiming this at someone, and I moved my eyes around without moving my face. Everyone was riveted, because, after all, this was the tsarina speaking to a commoner. But a face set in iron—a man in his thirties, with thick graying hair—was the target. And as I took in the grandness of his uniform and the pride of his stance, I knew he was an enemy of Caroline's and therefore an enemy of mine, at least for now.

When Caroline had decided to make a soapbox out of this, I wished she'd taken my inexperience into account.

But Felicia squeezed my hand. "Vasily, son of Alexander," she said, I swear without moving her mouth. So Proud Man was the son of the grand duke who wanted to give Alexei the heave-ho.

"I will do my best, Miss Rose. Captain McMurtry," the tsarina said, only slightly more loudly.

An American-born man popped up at the tsarina's side. "Tsarina?" he said, with absolute attention. He was a handsome man, lean-faced, with reddish hair. He was wearing a blue uniform covered with ribbons on the chest. He looked good in it.

"Captain McMurtry, this is Miss Lizbeth Rose, who saved my life this morning in the gardens. Can you find out why Prince Ilya Savarov, who spent so many days and nights in my husband's service, is in jail? And why his family has not been notified of the charges against him?"

"Of course, Tsarina." The captain bowed as if he'd been born with a hinge in his spine. He was gone from the room so quickly it was like a magic trick.

Now that I had put in my two cents, I had nothing to say to

Caroline. Luckily, she felt the same way. She turned to chatter to one of the other ladies, this time in a language that wasn't either Russian or American.

Xenia Alexandrovna, the white-haired woman from the park, took pity on me (needless) and felt it her duty to ask me questions about my trip to San Diego and what life was like in Texoma. Then she slipped in a question about Eli, whom she called Prince Ilya. "You must have known Ilya for some time, you're so dedicated to his freedom," she observed, and looked at me expectantly.

We were both surprised when Felicia answered. "Eli owes my sister his life, as do I," Felicia said. "My sister is famous." She sounded as proud of me as I was of her.

I had to concentrate on holding my face still. I wanted to grin down at her. For someone I'd wronged, Felicia was being a great advocate for me.

"Famous?" the white-haired woman said gently. But the way she looked down at Felicia was not gentle. I pulled my sister a little closer to me and put my arm around her.

"Lizbeth is a great shot," Felicia said. "That's why she's a professional."

"A professional . . . shooter?" Xenia Alexandrovna did a good job of looking puzzled.

"Yes," Felicia said simply.

The lady looked up at me in polite inquiry. "I'm a gunnie," I said. From her blank look, she didn't understand. "I get hired to shoot," I said.

"At targets? In a circus?" Xenia Alexandrovna was incredulous.

"To protect people. Or things. Sometimes that involves shooting other people. Naturally," I added, because it was.

"So under other circumstances, you might be the person hired to attack the tsarina."

"Under no circumstances. I am not an assassin."

"But if you were sending your beautiful necklace," Felicia said, "perhaps as a gift to your sister or your daughter, you would hire my sister to make sure no one snatched it along the route."

The grand duchess's necklace was pretty, for sure. I'd never seen pearls before, but I thought that was what they were.

Xenia Alexandrovna looked from Felicia to me thoughtfully. "I see. That's a fine distinction."

"However, it's real clear to me," I said through my teeth. I was still smiling. But it was beginning to be a strain.

Felicia reached up to my hand, which was resting on her thin shoulder. She squeezed it. No gentle pressure, either. A real pinch. That brought me back to earth. "Of course, it really doesn't matter what you think of me. What happens to Eli is the important thing. That's why I'm here." Back on track.

"But why?" persisted the white-haired lady. "Why is saving Eli your mission?"

"He brought me from Mexico to here," Felicia said. "My sister always pays her debts."

I nodded. "That's true," I said. As far as it went, anyway. Felicia was a smooth liar.

I was real glad to see Captain McMurtry appear at the tsarina's side. He had to wait for her to finish her conversation with a very young woman, then he had to bow when she turned to him, and all those moments I was burning to hear what he had to tell her.

Caroline beckoned to me, so I stepped closer, still with Felicia, who wasn't about to miss this. Captain McMurtry looked at me with a lot of calculation. "Tell Miss Rose what you have learned," Caroline said.

"I called the jail. Eli Savarov is a prisoner there," McMurtry said. "The charge is murder."

If they expected me to faint or something, they were disappointed. Didn't matter to me if Eli had been charged with torturing bunnies. "I can go and see him?" I said. "I have permission?" I looked at the tsarina, trying like hell to look humble and worried. The worried part wasn't hard.

"Yes, of course," Caroline said, pleased to be asked. "You shall go now, and Captain McMurtry shall go with you. I see your little sister's class has left to return to the school. Perhaps you had better drop her off along the way?"

Felicia was unhappy at being discarded, as she saw it, but what could I do? This was the tsarina telling us what she wanted. And I was far from sure Felicia should go into the jail, anyway. I would rather not have Captain McMurtry with me, but it might save me from being killed or imprisoned myself, having a royalty-approved escort.

"Of course," McMurtry said. "Miss Rose, are you ready?"

"I am," I said, and that was the most I'd ever understated anything. "Your Imperial Highness, I am real grateful."

"Then we are even," Caroline said, with a smile, pleased with her turn of phrase. "That's how Americans put it, am I correct?"

"Yes, Your Imperial Highness, you are quite correct," said one of the ladies. Suck-up.

I thought of trying a curtsy, decided I would look like a fool, and bowed like the captain. And we left.

CHAPTER ELEVEN

When we came out of the front door of the residence, or palace, or whatever they called it, a car pulled around immediately. Felicia tugged on my hand and shook her head. She did not want us to get in that car.

"That car's got a low tire," I said. "Captain McMurtry, don't you think we should take the next one?"

I looked up at him. He was a tall man. He was looking down at me with a doubtful face.

He could look all he liked. I was beginning to understand my half sister was the best ally I could have at my side.

"If you think so," McMurtry said, giving the tire, which was perfectly all right, a quick glance. I didn't care if he thought he was humoring me, as long as I got my way. Felicia's way.

McMurtry made a *go on* gesture, and the driver, a squat white-haired man, glared at him and waved his own hand at the passenger doors, indicating we should get in.

I bent down. "No," I said clearly. "*Nyet.*" I'd learned that from Eli.

The driver actually spat, which was a mistake if he'd still hoped to get us in the car somehow. McMurtry became as determined as I was. He said a few words in slow Russian to the driver, who had no choice but to pull forward without us. McMurtry beckoned to the next car in the rank, which obediently swung into place.

I waited a second to see if Felicia was going to nix this one, too, but she opened the front door and climbed in, leaving me and McMurtry to take the back seat. This driver was also Russian, and Felicia had a cheerful conversation with him. I had no idea what they were chattering about. McMurtry told the driver where we were going, and off we went.

When we came to the civilian parking area, I asked the driver to stop for a minute. We were close to Felix's car, and he was looking at us doubtfully. He rolled his window down.

"One second," I said to McMurtry, and beckoned Felicia to come with me.

"You sending me with him?" she said.

I nodded. "Thanks for all your help in there. And you sang great, too."

Felicia grinned. "Tell Eli I said hello, and give him this." She reached in her pocket to get a turquoise nugget. It was polished and gleaming. She held it so no one could see it but us two.

"What does it do?" I was a little worried. No, a lot worried.

"It will blow up." She was pleased as punch.

"You made it yourself?"

"I had supervision," she said haughtily.

I had a lot I wanted to say, but I bit it off. She'd been so great at the palace. I wasn't going to hop all over her now. "Thanks, sis," I said. We hugged briefly.

While Felicia went around to scramble into Felix's car, I bent down to talk to him. "We're going to the jail to see Eli!" I said. "Captain McMurtry tells me Eli's been charged with murder. I don't know who he's supposed to have killed. Felicia can tell you every-thing before you drop her off at school. Why don't you come to the jail afterward? Just in case."

"You have succeeded better than I ever imagined," Felix had the decency to say. Really surprised me.

"I couldn't have done it without Felicia."

"Death to the enemy!" Felicia said, with her big grin. I hoped none of the guards could hear her.

"You're not eleven years old," I said with certainty, the idea com-ing out of my mouth before I could even think about it. "How old are you, really?"

My sister just smiled. "Captain's waiting," she said.

I had to put Felicia on the back burner. I got back into the court car. Eli. He was what I had to think about right now.

"How long you worked at the palace?" I said when we were under way. I didn't want to fuss and fidget all the way to the jail.

"Four years now. My full name is Ford McMurtry, and I was formerly of the US Navy. Now I'm aide to the tsarina and a member of the Holy Russian Army." He shook his head. "Incredible. You?"

"Lizbeth Rose," I said, though I was sure he knew my full name. "I'm from Segundo Mexia in Texoma."

"You're a gunnie."

"Yes. I work on protection crews."

"I should take you out to the range," Captain McMurtry said, and there was a little sliver of amusement in his voice. I didn't like that, but I swallowed it. After all, I was on my way to see Eli.

"That would be great," I said. "My guns are in the hotel safe."

"What do you carry? I've got a Colt M1911. It's accurate and reliable."

We talked guns all the way to the jail. It was the best conversation I'd had since I'd gotten on the train.

We were close to the spot where I'd stood to try to contact Eli by sending him brain waves or thoughts or whatever I'd been doing. *Longing.* That was what I'd been sending him. If someone had asked me to predict how I'd feel at this moment, I would have said I'd be too excited to hide it.

Instead, I was having the shivery feeling that meant trouble was coming. A lot of thoughts about what that trouble might be jostled around in my head. Eli might refuse to see me, he might be dead, they might have tortured him, they might lock me up somewhere else . . .

I was hard put to control my breathing as we got out of the car. The driver had pulled right into the curb and placed some kind of government card on the dashboard. We crossed the sidewalk. We walked under the archway. I watched my feet cross the paved court to the check-in desk, which was enclosed by glass reinforced with bars. There was a circle cutout that you could talk through. There was a metal disk that the clerk could slide across the circle when there was no one waiting with a question.

I took it all in, clenching my hands at my sides so they wouldn't shake.

The uniformed cop on duty, an overweight fellow who must have been retirement age, looked Captain McMurtry and me over. He had no opinion of us at all. Slowly, he slid aside the metal disk, having decided that we weren't going to shoot him outright.

Captain McMurtry said, "This lady is authorized to visit one of the grigoris. Eli Savarov." He held out some kind of business card. "I'm aide to Her Imperial Highness, and I'm here on her behalf."

The policeman looked doubtful. He tapped his name, sewed on his shirt. "Sergeant Seth Rogers," he said. "Well, Captain. Not many visitors get cleared to go down there. Or want to. Those're danger-ous people. If they're really people at all! Devils or demons, more likely." Rogers looked like he'd bitten into a lemon.

"Whatever your opinion, Her Imperial Highness has given this lady and me permission to see Savarov." McMurtry wasn't giving an inch.

Rogers grimaced and pulled a ring of keys from one of the hooks on the wall behind him. He pushed a button on the wall, and I heard a bell ring somewhere else in the building. After at least five min-utes, a woman came down the passage behind the counter, in no big hurry at all. She, too, was uniformed and stout. She was not armed.

"You rang?" she said, smiling at Rogers in a flirty way.

"These people are from the palace," the policeman said. "Here to see one of your prisoners."

I leaned forward a bit to read her name tag. It read HUBBLE. She had bleached her hair and mashed herself into a really tight under-garment.

"That don't happen often," Hubble said. She turned her atten-tion to us. "Well, come on, you two. You got to sign some papers before I take you down there."

"Sign what kind of papers?" Captain McMurtry sounded both skeptical and bored.

Hubble didn't seem intimidated. "Saying we don't take respon-sibility if anything happens to you down there. It's at your own risk." Hubble seemed to enjoy the idea of something happening to us.

"You go down there?" I said. I didn't want any more of this delay.

"Every damn day."

"You look okay to me." Except like she never took a step if she could get someone to carry her.

"Sorry, honey, I don't swing that way."

If she meant to insult me, she had the wrong woman. We're poor in Texoma, but we don't care who goes to bed with whom. At least, most of us don't. I felt Captain McMurtry stiffen beside me as if he expected me to explode into action, but I gave Hubble a bland face. She waited for another moment, still hoping for a reaction, and then she presented us with a clipboard. We signed. McMurtry read the document. I didn't.

Hubble didn't search either of us. I found this shocking. Not only was McMurtry openly carrying a sidearm, but I had a knife or two hidden on me. I'd tucked 'em here and there while Veronika was out of the room. I hadn't been searched at the palace, which wasn't such a shock since I was an invited guest. But I was about to enter a jail, where *any* weapon would be a prize. Even the turquoise tucked behind my belt.

There must be rules about patting down visitors. Had to be. What a loafer Hubble was! Even if she believed McMurtry was beyond suspicion (right!) because he was a Russian Army officer, I should have been given the once-over.

I dared not meet McMurtry's eyes, lest he read my thoughts and search me himself.

We walked behind Hubble until she came to a door. Ambled, more her speed. She carried the keys given her by the reception cop. They swung from her finger, making an irritating jangle. When she unlocked the metal door and swung it open, I saw that it led downstairs.

Looked to me like this part of the jail had been added on or adapted after the original jail had been built. It was specially for the housing of grigoris. I don't know why they thought grigoris would be easier to take care of if they were underground. (Earth grigoris probably loved the location.) I was right behind Hubble, and she didn't move fast enough to suit me. I wanted to shove her so bad it made my hands itch. It wasn't that I wanted her to die, it was that I wanted her out of my way.

There wasn't a jailer at the foot of the stairs.

If Hubble's lack of reaction was any judge, that was the normal state of affairs.

McMurtry said, "Where is the officer on duty?"

"We tried keeping people down here, but they went crazy." Hubble shrugged. "So we just come down when we have to, like now."

"You didn't get another grigori to guard them?" I was truly shocked.

"What, hire one of them?"

If I hadn't been about to see Eli, I would have turned around and gone right back up those stairs, and I would have done it in a hurry. This place was not safe. We reached the bottom, and I gave McMurtry an urgent look so he'd be alert. I was preaching to the choir. His eyes were wide, and his shoulders were tense.

The cells were all painted beige. The walls to the side were solid. The doors were solid until waist height, then they were barred all the way up to the ceiling. The bars had not been painted.

The floor was bare concrete. There was a drain in the middle of the passageway between the cells, which was six feet wide. The inmates couldn't touch, even if they were tall and held their arms out as far as they could extend. There were narrow benches down the middle, for visitors.

The first cell to our right held a woman. She was broad and brown-haired, and her teeth were bared in a corpse smile.

"Step away from the bars, Svetlana," Hubble ordered.

Svetlana Ustinova moved back about an inch. Hubble seemed to consider that enough. What an idiot.

The first cell to the left was empty. The second cell to the left held a huge man who must be John Brightwood. He had a crazy tangle of blond hair and a reddish beard. He started laughing when he saw me. I didn't know why, and I didn't care.

The third cell to the right held another woman, must be Jane Parvin. She was tiny, with dark hair and a meek expression. Didn't fool me for a second.

"Dear Louise Hubble," she called, with one of those English accents that make you sound rich, "please bring me a canteen of water."

"Water time in an hour," Hubble said.

The last cell to the left held Eli. He was standing back from the bars, waiting. When he saw me, he was stunned. It took him a second to be sure it was me—the dress and so forth. Then he was at the bars, his hands extended through them. Before Hubble could stop me, I was holding his hands in mine. We didn't have to say anything.

"Ain't this touching?" Hubble, of course.

I ignored her. Here was Eli. We were holding hands.

I felt like I had grabbed an electric wire. I buzzed and crackled with life.

"How did you know?" Eli said finally.

"I got a letter," I said. I left out Felicia. Hubble was standing right beside me, and I couldn't give her anything to report. "I came directly."

"Is Peter all right? He came once and then not again."

"They won't let him back in. They won't tell your mom why you're in here. The tsarina didn't know. She got Captain McMurtry, here, to call the jail and find out the charge. Then Captain McMurtry and I came here to verify you're a prisoner."

"No one knew? How is that possible?" Eli's hands tightened still further on mine. I didn't care.

"Who is this little bit of fluff, Prince Ilya?" The voice was sarcastic and English.

McMurtry was just close enough. Before he realized it, I unsnapped his holster, pulled out his gun, and pointed it at John Brightwood. "I'm the fluff that's going to shoot your dick off," I said.

Svetlana Ustinova laughed. "And what would John be without his dick?" she said.

"Brightwood," Eli said, in a level voice. "This is Lizbeth Rose."

The English grigori actually stopped laughing. "This little gal? She's the one killed Marty and Varvara?"

McMurtry was tolerating the situation. But that wasn't going to last long. He'd realize I'd taken the only firearm in this area.

"Tell me," I said to Eli. "We can end this now." I'd shoot McMurtry first, because he was capable. Then Hubble, to shut her up. Get the keys from Hubble. Unlock Eli's door. Maybe the others' doors, too, to confuse the issue.

"I'm going to regret this, but no, Lizbeth."

I thought he was wrong, but this was his country. I returned the gun to McMurtry, who snapped it into his holster. While McMurtry's eyes were on his gun, I slipped the turquoise from behind my belt and into my hand. My other hand went right in front of Hubble's face, and I snapped my fingers. Hubble had been mouthing off, but she glared at my fingers and ignored everything else, which had been my goal.

"Pretty sure about the regret, Eli," I said. "We could be out of here." I took his hand again and pressed Felicia's turquoise into his palm.

"Where would we go?" Eli's eyes were sad, and the blood was wrung out of my heart with his desperation. He let go of my hand, his fingers closing over the smooth turquoise. For the first time, I took in what he was wearing: sort of pajamas, to my eyes, a loose top and pants with no belt or suspenders, no socks, just some kind of slippers on his feet. "We have to make the best of this."

"I understand." I didn't, not really; but it was time to leave, no matter how much I wanted to stay with him. "What shall I tell the tsarina?"

"Tell her I have been imprisoned here for weeks without being charged with a crime," Eli said. "The jailers keep telling me we'll all be going before a tribunal of our peers, but that hasn't happened yet, and no one seems to know when it will."

"Were you brought in the same time as Eli?" I asked John Brightwood.

"Two days before," Brightwood said. "Jane and Svetlana the day after me."

"Tell the tsarina we are loyal," Svetlana called.

"Tell her we cannot protect her if we are in jail!" This from Jane Parvin.

Captain McMurtry wanted to wrap this up. He told them, "We've heard everything you've said, and we'll tell the tsarina and the tsar."

"You've been charged with murder," I told Eli, at the moment a silence had fallen.

"The murder of . . . who?" Eli said, finally.

"I got no idea. I'll try to find out."

"All right!" Hubble shouted, her authority finally seeping back into her. "You four shut your damn mouths. The tsarina don't care about you."

I turned on the woman. "She does care. She sent me here to see what was happening. And I will tell her." If she chose to take that as a threat, so be it.

Eli slid the amulet into his pocket while everyone else was looking at me. His hand was open when I glanced back at him. I had done everything I could do.

Hubble yelled, "You, Rose! Out, now! And McMurtry, you with her."

"I'm staying at the Balboa Palace," I told Eli. "I'm in touch with Felix and your family and Felicia." There was more I wanted to say, but not in front of all these people. I had the little black velvet bag around my neck, hidden in the dress. I pulled it up a little for him to see. "Good-bye for now."

"For now," Eli said. And all of a sudden, he smiled.

Turning and walking away was even more painful than I had imagined.

But I did it.

CHAPTER TWELVE

We got back to Imperial Island much faster than we'd gotten to the jail, or so it felt to me. I had a lot to think about, and Captain McMurtry hadn't had much to say on our way, not that I cared.

Maybe I'd angered McMurtry by drawing his gun. Maybe he'd been scared of the other grigoris (I'd be interested to know what charges the other three faced). Maybe the captain had been as astounded by the stupidity of Hubble as I'd been. Had the San Diego PD chosen their most useless officer to oversee the grigoris, because it wouldn't make any difference if she died? Or had Hubble been selected because two of the grigoris were women?

"Hubble is a null," McMurtry said, as if he'd been reading my thoughts. "They had to find a null to guard the grigoris."

I'd forgotten what that meant. But I wasn't in an asking-questions kind of mood. "She's the most incompetent guard I've ever seen," I said.

"Bottom of the barrel," McMurtry agreed. And we fell back into silence.

For my purposes, it was good she wasn't better at her job. But for Eli's protection and well-being, Hubble needed to be smarter and more alert.

I'd gotten control of myself by the time I arrived back in the room where the "best" people were still gathered. Lucky I had, because I saw the tsarina hadn't been waiting with bated breath for my report. Vasily, son of Grand Duke Alexander, was standing in front of her, and his mouth was moving. Caroline looked at him intently, but I was pretty sure she was hearing *Blah blah blah*, since she wasn't reacting to his words at all.

The man seemed to talk forever. Finally, Caroline was able to beckon Captain McMurtry forward when Vasily's lips stopped flapping. McMurtry took my arm and propelled me over to the tsarina. I had to resist the impulse to yank my arm away from his grasp. Not used to people taking hold of me.

Following McMurtry's lead, I bowed to Caroline. I didn't miss the sneer on Vasily's face as I straightened. Caroline glanced at the man but didn't seem to find a way to tell him to get lost.

"Did you find Ilya?" Caroline asked.

McMurtry squeezed my arm a little. So I was supposed to answer, not him.

"Yes, Your Imperial Highness, Eli is in the jail. There's a special group of cells for holding grigoris. There are three others in there." I wasn't surprised that a lot of people in the room had fallen silent and moved closer. Who wouldn't want to know what the tsarina was worried about?

My information appeared to be shocking to everyone in the room, though that couldn't be the case.

"Who are the imprisoned?" Caroline said. If this wasn't news to her, she was doing a good acting job.

Captain McMurtry took a turn answering. "Four, your highness. Eli, Jane Parvin, Svetlana Ustinova, and John Brightwood."

"This must be brought to my husband's attention," Caroline said, and the captain sort of loomed over her, obviously hoping to get the job. It worked. "Captain McMurtry, since you accompanied Miss Rose to the prison, please go inform my husband about what you saw."

McMurtry bowed and departed.

I was envious of royalty's ability to get results. All of a sudden, I was tired of being here, tired of wearing someone else's clothes, and I was definitely in need of some thinking time.

I wondered how to excuse myself. The white-haired woman was near me, and I sidled over to ask her how to leave. It would be bad to simply walk out. There had to be a procedure. I got in Xenia Alexandrovna's line of sight and raised my eyebrows.

"Miss Rose begs for your permission to depart, Caroline," Xenia Alexandrovna said quietly. "She wants to tell Eli's mother and sisters about what she's discovered."

"Oh, of course!" Caroline really didn't want me to leave without further talk, I could tell, but she realized that Eli's family should come first. I was kind of amazed. Myself, I'd really wanted to leave so I could tell all this to Felix . . . and my sister, if he hadn't taken her back to the school yet.

I bowed again and eased my way back until I figured the crowd obscured me. Then I made haste to leave the palace, and this time I didn't need anyone to lead me to the front door.

I didn't worry about who drove me to the civilian parking lot this time. I'd seen Eli. I figured that was what they hadn't wanted me to do.

I'd wondered what I'd do if Felix hadn't followed us back. When I spotted his old car, I felt relieved. He was alone. I was relieved and sorry. I'd had some questions for my sister, but today had been a big old mountain, and I needed to climb down before I tackled Felicia.

I'd no sooner set my bottom on the seat than Felix said, "Did you see him? How is he?"

And at that moment, I understood everything.

I stowed it away to think about later.

"He seemed okay," I said. "No signs of torture. The same grigoris are in with him that Peter named: Ustinova, Brightwood, Parvin. They're in staggered cells, so they can't look directly at each other." I wasn't surprised that Felix had a piece of paper to hand me, along with a pencil. I drew a sketch.

"Where are the toilets and sinks?" Felix asked.

"At the back right corner of each cell. The mattress is on a metal ledge, attached to the wall." I'd never seen such a thing. I'd only been in one jail as a prisoner, and Eli's cell had been real nice compared to that one.

We went over the security, such as it was.

Felix looked disgusted at my account of Hubble, and he said, "She has to be a blank, a null. That's the only reason they'd send her down there, unless they wanted her to die."

"McMurtry said she was a null. What's that mean?"

"Blank cartridges have no explosive force, am I correct?"

"More or less."

"There are humans who are like that. Blanks, nulls, voids, whatever you call them. They can't be affected by magic, and magic can't be worked in their presence."

I had never heard of such a thing. "It must be rare," I said.

"Very. Thank God." There was a pause; we were both thinking.

"Did you believe that Captain McMurtry knew about the first driver, the official one in the palace employ?"

"The one Felicia told us not to ride with."

"Yes."

I tried to recall McMurtry's reaction. "I didn't think he was in on anything. He seemed . . . willing to go along with Felicia's warning. He didn't ask any questions. At the time, I was just relieved."

"So you think he is sincere. Not in on any plot."

"That's a big thing to give an opinion on, based on a car ride together. I did think he was being straight with me, with us. I think he's driven by ambition to rise higher in the imperial service, so he's looking out for opportunities to do that." I looked around me. "We need to get out of this parking lot. No one else is sitting in cars talking. They get in, they leave."

Felix kind of shook himself and turned on the engine. We drove back across the bay. "Do you want to go with me to the Savarovs' house?"

I did and I didn't. I wanted to return the dress and retrieve my own clothes. I wanted to tell Veronika about Eli. But I also wanted to think about everything that had happened this long day, and I wanted to eat. Now that I'd seen Eli, alive, breathing, knowing me, I had felt something relax inside me.

"They'll be waiting to hear," I said. Couldn't decide.

"Let's go there." Felix turned left and began to make his way to the house on Hickory.

We fell into silence. I wanted to ask him about Felicia, what he thought about her age and her abilities. I had thought I was sending her to the Rasputin School so she would have a safe place to live and food to eat while she grew up and learned how to make some kind of living in a city with more opportunities than Ciudad Juárez or Segundo Mexia. Instead, I had sent her to the place where she could learn how to be a grigori herself. Did the teachers at the school know about Felicia's talent and true age? Or had she fooled them like she'd fooled me?

I didn't think Felicia had set out to deceive me. After all, we'd had so little time together before she'd had to leave with Eli. She'd just let me believe . . . what seemed likely to me. And her letters to me had been monitored, at least in the beginning. I shook my head in admiration. I'd been gotten, good and proper. My sister was smart and unpredictable. She'd given me the turquoise to let me know what she was, and I hoped Eli could figure out what it did. Whatever the spell in the stone, it wouldn't work around Hubble.

As Felix had done before, he drove to the parking apron behind the Savarov house. I wasn't surprised that their yard lights—if they had any—weren't on, and only one light was visible in the back of the house. How could they be sure we were coming tonight? They'd probably figured we'd been arrested, too. And I still had to tell the three women everything that had happened. As I climbed out of Felix's car, I was tangled in my thoughts and very tired. From the slump in Felix's shoulders, he felt the same.

And that was when we were attacked.

CHAPTER THIRTEEN

Fighting for your life clarifies your thoughts and gives you a boost of energy. Without that, you would die.

My body reacted before my mind could tell me, *She's trying to kill you.*

I pulled up my dress, pulled out a knife, and flung it. If my body hadn't done that (all on its own), I would have been a dead woman. Katharine Demisova died instead. As she fell, I recalled her name and put it to her face. She was the grigori who'd been waiting, along with Derek Smythe, outside the Balboa Palace when Felix had dropped me off the other night.

I have to admit it was a lucky throw. She'd heard I was a shooter, so she'd squatted to let the shot go over her. So the knife had taken her in the throat rather than her ribs. I took a second to be surprised and grateful before I turned to help Felix. He hadn't been as lucky. Derek Smythe was not at all surprised by Felix's magic. Derek was primed to combat it.

He was not primed for being tackled from behind. Which was what I did.

The grigori didn't have time to catch himself. He yelled as he went down, and his homburg flew off as his head hit the ground. I grabbed his greasy hair with my right hand and slammed his face into the pavement. Felix pointed a finger at Smythe's head, whispering a few words.

Then Smythe lay still forever.

As Felix and I stood there panting in the dim backyard, lights began to come on in the house, and I could hear Lucy's voice calling to her mother.

The big light came on over the garage door.

Veronika, Lucy, and Alice poured out of the back door in their dressing gowns, each armed with a knife. I was astonished, as much as I had energy to be. The women weren't as helpless as I'd thought.

When they recognized us, the three stopped in their tracks. They looked down at the bodies on the ground. They looked back at us. They did not faint. They did not vomit.

"I saw Eli. He's alive and well," I said.

And that was the most important thing.

On the way back to the hotel, I thought how strange it was that no one else's lights had come on. Had all the neighbors been pretending the backyard attack did not wake them?

In fairness, the fight itself had been quick and quiet. But Lucy, Alice, and Veronika had come out of the house shouting. And when the big light over the garage door had come on, I'd felt like it could have been seen from the moon.

Since the neighbors were ignoring any hoo-rah from the Savarov house, I hoped they'd also been blind to Felix and me loading the bodies into the trunk of his car.

We couldn't think of anything else to do with Demisova and Smythe. We couldn't bury them in the backyard. Lucy suggested we pitch them over the fence, because their neighbors to the north had some vicious dogs, but she got voted down. "Maybe the dogs would eat them," Lucy said. "Or maybe the dogs would get blamed for the killing of them."

I thought it wasn't a bad plan, and at least it would be easy and quick. But no one else was in favor.

"Too close to home," Veronika said.

"Mother, no one will marry us," Alice said. "We might as well."

Veronika's mouth set in a hard line. "Not here," Veronika insisted.

"No, Lizbeth and I will remove them," Felix said firmly. "They were here to kill us, so we are responsible."

Maybe because I was tired, very tired—today I'd killed a dead man, saved the tsarina, gotten dressed up by Eli's mother, gone to court, gotten a killer turquoise from my little sister who probably wasn't so little, visited Eli, and killed a grigori—I thought this was a funny conversation. I had to bite my lips to keep from laughing.

Felix shot me a grim look.

He opened his car trunk and went to Demisova's head, waited for me to pick up her legs, and in she went. Smythe followed. "Ladies, please turn away," Felix said, and I knew he didn't mean me. He had to close the trunk, and the bodies were going to suffer for it. I had to help him push down. Finally, we heard the trunk latch engage.

"I'm sorry about the dress," I told Veronika. "I'll get it cleaned and return it."

"Please don't bother," she said courteously. "It's yours now."

I wasn't going to go down a list of items of hers I was wearing or carrying and ask her about each item. "Thank you," I said.

We agreed I'd return the next day and tell them everything. "Where's that Natalya?" I asked. Seemed strange the maid wasn't out here with us.

"She doesn't live here, thank God," Lucy said. "She comes in the morning at seven, and she leaves in the evening at six."

I liked this girl more and more.

"She's a spy," Alice said, like she was mentioning Natalya had gray in her hair.

"I figured."

"But she does put in a good day's work, and we could do worse," Veronika said. "We'll come out in the morning, early, and check the gravel for blood."

My first impression of Eli's mom and sisters had been wrong. Not that they weren't very different from me. They were. But in some ways, we did think alike. They went back in the house, and Felix and I set out on our last task of the night.

We threw the bodies into the water, I don't know where. This had never been a choice anywhere else I'd been, so I was real pleased with how simple it was.

I was so glad to see the Balboa Palace I could have clapped. The night clerk stared at my dress in amazement as I passed him on the way to the elevator. The same glum woman took me to the third floor and stared at me, too. I was glad to hear the elevator doors slide shut behind me. I opened the door to my room, standing to one side, knife in my hand.

There was no one waiting for me.

I shucked off all my borrowed finery, washed my face and brushed my teeth, and crawled into the bed. I pulled the blanket up. I looked over to the door to check that I'd locked it, and I turned out the bedside lamp. But it took me a while to sink into sleep.

I'd finally seen Eli. He'd smiled.

It was full sun the next day when the knocking on the door

woke me up. I crept over to listen. One person outside, as far as I could tell. I pulled on my blue jeans and a shirt and opened the door cautiously. Peter.

"Where have you been?" I said. "I expected to see you yesterday. I saw your brother. Have you been by your mom's?" I stood back to let him in.

"I did go by this morning," Peter said. "Lucy was outside in her bathrobe hosing down the gravel in front of the garage, and she wouldn't tell me why. Why?"

That was a poser. If his sister didn't want to tell Peter what had happened, maybe there was a reason. Peter was hotheaded, sure enough, but he was also devoted to his brother.

"Have you had breakfast?" I said.

"No, not yet."

"Then let me finish getting dressed, and we'll get some." I realized that I was very, very hungry. I hadn't eaten much the day before, and I had done a lot of things. I went into the bathroom, got myself set for the day, and emerged feeling like Lizbeth instead of a lady going to court.

We left the hotel and went to a pancake place across the street. It was full of people drinking coffee and eating to start up their working day. None of them wore uniforms or grigori vests. I checked.

After we'd ordered and I'd had a sip of coffee, Peter said, "I thought I was going to be in on every plan."

"I thought you were, too. But Felix told me where to be and what to do, more or less, and that ended up with me getting to see Eli."

"Mother tells me you saved the tsarina's life." Yeah, he was pouting.

I raised my hand and tilted it back and forth. "In a sense."

Peter waited for me to explain. He was not my favorite person to be with in the morning, I decided. There were things I didn't want to say out loud where anyone could overhear, no matter how uninterested the other customers seemed to be in our conversation. And Peter should know that. Instead, he was doing everything but tapping his fingers on the table to let me know how impatient he was.

"I'll tell you later," I said. Used the voice that would let Peter know I wanted to make something real clear.

"You and Felicia are friends, right?" I asked instead, to change the subject.

Peter looked startled. "Yes, we are," he said, real cautiously, like I might be trying to trap him.

"How old do you think she is, really?"

Peter's mouth literally hung open for a few seconds. "I don't know," he said, in a tone that let me know he was thinking about it for the first time ever. "She looks real young, but she acts a lot older." He considered it. "I'd average it out, say she's thirteen or fourteen." Then he realized that, to his mind, I'd asked a strange question. "But you should know."

"You've spent way more time with her than I have." I hadn't known Eli had kept the story of Felicia and her circumstances to himself. I pondered the reasons he'd done that.

Peter gave me a blank look.

"What do you see in your future, Peter?" I hadn't known what I'd ask him until it popped out of my mouth.

"I will be a grigori, like Eli," Peter said, as if that were the stupidest thing anyone had ever asked him.

"But your older brothers and your father have disgraced your family. Do you . . ."

"Understand that may affect my career? Of course I understand it."

Here was the bitterness. I waited for him to go on, and he did.

"But what else can I do? This is what I am. And now that Eli has been arrested, the care of my mother and my sisters is on my shoulders, since my half brothers will only shuffle Lucy and Alice off their hands like cards. To whatever friend of theirs needs a noble wife."

I waited some more.

"Eli and I, once he is out of jail, will bring our family back into good repute."

He really said "good repute." I waited, because there was more to drain out of this sore spot. Though Peter was doing a good imitation of someone who was facing facts . . . he hadn't faced them all.

"You're assuming Eli gets out of jail," I said, when I ran out of patience.

Peter's face had been still, but it froze harder. "Why would he not?"

"Because he was jailed on a murder charge."

"Murder?" Peter looked even worse now, like someone struggling to get out of a nightmare.

"Yes."

"He told you." Peter looked really upset and angry, as well.

"No. You're going to." I wasn't sure I could kill Peter, since Eli loved him. But at the moment, I felt like giving it a try.

Peter lurched to his feet and walked out the door. I threw some money on the table and followed. We walked in silence back to my hotel and went up to my room.

I was relieved, because this was the only place we could be sure we wouldn't be interrupted. I was tired of Peter's moods.

When we were inside, we sat on the two wooden chairs set on

either side of a tiny table. Peter threw himself back. His body said, *Look how miserable I am!* I crossed my arms across my chest and waited.

Finally, Peter quit waiting for me to ask him what was wrong. "I killed Ivan Nichinko," he said.

"Am I supposed to know who that is?"

"No," Peter said grudgingly. "Ivan is—was—a friend of Bogdan's, my older half brother, and while I was escorting Lucy and Alice to their library visit . . . they go once a week . . ."

I might give Peter a good slap.

"We encountered Ivan. I thought it was by accident, but now I think he planned it. Maybe our brother told him the girls' routine. There's an obvious route."

I nodded, hoping that would hurry Peter along.

"We had to speak to him," Peter said, looking down at his hands. "We didn't have a choice."

They'd had a choice, but Peter would never believe that. Not the way he'd been brought up.

"I didn't want to. Not only is he a boor, but Ivan had been paying attentions to Alice, who is twenty years younger than him. Alice gets very nervous when she has to speak to him. He likes—liked—to *scare* her. That afternoon he crossed the boundary as no man should with a respectable girl. Not trying to *interest* her, or *charm* her . . . to *seduce* her. Like she was no one who counted."

"He put his hands on her?" I wasn't clear what had happened.

"He said . . ." Peter made a strange face. "He said he could smell her sweet . . . female smell. I thought Alice would vomit. Or run."

"Did you kill him then and there?" I had uncrossed my arms. I was feeling a little better about Peter.

"I didn't want to do that in front of the girls."

Who were just about women, especially Lucy. After last night, I would not underrate the Savarov ladies. I nodded, to get Peter started again.

"Ivan lives—lived—not too far from Felix. It wasn't hard to find. I hid in his backyard that evening, and when he returned from his dinner . . ." Peter was breathing in deep, gusty lungsful. He sure was emotional.

"You killed him. How?"

"I pulled the blood out of his body."

"Which is something Eli can do." I could see where this was going.

"Yes. That was my mistake."

"That was one of your mistakes."

"I had to do it!"

"I don't dispute that," I said. No point, it was done. "But if you felt you had to do it, you should have waited a week or two. I guess Ivan wasn't by himself when he had this conversation with Alice?"

Peter turned red. "One of his friends was with him."

"There's your big mistake. You should have killed the friend, too."

Peter's mouth hung open. He had not expected that piece of advice. But it was golden.

"That would have left you free and clear, and you could have warned Eli to have an alibi for that night. Learn from your mistakes."

Peter was vastly relieved to have gotten this off his chest. I could tell he was delighted I hadn't told him he was a bad, bad boy for defending his sister's honor. I did have some issues with that, as you can imagine. Alice should be able to defend her own honor. It was her right. That having been said, this asshole Ivan had needed a takedown, though Peter's response had been pretty drastic. Hot-tempered and young.

"Would you have done the same thing?" Peter said. "When you were my age?"

"I don't have any sisters," I said, and then corrected myself. "I grew up as an only child. But if someone had said such a disgusting thing to me . . ."

Peter nodded vigorously.

"I might have shot him somewhere that wouldn't have killed him. Like his crotch. Or a foot or knee."

"When you were sixteen?"

"Sure. Why not?"

"You . . . were shooting people then?"

"That was the year I joined my first crew."

I didn't know why Peter was so taken aback. The boy was looking at me with different eyes. Didn't like what he saw. Good. One problem out of the way.

"So who's the witness?" Maybe this situation could be salvaged.

"Dima Zaitsev. He's a carpenter, working on the royal island now."

"Where does he live?"

"He rooms with a family close to the waterfront," Peter said. "I don't know the house, exactly."

"How much do your half brothers know about this?"

"I'm sure it was Bogdan who urged Dima to report the words I had with Ivan to the police after Ivan's body was found."

"But Bogdan would have figured it was you who did the killing, wouldn't he?"

"Bogdan doesn't know me very well," Peter said. "But he knows Eli is dangerous to him. Bogdan and Dagmar want Eli out of the way."

"Why?"

"Because Eli stands between Bogdan and Mother and the girls. Now that our father is dead, and was exposed as a traitor, Bogdan and Dagmar have had a much harder time making their way in society. In fact, they won't, unless they somehow get a lot of money. That will open a few doors. The only easy money they can see is money they'd get from the house sale, if they could force Mother and the girls to move. And if they sell the girls in marriage. As long as Eli is around, that won't happen. They weren't reckoning with me." Peter's back straightened. He was the man who had dealt with the problem, in his own head.

"You, who so bravely got Eli arrested," I said.

It was like I had hit Peter. I was a little ashamed (because it was so easy) and a little angry (because he was missing the point). Peter was not taking the burden of what he had done, only the credit. He expected Eli to squirm out of his situation, some way or other.

"I didn't think that would happen. The arrest." Peter hung his head again.

"It's hard to believe you really thought that, since you just gave me a reasoned-out statement of why it would. You commit a murder using Eli's technique—one no one knows you can do, I'll bet—and it's the murder of a buddy of your half brothers, who are looking for an excuse to get rid of Eli. And you left a witness."

Peter looked so miserable I almost felt sorry for him . . . but only a pampered teenager would imagine that he was blameless. Right? And this had caused the arrest of my Eli.

"Does your mother know all this?"

"No," Peter said, choking. "No. Even the girls . . . but maybe they suspect."

This was beginning to feel like kicking a puppy, but he had been so stupid about the whole thing. I couldn't even be around Peter now.

"I'm off," I said. "I'll talk to you later when I've thought about this."

"You'll . . . you'll save Eli? Still?"

"I'll do everything I can. Doesn't have anything to do with you," I said.

He stood up, looked at me helplessly for a moment, and left without another word.

I needed to walk myself, so I waited until Peter had time to be a few blocks away before I got to the street. I'd been awful hard on the boy. Eli would have been upset, probably.

On the other hand, Eli could have been by my side at this moment if Peter hadn't acted like a fool.

Dima Zaitsev had to go. And it couldn't look like death-by-wizard—which was lucky, because I'd have a hard time imitating a wizard.

I felt powerfully unhappy. This was not the way I operated. I hadn't ever killed someone outside of work, true. But there was a difference between defending your cargo and killing someone to shut his mouth. Also, this wasn't the first time I'd had to assassinate someone when I was working for Eli.

I cast around for a way to feel better, and I found one. Eli was my cargo. My job was to defend my cargo.

There was so much truth in this that my world righted itself, and I felt steady. Zaitsev had to go.

Back in my hotel room, I checked my telephone book, but

Zaitsev didn't have a phone. And I didn't know where he roomed. I could have stood by the ferry when it came back from the royal island, scanned the faces, and followed him home . . . if I knew what he looked like.

I knew someone who did.

The hateful Natalya answered the telephone. "Savarov residence," she said, as if she was daring me to ask for something.

"Lucy, please," I said.

"May I tell Miss Lada who is calling?"

This was probably standard, I felt sure, but it felt snide and personal.

"This is her friend Amanda," I said.

Without another word, Natalya put the phone down on something wooden and hard. She was gone quite a while. Maybe she'd stopped off on her way to Lucy's room to clean the bathroom.

I heard footsteps. The telephone was lifted. "Hello?" Lucy said, with a big question in her voice.

"Hi, Lucy. It's Lizbeth. I didn't want to tell Natalya the Spy it was me," I said. "She probably guessed from my voice."

"Or from the fact that very few people call us anymore."

"I need your help," I said.

"Really?" Lucy sounded not only interested but surprised.

"What time did that really unpleasant meeting outside the library happen?" I was willing to bet money that Veronika didn't know about the incident. I was being cautious in my words so Lucy would be cautious, too.

"Oh! The last time Peter escorted us there?"

Had there been more than one? "Yes, that one," I said. "Was this a normal thing? Being . . . accosted?"

"Normal for *them*, Dima and Ivan. That was why we asked Peter to go with us. I had taken as much insult as I could, and Alice was getting very . . . ah, anxious about it. But we didn't want Mother to know. We usually go to the library about nine. We like to be there early. Fewer people to snub us."

"A weekday or on Saturday?" I assumed the library was closed on Sunday, like almost everything else.

"It was a Thursday. We always go on Thursday."

Sure, because why make it harder for people who wanted to lie in wait? "All right, here's what I need," I said. I'd gathered from scraps of conversations that there were various shifts of workers on the royal island: construction workers from six to noon, the second shift from noon to six, six days a week. There were also cleaners who came in at night to clean halls and offices and kitchens, and cleaners who worked during the day on bedrooms and the personal areas. If the Savarovs had encountered carpenter Dima in the morning, he must work the afternoon shift. So we could catch him. I explained my reasons to Lucy.

"I can't go out by myself," Lucy said.

"Even if you're meeting me?"

"No. Not done." Lucy didn't sound angry about this, just factual.

I thought if Lucy was such a pariah, she could do what she damn well pleased, but I didn't say that. Not my life. I cast around for a way to get around this. "Could you go out with Felix?"

"Yes, if you were with us."

"I'll talk to him and get back with you."

Telephones were handy things. I talked to Felix in the next five minutes and explained the whole Peter issue, what I'd concluded, and what I thought we could do.

"So you and Lucy and I will watch for this Dima, and you'll kill him," Felix said. At least he sounded workmanlike about this.

"Not then and there, but yes, that's the plan. There won't be a witness who can incriminate Peter, 'cause he won't be anywhere around. And Eli will be in his cell. So Eli won't be obliged to take the weight for Peter. He'll be released." It seemed simple to me.

"There are some flaws in your reasoning," Felix said in his extra-dry voice. "But I agree that Dima being out of the way would be a good thing. And of course, spending time in your company is always entertaining."

I was sure he was making fun of me, but I didn't care. "You'll get to spend time with Lucy."

"And that's the consolation. When and where?"

"You and I have to go together to pick Lucy up at her house. Lucy says she has to have both of us. Seems you have to protect us by just being a man, and I have to protect Lucy because you are a man. Let's try to catch Dima when he gets off shift at six this afternoon."

"I'll pick you up at four forty-five. We have to get across town and back to the pier."

"Okay."

Felix hung up. I guess saying good-bye would have been too much trouble.

That left me with a hunk of empty time. I'd have liked to spend some time with Felicia, but since she'd missed a lot of class hours the day before singing at the palace, I didn't want to disrupt her school hours today. I could not do any of the things I'd normally do: hunt, shoot at targets, clean my cabin, do my wash, take care of my neighbor Chrissie's baby. Since my last crew had fallen apart—all but one were dead—I'd taken to helping Freedom, son of my friend Galilee, who had started making furniture in a shed in his backyard. Father-hood had improved Freedom's character, and there was something satisfying about making things that people could use.

I went to the zoo. The desk clerk had told me it was a marvel. I'd never seen a zoo.

Two hours later, I knew I'd never go to one again. No matter how interesting it was to see animals I'd never seen before, it was depressing as hell. All the animals reminded me of Eli, shut in a cage.

I sat on a bench and stared at a bear pacing back and forth until an old man asked me if I was okay. I said, "Yes," but I knew I wasn't. I took myself out of the zoo and walked back to the area of my hotel. I'd dropped Veronika's dress by a cleaner's, and I picked it up and hung it in my room's wardrobe. It was the only thing there.

Since I was tired of thinking about getting Eli out of jail, I thought about how I stuck out like a sore thumb on the streets. Not enough that people would start laughing and pointing, but a lot of people gave me a second look, and that wasn't good.

As I had noticed my first day in the city, there were women wearing pants, but they weren't my kind of pants. I figured anything with legs was easier than a skirt or a dress. I hadn't wanted to be in the city long enough to need to blend in, but here I still was.

So I went shopping.

I had only been in a women's store once before, and it hadn't been a good time. So I sort of crept in and tried to look at pants by myself, but that didn't work. The middle-aged gal was on me like white on rice. I have to admit she was a lot of help.

"You're from out of town," she said brightly. "Can I help you?" She didn't sound superior or disgusted.

"I want to blend in," I said. Might as well lead with my chin.

"No harm looking cute while you blend, right?" She smiled at me. "I'm Margaret."

"Margaret, I'm Lizbeth. I figure I need some pants, a blouse, a jacket, and some shoes. Walking shoes."

"Then we better get to work. We don't sell shoes, but there's a ladies' shoe store on the next block, Florence's City Steppers."

An hour later, I got back to my room with my two bags. I'd had to insist on flat shoes, but I'd gotten them. And socks. And very roomy gray pants with a white blouse, and a navy jacket. My old belt would do, I figured. I'd almost gotten a hat, but I'd added the price of my purchases in my head and put it back on its rack.

I was all fixed up when Lucy and Felix pulled up to the curb. Felix kept looking past me until I got in the back seat.

"You look so nice!" Lucy said. "Mother won't let us wear trousers."

"These your own?" Felix said. He was being snooty again. I didn't understand Felix.

"Yes, bought and paid for," I said, lest he should think I'd stolen them.

Lucy kept up a conversation while Felix drove in grumpy silence down to the island ferry. There was a big car lot outside the gates to the ferry entrance, and he had to park far from the docking area.

Lucy had a hat on, which was good, because maybe she wouldn't be as recognizable. As we walked to a spot closer to the gate, she said, "My mother has petitioned for Eli's release. She filed the petition with the proper judge this morning."

"On what grounds?"

"Because he hasn't been formally charged in court, like American law demands, and that's still the law here . . . though our Russian justice system . . ."

Here Felix made a rude noise.

"Hush!" Lucy said sternly. "As I was trying to say before Felix so rudely interrupted me, Lizbeth, our system of laws from Russia is very different, and there's still a lot of talk and—palaver?—about whether the tsar will agree to the American system in place or whether everything will change. There's been time. I think Tsar Nicholas was reluctant to, uh, rock the boat."

"If Alexei has a brain, there will only be minor alterations," Felix said. "He is in place as emperor, but if he starts making life miserable for the people, instead of adding glamor and stability, he may find himself back on a boat."

"I agree," Lucy said.

Felix turned to look at her in astonishment. "You do?"

"Why are you surprised? I, too, have a brain."

I was a couple of steps behind them. I grinned to myself.

"Of course you have," Felix said, in a much quieter and more civil tone.

"Ferry's here," I said, and we picked up our pace.

CHAPTER FOURTEEN

We wanted to see without being seen. On the busy water-front, that was harder than I'd imagined. I picked a spot between the first two rows of cars, which was camouflage, but there was no way to pretend we weren't watching the people get off the ferry. To make it more difficult, there were two ferries, and as soon as one unloaded and started back to the island, another docked in its place. So that we wouldn't present the same grouping, we moved around from time to time briskly. We wanted to look like we had a reason to be there. We didn't want the guards who checked everyone going onto the ferry to notice us and ask us our business.

This late, few people were going to the island: night watchmen, cleaning crews. But there weren't enough of them to provide any kind of smokescreen.

At least the evening was dark and shadowy.

I was glad of my new jacket. Rain was coming soon. The air had turned misty and clammy. I felt damp down to my bones. I wondered if I were coming down with something. I was so seldom ill that I hardly remembered the last time I'd felt bad with anything other than a gunshot or a wreck. I knew a healing spell that Eli had taught me, and there was a little magic in me from the man who'd raped my mother. I chanted the spell silently, hoping it would work, and after a few minutes I did feel better.

People poured off the ferry, men and women alike. Some of them got into automobiles, some of them got on the cable cars making a stop at the entrance to the car park, some of them trudged off into the streets of San Diego. Our cover was vanishing. Soon we would be obvious.

I was ready to kill Dima Zaitsev. I'd steeled myself to do it. I was trying not to think about how unhappy I felt. This was what I had to do to get Eli free. He would do the same for me, I told myself. I could not be any less strong.

I had my hand around the hilt of the knife in my jacket pocket. I hoped to draw this Dima into a shadowy area between parked cars so what I was doing wouldn't be too obvious. Or I could follow him for a few blocks, catch him in a lonely place. If only he didn't cry out . . . I set my teeth and told myself to stop the foolishness.

Then Lucy turned to Felix and said, "There he is, with the beard."

Before I could fix on my target, Felix plunged into the crowd and joined the people walking toward the road. He came up behind one of the men—big, heavy, muffled in a dark coat and cap. Felix got very close to the man's back. In the uncertain light, I saw Felix's mouth move. The man, a tall, heavyset guy with a thick dark beard, started to turn. He opened his mouth as if he were going to say something to Felix in return. The words never came out. His body collapsed to the dirty pavement. Felix sidestepped the fallen man and kept going. Felix jerked his head to make sure we would follow.

I took Lucy's arm to speed her up, as the next person to come along, an elderly woman, stumbled over the body. The woman didn't exactly scream, but she shouted. The guards came running, except for those directly at the ferry gangplank. A number of people simply circled the body and kept their course, anxious to get home and eat and sleep.

As Lucy and I hurried along with them, I talked myself down.

I hadn't had to do it. I had turned myself into iron to get it done, and now I didn't have to kill Dima Zaitsev. It was silly, it was *ridiculous*, that I felt shocked and shivery. It took all I had to keep myself in motion. If I faltered, I would make myself notable, and Lucy, too.

We caught up with Felix and walked along in step. He wouldn't be able to keep it up for long. Death magic took a lot of energy to perform. When he stumbled, I took his left arm while Lucy took his right.

Lucy didn't exclaim or raise a ruckus. Except for a little gasp when Dima had folded to the pavement, she had stayed silent.

None of us spoke for at least three blocks. The crowd thinned as workers branched off to go home. Finally, we stopped and leaned against a shop window.

"I'll go back and get the car," I said, holding out my hand for the keys. It was the least I could do.

Felix fumbled in his pocket and dropped them into my hand.

"Thanks," I said, and he could take that as he wished. Then I took off walking so Felix didn't have to respond. Maybe I was having some of the same reaction as the grigori. I'd hardened myself to do something I didn't want to do, but I'd meant to succeed anyway. Now I felt a hole where Zaitsev's death should be.

A man grabbed my arm. He was rat-faced and stank. "How much for a trip into the alley over there?" he said.

"More than you can pay," I said, and yanked away from him. I'd been sure he'd been going to accuse me of causing Zaitsev's death.

Rat-face stared after me as I went to Felix's car. Maybe he decided that if I could afford a car, I really would charge him too much. He spat and walked away. Not for the first time, I was glad I didn't have to be a whore.

I drove to the corner where Felix and Lucy waited. Felix got in the front seat, where he leaned back, his eyes closed. After a moment, Lucy got in the back. She huddled in a damp heap, her lips pressed together.

I had to do some thinking and figuring, but I made it to Felix's little house.

Lucy said, "Where is this?" She leaned forward, tiny wrinkles in her forehead.

"This is Felix's house," I said.

"Oh! I can't . . ." She took a deep breath. "I can't go into a single man's house, especially at night. Even chaperoned."

I grabbed hold of my temper with both hands. "Then we'll drop Felix off here, so he can sleep. And I'll take you to your house and return here."

"But you should not be here, either!"

"We'll talk about this later." I went around to the passenger side and began hoisting Felix out. Then I held out the keys to Lucy. "If you can get close to the back door without losing your good name, unlock it for me. You don't need to come inside."

I felt like a heel when I saw her eyes were shiny. Until this moment, Lucy had been a champion. She snatched the keys from my hand and stomped up the back steps. After a little fumbling, the girl unlocked the back door and pushed it open. She even reached in and turned on the kitchen light.

I was glad Felix was small as we wove through the kitchen and

into the living room, turned left to go down the hall to the bathroom
and the two bedrooms. It was easy to tell which was Felix's, since the
other one had nothing in it. I wasn't at all surprised to hear Lucy's
footsteps behind me, since she was bound to be curious about a bach-
elor's house, and especially curious about this one because she knew
Felix was interested in her.

Since I wouldn't put it beyond Felix to play dead if he wanted
to listen to what Lucy and I said, I made sure he was out the minute
I eased him onto the bed. I took off his shoes and his jacket (which
involved rolling him from side to side, at which Lucy giggled) and
arranged him on the bed in what looked like a comfortable position.

Lucy was having a good old time looking at Felix's bedroom,
which (like the living room) was neat without being really clean. His
closet door was open, so we could see his three pairs of shoes lined
up, his coat, and some pants and shirts. The top of his chest of draw-
ers held a dish full of coins, some pretty rocks, and a brush and comb
set neatly beside a small mirror.

"I need to use the bathroom," Lucy whispered.

"Go right ahead," I said in a normal voice. Felix wasn't hearing
any of this.

Lucy shut the door behind her, and I heard her say, "Ugh!" Felix
needed to learn how to scrub a toilet and a tub.

I pulled a blanket over Felix, who looked like a nice person
when he was asleep.

I drove Lucy home. We didn't talk much along the way. I was
sure she'd ask questions about how Felix had killed Dima Zaitsev,
but not a one passed her lips. That made me wonder.

I drove to the back door of the Savarov house, which was dark
and silent.

"Good night," Lucy said stiffly. "I didn't mean to be so prissy." And she marched to the kitchen door in the light rain, which had just begun falling.

I waited until she was safely in the house before I turned Felix's car in a circle and left. I'd gone a block or two and was waiting my turn at the stop signal by the corner grocery. I figured I would leave Felix's car at his place, then walk to the Balboa Palace. I glanced over to read the clock in the grocery window. Though this had been another long, long day, the clock read 7:30.

The light changed, and I pushed down on the gas pedal.

And a question popped into my brain.

It was just seven thirty. Why had all the lights been off in the Savarov house?

I even drove a couple more blocks before I turned back, simply because I was tired and didn't want any more problems to solve. I parked on the street. I wanted my guns so bad it hurt.

I snuck up to the house on the grass and slipped into the back-yard. I couldn't avoid the gravel entirely, but I did my best to step softly.

I double-checked the house. There was a very dim glow in Veronika's upstairs bedroom window, like a night-light. That was all.

Absence of light. Absence of sound.

Though Lucy had just returned to the house from a very unusual outing, her mother and sister were not asking her a million questions.

The rain had stopped, but I could feel it in the air. I wished for thunder, but I didn't get it. Got lightning, though, which helped me get right up to the kitchen door without falling on my face. I remembered Lucy had opened the back door without unlocking it. I hoped I could get in.

If I had let Eli's family get killed . . . I couldn't face the thought.

I was quiet as a snake. I turned the doorknob so, so slowly. Unlocked! Crept inside, keeping down. Lucky I had planned on killing Dima Zaitsev, because I had a good knife.

I took my shoes off in the kitchen. I crept to the door leading to the dining room. There was a small glow at the edges. Flickering a little. A candle.

I scoured my head for my memory of the room. I'd walked through it once. A gleaming table with seats for six. A sideboard. Pictures on the wall. Two windows to my left. Curtains must be drawn tight, or I would have seen the candlelight when I'd skirted the house.

I eased the door open a couple of inches. Looked through the crack.

The chair at the foot of the table closest to me had been pulled out of place. But three of the chairs on the long sides of the table were occupied, and the one at the far end was, too.

John Brightwood, the giant grigori who'd been in prison with Eli, was facing me. He had a heaped plate in front of him—chicken, bread, cheese. He was eating with his fingers, wiping them on the table itself. Veronika, Lucy, and Alice were sitting in the side chairs.

The three women watched him. But their bodies didn't make the slightest twitch. Brightwood had frozen them in place.

He had uncovered their breasts and left them sitting there, bare to him and to one another. For these women, this was the last word in humiliation.

I would kill him for this.

Now I regretted giving Eli the spelled rock. I needed to be able to surprise Brightwood. I had no gun. And Felix was out of it for the night. *Dammit.* Not a word I used often, but tonight it fit the bill.

All I had was my ability to resist magic. And a knife. I set myself to action.

I needed to move swiftly, and I needed to shock him. I worked out what I would do.

"Your tits are sagging a bit, Veronika," Brightwood said, pointing a chicken leg at Eli's mother. "Probably breastfeeding all those babies. Who sucked the hardest? Eli? Peter? Or one of these little gals?"

I flung the door open, screamed as loud as I could, and leaped onto the table on my stomach with all the force I could muster. I slid across the polished surface like the wood was greased. My knife arm was extended as I slid, and I sank the knife right into Brightwood's chest, just below the breastbone. He'd had a second to drop the chicken leg and raise his hands, and he fired some magic that skidded past me.

Then John Brightwood looked down at the knife protruding from his chest, half-smiled, said, "Bitch." And died.

I had food all over my arms and face. I pulled the knife out of his chest.

I scrambled backward off the table, not wanting to knock into the three women . . . who were all looking behind me, eyes wild. I whirled to find that Natalya had been standing there the whole time.

Brightwood's spell had hit her, maybe not full force. It hadn't disabled her. The older woman jumped at me, a candlestick in her hand, her face all twisted with rage. She swung hard, aiming for my head, but I squatted and came up under her raised arm. Stabbed her. Yanked back.

Natalya shrieked in pain, and blood bubbled out of her mouth and spotted her uniform. Her arm hung uselessly from her shoulder like it didn't belong to her.

I hung back to see how much fight was left in her. But Natalya was done. She sank to the floor, her back against the wall, and after a few moments, she died, staring into some dark hole I could not see.

CHAPTER FIFTEEN

The Savarov women recovered from the spell Brightwood had put on them pretty quickly, maybe because he was dead.

Alice fell to pieces. She started crying as she pulled her blouse together and fastened two of the buttons.

Lucy got up, though she was shaking like a leaf. She put her arms around her little sister. Veronika pushed back from the table, took care of her clothes, and said, "Alice, take care of your sister's dress." Since Brightwood had ripped Lucy's dress, there really wasn't much that could be done, but Alice pulled herself together enough to help Lucy pull up her bra. Lucy finished buttoning Alice's blouse. Brightwood had been in control of himself when he first got here, but by the time Lucy came in, he was drunk on his power over the women, and he might have been drunk, period. I noticed an amber bottle by the plate of food.

"Thank you," Veronika said, turning to face me. I had slumped down in a chair, the knife still in my hand and dripping blood.

"My job," I said.

"How is that so?"

"You're Eli's family."

A large number of expressions crossed Veronika's face, one after another. I couldn't name them all. She took a deep breath and nod-ded. Now she knew.

"You up to talking?" I asked, when I could be sure my voice was steady.

Veronika said, "Yes." Alice was still sobbing, but other than that sad sound, the house was silent.

"Did John Brightwood tell you how he got out of jail?"

"He said he had gotten time off for good behavior," Lucy said.

"He said Eli had told him to come to our house," Alice said, looking at me with a wet face. She hiccupped a few times.

"He said a lot of things," Veronika added.

"Did you know who he was?" I was trying to keep my voice real even and calm.

"I had heard of him," Veronika said. "At court. How bad he was. But he, Brightwood, was also in jail for murder, like Eli, and I know my son is a good man. There was a chance Brightwood might be also."

"So you let him in."

"No, Natalya did. We only knew after he was inside, and Nata-lya called up the stairs to tell us we had a visitor from the jail, and Alice and I thought it was Eli. We came down the stairs running. But it was Brightwood."

There was a long silence. Alice quit crying, Lucy straightened up and closed her eyes, and Veronika looked like she wanted to be anywhere else.

"So how you want to play this?" I said.

They all looked puzzled. I felt like being anywhere else myself. I took a deep sigh.

"We got to hide the bodies." I was doing a lot of that lately on behalf of the family. "You can call the police in the morning and say you found a lot of blood downstairs, that someone must have broken in after you went to bed, and your maid hasn't shown up to work." Then I had a better idea. "Or you can call 'em right now. Say that John Brightwood broke in and stabbed Natalya, but she stabbed him back and killed him. I'll go back to my hotel now if you want to do that. I'll need a new blouse to get there without someone calling the police on me. Or we can all tell the truth."

Alice and Lucy looked to their mother. Veronika looked at me, then at the bodies, then at me again.

"Brightwood came here because he got released," Veronika said, thinking it through as she spoke. "And he got released even though he is very dangerous. *Was* dangerous. And bad. And his first thought was to come and degrade us? Whom he had never met? I don't think that was his idea."

"I don't, either." In fact, I'd never even considered it.

"So . . . Lizbeth . . . why do you think he came here?"

Veronika'd said my name kind of carefully, like she hadn't expected it to be in her mouth.

"I think he was released to do this," I said. "I think he made a bargain with someone who wanted your house to be his first stop."

"Who would be so evil?" Lucy said. All her fear turned into rage. "And why?"

"You have to know this ties into your . . . Prince Savarov's plot with the grand duke. Alexander. I don't know the tsar, but from what Eli's said about him, I don't think Alexei would do this." Eli might be fooled, or he might have only told me the good stuff. But I didn't think either of those was completely true.

Veronika gave this some consideration. "I agree, but I don't see what killing us, or raping us, or whatever Brightwood intended, would do to further Alexander's ambition. He would have to have an overwhelming number of people on his side to depose Alexei, especially now that there's an heir."

"What if the baby died?"

The three women gazed at me, their mouths open. "Kill the heir?" Veronika said, her voice faltering.

"Brightwood would have had no problem with killing a baby," Lucy said.

"Please, can we move to another room?" Alice said.

"Sure," I said. "And we need to be thinking more about who sent Brightwood here, and if they're going to check up on him. Right now, we need to make up our minds how to handle this."

We moved slowly into the front parlor and took seats.

Lucy said, "I'll vote, like an American! I vote that we tell the police they stabbed each other."

"Whoever sent Brightwood will know that's a lie," Alice said. She was looking a lot better now that she couldn't see the bodies.

"That might be a good way to find out who it was," Veronika said.

"Makes sense. So I need to change and get out of here. My new clothes!" I looked down at the blouse. It wasn't ruined, but it sure wasn't wearable.

"We will soak it in cold water and get the blood out," Veronika said. "You don't want to try to do that in your hotel room."

She was right, I didn't, so I went upstairs with her and gave her my blouse in exchange for one of hers. I watched while she ran water in the sink and dropped the blouse into it. I suggested she and the girls change into their nightgowns and bathrobes, since it was late enough now to make this reasonable. When the blood came out of my blouse, the girls could put their clothes in the washing machine with the blouse, so they could soak and wash in cold water. I was pretty good at getting out bloodstains. I had to be.

"Give me ten minutes to get out of the area," I told Veronika. "I've got Felix's car. We'll talk tomorrow."

"God willing," Veronika said.

"God willing," Alice and Lucy said in unison, as I scooted out the back door. They'd turned on more lights, and I had an easier time of it getting to the car.

It was more a case of our enemies being willing than God, I thought.

I figured police would be quick to answer a call from Hickory Street, so I wasted no time starting back to my hotel. When I got to the corner store, I looked at the clock again. It was less than an hour since I'd stopped there before.

I had to pay attention to my driving. I felt very cold and shivery. If you had to take out a threat, you did, but that had been very close work. Give me a gun to shoot, anytime. Guns were better. You could do the job from farther away.

I tried not to think how near I'd been to dying. If Brightwood's spell had hit me. If the women hadn't warned me to turn to see Natalya. Gunnies didn't live to be old, as a rule, but I wasn't ready to go. Tonight it had been real close.

And what if I hadn't had a feeling things weren't right in the Savarov house? What if I hadn't turned around?

The world owed me a favor for taking out John Brightwood. I smiled at the thought and felt a little better.

I should have left the car at Felix's and caught a cab or walked to the Balboa Palace. But I didn't have the energy. There was a small parking lot behind the Palace, and I found a place for the car there. I walked around the hotel and came in through the front door, as I always had. No point asking for notice.

I crossed the lobby at a brisk pace. After all, I might have missed some blood in my hasty washing-up in Veronika's bathroom. But the desk clerk called, "Miss Rose!" It would have looked strange if I'd ignored him. And I didn't have my key.

I went over to the desk. There was an envelope in the little cubbyhole with my room key.

My friend the clerk handed it to me with a smile, and I smiled back and scuttled away with the letter and the key.

Safely in my room, I took off my new clothes and hung them up, checking them over as I did. A spot on the pants; I'd have to take care of that in the morning. I ran hot water in the tub and climbed in, letting the heat and the lightness of being in water put me in a better frame of mind. I soaked until the water began to cool, and then I bathed and washed my hair. Then I worked on the spot on my pants.

I felt so much better. I opened the letter. It was from Her Imperial Highness, Caroline. No wonder the clerk had been smiling so big. A flunky from the palace had probably delivered it, in some kind of uniform. *Thank you again for saving my life*, Caroline began. *I hope you had a wonderful visit with Ilya Savarov. I have talked to Tsar Alexei about Ilya's imprisonment. He promises to discuss it with his great-uncle, who is the head of state security. Captain McMurtry returned to the city jail to try to get more information about who ordered Ilya's arrest. He tells me one of the grigoris had been released, without a trial or hearing of any kind, a man named John Brightwood. He is not a friend of Ilya's; you might want to keep an eye out for him. As to who was responsible for letting Brightwood out, Captain McMurtry tells me one of the junior adjutants brought a notice of release. This adjutant was an assistant to the aide of Grand Duke Alexander.* The letter was signed *Caroline* in a flourishing hand.

I began laughing, and I couldn't stop. I kind of wound down, like a clock.

CHAPTER SIXTEEN

I didn't sleep long enough, but I slept heavily. You would have thought I'd wiped my thinking slate clean during the night, but the first thing on my mind was how ignorant Tsar Alexei must be. His great-uncle, the man who'd tried to kill Alexei to supplant him, was the man in charge of state security. How's that for stupid? Alexei ruled a chunk of the former America, but he didn't seem to have a clue how to ensure his own safety and that of his wife and child. Someone needed to take him in hand.

As I dressed, I realized I should be counting my blessings. Since no one had shown up to arrest me in the night, Veronika and the girls must have convinced the police no one else had been at their house.

The minute I thought this, there was a knock on my door.

I stuffed my shirt into my jeans and answered it.

Both Peter *and* Felix barged in without asking, steam practically coming out of their noses. Peter's mom had called him lest he hear the news from someone else, and Peter had called Felix, who had had to get a trolley to reach the hotel, whereupon he'd seen his own car parked outside. The moment I shut the door behind them, they launched right into telling me the official story, *yackety yackety yack*. All horrified and angry that neither of them had been there to defend the women.

I sat on the bed to pull on my socks and boots and let them get it out of their systems. I didn't even try to get a word in edgewise.

When they ran down, I said, "I don't know why you're mad. I killed Brightwood and Natalya. They were holding your mother and your sisters hostage. They were scared, and they were humiliated, but they're okay, and they're tough women. They're going to be fine." I was pretty sure I was right. Maybe I only wanted that to be true? No. I was right.

"My mother and my sisters were *abused*. By an air grigori!" Peter said, so angry his jaw looked like iron. "From Eli's own guild!" He hadn't taken in anything I said.

"I know. I was there. I killed him."

And Peter took a deep, shuddering breath. The fire died out in Felix's eyes. All the heat left the two men. I still couldn't figure out why they'd decided to bring all this anger to me, but at least their brains were cooling off.

"Thanks," Felix said. He still sounded stiff. "Thank you, Lizbeth Rose."

"You're welcome, Felix." If Felix didn't watch out, he might end up thinking I was worth the air I was breathing.

"So the tsarina tells me that Grand Duke Alexander is in charge of security," I went on, when neither of them seemed to have anything to add. "And since he's the one who wants to replace Alexei, I think that's the dumbest thing I ever heard. The grand duke's the one who let Brightwood go. Don't you think we need to get rid of him? If you cut off the head of the snake and jump way back, you're going to have a dead snake."

"Kill Alexander," Peter said. "That's a wonderful idea!"

For a second I thought he was mocking me, but he was sincere.

That gave me pause. If Peter thought something was a good plan, I had better take another look.

"No one can get close enough to the grand duke to kill him," Felix said. He was hissing like a snake himself.

"What's stopping them?"

"He has grigoris like Brightwood around him at almost all times. He has an armed bodyguard, too. Alexander has been around long enough to make a lot of enemies, and he is no fool." Felix looked broody for a moment. "No fool at all."

"You're a reanimator. Can you turn that around? Like you did with . . . before?" I didn't want to name names with Peter there. He was too rash.

"Only if I wanted to die in the attempt. It may come to that, but not yet." Felix scowled at me.

"Felix is known to dislike the grand duke," Peter said, sounding unexpectedly grown-up. "Me too. Maybe after saving the tsarina and telling the court you wanted to visit Eli, you've put yourself in the enemy camp publicly. The only person we know who is unknown to the grand duke is Felicia."

The silence was thick and deep. It took a moment for Peter's words to sink in. I admired the sharpness of the idea, while I hated the idea itself. I began to wonder how it could work. "Are you—I hope you're not telling me—that the grand duke likes little girls?" I said, and my voice was warning enough.

Peter was startled. His eyes, so green like Eli's, opened wide. "God, no! I have no notion what he likes to take to bed! But he and his wife have several sons and daughters, so . . ."

"So how do you imagine this scarcely-an-idea might work?"

"I think we'd have to talk to Felicia."

We all looked at something else in my small room while we considered that. "If my sister was a normal eleven-year-old, I wouldn't even consider this," I said. "But she's not. I guess I can call the school and ask to take her out." We scrabbled in our pockets for the right coins, and I walked to the end of the hall to call the school.

There were two rings, and then the phone was picked up. I recognized the voice that said, "Grigori Rasputin School." Tom O'Day, the grigori from Texoma.

"Good morning. This is Lizbeth Rose, Felicia's sister. I'd like to arrange to take Felicia out for the afternoon and to have dinner. I'm not in town for much longer."

"I'll talk to Miss Drinkwater," O'Day said, without sounding like he cared one way or another.

"Thank you. I'll call back in an hour."

"Good-bye, Miss Rose."

Peter had a class to attend. He left, and Felix and I waited. Felix began to write in a little notebook he carried in his pocket. I did not ask him any of the questions I wanted to ask. They were too personal. The last thing I wanted to do was to lose the only strong ally I had here in the Holy Russian Empire.

"I thought I'd hear from Veronika or Lucy today," I said, when I got up to walk to the window. Outside, the sky was dulling. Maybe rain . . . again.

"Probably the police are still at the house," Felix muttered, not lifting his eyes to mine.

"Why?"

"Still asking questions, maybe getting a seer to look at the bodies."

"They do that here? That's not good!"

"Only if you believe in seers," Felix said.

I wanted to smack the sneer off his face. "Why would I not?" I said. "After what I've seen."

"Did Paulina really turn into a zombie?" Felix had a look of professional curiosity.

"Yes."

"I am not surprised that you think seers are real," he said after a moment's consideration. "But sometimes when a reanimator is on hand, they lay a spell on the dying, that they'll rise again. I think one of the grigoris you killed in Mexico was a reanimator, like me. If I were to guess, I would guess that was Clemence Parry, since I haven't seen him in months."

I shrugged. Might have been. I'd killed a lot of grigoris in Mexico. All of a sudden, I wondered why. "Felix, who were they after, you think? If they were after Eli, why? Because he was bringing help for the tsar? Or were they after Felicia, because she had the right blood? And if Alexander sent them . . . that was a lot of grigoris sacrificed for nothing. Because Eli lived, and Felicia lived, and I lived." I stopped, struck by that question, which had never crossed my mind until now.

"Alexander doesn't care how many people die in his service," Felix said. "He considers his cause just. How is that any different from you? Do you care how many people you have to kill to do your job?"

I sat on the side of my bed and looked at Felix, considering. "When I sign on with a crew, I've promised to do my job. Whatever that involves. And some of it I haven't liked very much, I can tell you that." I looked at the clock on the bedside table. "Time to call the school."

I went into the booth at the end of the hall, sat on the small bench. I looked down at the slip of paper where I'd written the school number. I got out the correct coins. I didn't shut the door all the way, because it made me feel tight in the chest to be shut in such a tiny space. That meant the overhead light didn't come on to signal the booth was occupied, but I'd rather have dark and an opening than light and a closed space.

I listened to the phone ring at the grigori school. After it rang six times, I wondered where Tom O'Day had gone. I hung up.

A smartly dressed woman emerged from the elevator and let herself into her room. A heavy man opened his door and plodded toward the elevator. As he got on, someone else got off. The newcomer was a grigori—vest, tattoos. A woman in her forties, maybe, with short wavy hair and a big scar on her left cheek. I could not hear her steps as she passed the phone booth. Since the light wasn't on, she didn't even glance over to see if anyone was inside.

I hadn't locked the room door as I left. Felix was expecting me to return. She might get the drop on him. But what if she was a friend? I doubted that, knowing Felix, but maybe he had an ally or two.

I didn't even have a knife this time.

I tried to remember if the phone booth door squeaked. If it did, I'd have to be very, very fast. I slid my boots off. While the grigori was still walking, I pushed the folding door open as careful as I could be. It made hardly any noise.

Then I slipped out of the booth and followed her down the hall as silently as a ghost. She had reached my room and had her ear against the door. Enemy, then.

She saw me moving out of the corner of her eye and tried to turn in time to face me, but I was on her by then.

She didn't make a noise. I said "Felix!" real urgently, but quiet, because she was fighting like a cornered coon. We thudded against the door, and it opened, spilling us into the room. She was trying to get her hands free to work a spell, and I was determined she would not. I was also trying to keep her on top of me, which was not what I would have done if I hadn't expected Felix to help. I didn't want to be in the way of anything he chose to do.

He chose to say, "Lilias Abramova!"

She jumped so much I was able to punch her in the head. She went all cross-eyed for a second or two, and I rolled her over and sat on her, pinning down her wrists with my hands.

"A little help would be nice, Felix!" This Lilias Abramova was stronger than she looked.

"Oh, by all means," Felix said. He pinched some powder out of one of his vest pockets, dropped the powder on the woman's face, said some words, and she went limp. She was conscious, though. The look she gave me said as much.

"What are you doing here, Lilias?" Felix said. He sat down again, crossed his legs, looking cool and composed. But I could see the vein in his neck jumping around.

I climbed off Abramova with some relief and perched on the bed. That had been brisk. I took some deep breaths.

"I came to see what she was really here for," the grigori said. Her voice was deep, and she had a heavy accent. I didn't know what kind it was, some brand of English. "I had no idea you were involved in her doings. Your preference does not tend to run that way." She could roll her eyes, and now she did, from me to Felix.

"We are allies," Felix said.

"Ah. Because of Eli," Lilias Abramova said. She was wearing a gold wedding band.

"Did you think sneaking up to my door and listening would help you find out what I was really here for?" I said.

"I hoped it might." She was calm about this admission.

"And what was your goal in finding out why I'm really here in the empire? Did you want to help me? Kill me?"

"Captain McMurtry asked me to check on you."

If I'd been McMurtry, I'd have done the same thing. Didn't surprise me any.

"Does he doubt that I saved the tsarina's life?"

"No, he does not. But why you did it is another matter, and why you happened to be so conveniently on the spot to do it is yet another matter."

"A seer told me to be there," I said. "I asked how I could draw attention to Eli's dilemma, and the seer told me to be on the spot. I didn't know what would happen, only that I had to be ready to act. If I'd been there by accident, I would have done exactly the same thing."

The spell seemed to be wearing off, because Lilias Abramova was able to raise her eyebrows. "What seer?" she asked.

"Does it make a difference? I did what I was told to do. There I was. Caroline's life was spared. I was able to help Eli and his family."

"I'm going to sit up now," she said. "Do you object?"

"No," Felix said. He was smiling.

I held out my hand to help her, and after looking at it for a second, she took it.

"Who are you?" she asked.

"I'm Lizbeth Rose from Texoma. I'm a gunnie."

She made a face like I'd given her an answer in baby talk. "Why are you here?" Lilias Abramova said. "In the Holy Russian Empire? Instead of back in Fleabag, Texoma?"

"I have worked with Eli a lot," I said. "I heard he needed some help. I came."

"Who's paying you?" she asked.

A few different answers were in my throat, but out of them all, I picked, "I don't see that as being any of your business."

"Do you not?" She was definitely mocking me. I don't enjoy that any more than the next person, but I know who I am and what I'm capable of doing. Since we were giving each other steely glares, I raised her one.

"So Captain McMurtry, the tsarina's attaché, took it on himself to find out why the tsarina's life was saved by someone besides himself? Let's move this conversation along, Lilias. Felix and I haven't got all day, though you seem to."

"Oh? What are you doing next? Going to the zoo?"

"I been," I said, for what seemed like the tenth time. "I didn't like it. I got to go make my phone call, Felix. You okay?"

"I am." Felix wasn't taking his eyes off our visitor, though.

This time I made it down the hall and into the phone booth with my coins, dialed the school, got Tom O'Day again, and was glad to hear that the school agreed to my picking up Felicia and keeping her out until after dinner.

"Thank you," I said. "I'll be there within an hour."

O'Day hung up. What a charmer.

I went back to the room and found Felix and Lilias in an argument. That wasn't any large surprise.

Lilias told Felix he should trust her, and Felix wondered why he should.

Lilias said some things in a language neither Felix nor I could understand (from the look on Felix's face) and threw her hands up in the air.

"You!" she said to me as she stood, about to make her exit. "You tell him, since he won't listen to me. He needs help on this, and some of us are loyal. If you don't want to die, call me at the grigori dormitory."

I nodded. She had her hand on the door, but she stood, giving me one of those long looks. "I think you might," Lilias Abramova said slowly.

I didn't know if the woman meant I might not want to die or I might call her. I nodded again, just in case.

Lilias reached into one of her vest pockets, and Felix and I both tensed, but she pulled out a white card and handed it to me. It was a business card, my second one. On it was printed her name, underneath that FIRE GRIGORI, and underneath that a phone number.

"Thanks," I said, and Lilias left. I listened for her footsteps until I heard the elevator arrive.

Felix was looking off into space like he was pondering something, and I let him be while I got ready to go. "Time to get Felicia," I said, and he came out of his thoughts to stand and head for the door.

Felix did not talk on our drive to the school, and I left him in the car when I went in. Felicia was sitting in the lobby, or whatever they called it, chatting away with our friend Tom O'Day, who was even smiling. There was a spark in my sister that made people interested in talking to her. It was a spark I didn't have.

Felicia jumped up when she saw me and threw her arms around my waist. I hugged her back. Tom's face got blank again when he saw me. I didn't seem to be anyone's favorite person here in the Holy Russian Empire—except Felicia's, and I didn't know how much of that was manufactured for O'Day's benefit.

I signed a book to show I'd checked Felicia out of the school, and as I did so, I noticed a cluster of children in the hall, ranging from maybe nine years old to at least fifteen, boys and girls, all peering at me and exclaiming to one another in hushed tones. The hotel was cleaning my pants and new jacket, I hadn't picked up Veronika's dress from the cleaner's, so I was wearing my jeans and boots, Veronika's blouse, and my old jacket.

I hoped the children were saying good things about me, or at least that they couldn't find anything to tease Felicia about.

I grinned at them, and they all laughed. I took Felicia's hand like she was really the eleven-year-old she seemed. We went out together. It was about three in the afternoon, and the clouds had blown away. The far glimmer of the water made the afternoon seem like a festival, a far cry from yesterday.

Even Felix smiled when he saw Felicia, or at least his mouth moved a little. She scrambled into the back seat and said, "Felix, hello! What have you and my sister been up to?"

"We gained an ally," Felix said. "Or at least, we found out we had one. Do you know Lilias Abramova?"

"Only by sight." Felicia waited for the follow-up, but it didn't come. We pulled away from the curb and set out.

"I think we'll go to my house where we can't be overheard," Felix said. "Though they may have stationed someone close to overhear or to simply detail who comes in and who goes out."

While we rode, I told Felicia about John Brightwood and Natalya, and then about Katharine Demisova and Derek Smythe.

I got to say it felt strange talking about the people I'd killed . . . to my little sister. But in her years, however many there had been, Felicia had seen a lot of death in some strange and terrible ways. She'd seen me shoot a lot of people at the train station in Ciudad Juárez. So the unpleasantness was only on my part. Or I thought so until Felicia said, "I kind of liked Derek Smythe. He helped teach water magic at the school when Instructor Medvedev was ill."

I felt terrible until she added, after a moment of thought, "But he was a rule follower, and if he was ordered to do something, that was what he'd do, no matter if his sense told him it wasn't right."

"Derek Smythe didn't have any reason to like me, or to think I was above suspicion," I said, picking my way through the words. "So he didn't have any reason to balk at his orders. But I had to defend myself, and so did Felix."

"Where did you put the bodies?" Felicia asked Felix, sounding real calm.

"Least said, soonest mended," Felix told her primly. I couldn't help but laugh. Even Felix smiled a bit. "That's what the English say," he added.

"I'll summarize," Felicia said. "That's what they teach us in class."

"I'm ready," I said.

"Eli is in jail for murder, though he didn't do it."

I nodded.

"Since Peter's not a man yet and Eli's not around, his mom and sisters are available to be picked on by the older half brothers, Bogdan and Dagmar."

"That's right." Felix turned a corner. We were close to his house.

"Two wizards who were following orders began to trail you two. We don't know what their orders were, but since they were lying in wait at Eli's house, we can assume they were about to take action, and they did."

"Which was not successful," Felix said with some satisfaction.

"Not successful. They died," Felicia said. "And then you learned what Peter had done, since he can be a real idiot. You tracked the other witness, and Felix killed him so he couldn't testify against Peter truthfully or Eli falsely."

"Right," I said. This really sounded bad when you put it all together.

"And then Grand Duke Alexander freed John Brightwood and sent him to prey on the Savarov family," Felicia said.

We were all silent for a long moment.

"But you surprised him, Lizbeth, and you killed him," Felicia said. She sounded proud.

"I did, and that Natalya, too." Didn't regret either killing at all.

"And Eli has the pebble," Felicia said.

"Yes, last I knew."

"What pebble?" Felix said.

"I made a pebble full of power," my sister said, with not a little pride. "It should explode when it's thrown."

"Should?" I was worried, all of a sudden. "Did you try one out?"

"How could I? Everyone in school would know about it. You can't use those silently . . . though that would be pretty great."

"A boom without noise?" Felix grinned from behind the wheel. "That *would* be wonderful."

I was riding through San Diego with two lunatics.

"How can Eli decide when to use it if he doesn't know what it does?" I asked, pretty sharp. I didn't care for this smiling when Eli's safety was at stake.

"He's a grigori!" Felicia looked at me like I was the crazy one. "He'll know what to do."

"So grigoris can hold something that has a spell on it and know what the spell is?" *That* would be pretty great.

"No, but what else would I have given him?" My sister clearly thought I was being dumb on purpose.

I wanted to scream. I put my hands over my ears for a moment and tried to think about a plan for now. Then I covered my eyes instead. Helped a little. "So here's what we want to do," I said, sounding real level and sure. "No one is arresting us for anything right now, so we're in the clear. At the moment. I'm in good with the tsarina, not that she's that powerful, and Felix is in good with his guild, right?"

Felix shrugged. I had to let that go.

"Felicia, you're okay with the school. No one suspects we're going to try to bust Eli out of jail. The pebble may help with that. Or Eli may use it because something happens that we can't foresee." That made me gloomy. "Howsomever, we've got to be ready to get Eli out of the city."

"What about his mom and sisters?" Felicia said.

"That's a good question, and I got no answer," I said.

"I will propose to Lucy and give them my protection," Felix said. He sounded more like he was going to face a band of grigoris than propose to a girl he cared for.

I should have thought more about the expression on my sister's face. It wasn't a happy one. But it smoothed out almost before I'd been sure I'd seen it, and I was glad to forget it. Because if Felicia had some kind of crush on Felix, that would be just too messy. If I thought Felix was too old for Lucy, he was *really* too old for Felicia, no matter what her real age was.

And this was all besides my belief that Felix was unlikely to fully love any woman.

Peter arrived at Felix's little house very soon after we got there. He was fuming angry about something, but he was determined not to tell us what. I left him alone to brood in a corner of the sofa, while Felix made us some hot chocolate at Felicia's request and I went to stare out the front window. Because I had nothing else to do. I wondered where Grand Duke Alexander lived. I wondered how good his security was. I wondered if his death would really end the vendetta against Eli and his family. Would I have to kill his half brothers, too? At this rate, I could whittle away at the Russians for weeks until I'd arrived at a group I could get along with. And then it would be time to go back home.

All of a sudden, the sun was gone, the clouds gathered, and rain sprinkled down again.

Great.

CHAPTER SEVENTEEN

Felicia complimented Felix on the hot chocolate, and she got a lopsided smile for her courtesy. "Just like my mother never made," he said, and stood staring at Peter, who had refused a drink.

The rain made me feel cold, and I was glad to have my own cup in my hands.

"Peter, stop acting like a bear with a sore paw, and tell us what's got you all sulky," Felicia said.

I applauded her silently.

"If you must know," Peter said, as if we'd been begging him to tell the story, "one of my classmates heard the new director talking about expelling me."

I could see from the reaction this produced that getting expelled from the Rasputin School was rare and serious. Felix and Felicia both had their mouths open.

"Just because? Or for something in particular?" I said, to break the silence.

"She told one of my instructors that my family could no longer be counted as loyal to the Russian court," Peter said. "In her opinion, I'm no longer deserving of my education."

"Who told you this?"

"The student aide of the new head of the school, Emma Morozova. She was appointed after Boris Morozov, her father, died in his sleep last month."

"We wondered if he did die in his sleep," Felicia said. "Me and my friends." She did not seem upset by the possibility that Mr. Morozov's death had not been natural. The more I got to know my sister, the more I loved her . . . and the more frightening she seemed.

Peter nodded. "But people do just die. Especially old people."

Couldn't argue with that. But it did seem like a real suspicious time for Mr. Morozov to die, with Eli in jail and Peter at the school. Suddenly, an idea came to me. What if my sister was expelled, too? What if the school made the connection between me and the Savarov family and decided she needed to go? After all, it wasn't a secret. I'd talked about it at court.

"Anybody say anything to you?" I asked Felicia.

She understood without me having to explain. "Not yet. I think it would be harder to get rid of me since my blood is valuable to the tsar."

And I had more bad thoughts. "You know a child of Rasputin and a bastard of his died when they shouldn't have."

Felicia nodded. "I'm looking around me," she said.

That didn't seem good enough, but I had nothing else to offer her, at least not at the moment. I had to stay here to get Eli out. I realized that ever since Eli and I had found Felicia in Ciudad Juárez, she'd been in danger. I gave a gusty sigh. I'd truly thought I was saving her. Instead, I might have condemned her to an earlier death than she'd have faced in the slums of Mexico. Some big favor.

"Why are you looking so dark, Lizbeth?" There was a wrinkle between Felicia's eyebrows.

"I thought I was bringing you to a safer place," I said. "I wasn't."

Felicia jumped up and threw her arms around me. "No, don't think that," she said. "You did save me. I have learned so much here. The teacher who likes me says I am a sponge."

"A sponge, huh? Soaking up the learning." I put down my chocolate on the nearest surface and hugged her back. It kind of scared me, how smart and quick Felicia was. "Maybe you can come visit me in Texoma."

"We got time to talk about it," Felicia said stoutly. "We *have* time."

I sure hoped so. After a moment's more of clutching, we separated. "Now we have to make a plan," I said. "Peter, what's happening at your house? How are your mom and your sisters? When did you get there?"

"Mother called me early this morning, and the school gave me leave to go home. Then I came here, then I went to class, then I called home again and talked to Lucy. The police finally left our house an hour or two ago. Captain McMurtry came to advise Mother, and he's still there. He was a great help," Peter said, like he was holding a grudge.

"Then you must be glad he was there to help, and you must thank him," Felix said. He seemed to understand something I didn't.

Peter looked grim, but he nodded. "Yes, as you say. The police wanted to ask Mother more questions about the, ah, exposure Brightwood insisted on, and Captain McMurtry cut that line of questioning off. Alice has been very . . . distraught."

"Good thing the captain cut 'em off," I said.

"And they had a lot of questions about how Natalya came to kill Brightwood and how Brightwood got her in return."

"Natural," I said.

"They also wondered about some scratches on the table," Peter said, raising his eyebrows.

My belt must have gouged the wood as I slid.

"That Brightwood didn't have any manners," I said, and Felix laughed.

"Mother and Lucy and Alice are getting the house back together. Mother put an ad in the paper for another housemaid. Formerly, she would have called the Russian Society, which finds jobs for indigent people who fled from Russia. But she's afraid she might get another Natalya."

God forbid the Savarov women should have to keep house themselves. But I gave them a pass. They weren't used to it, and also it would look funny if they didn't keep the help they'd always had.

"So I need to see Eli again," I said. "He has to know what's happened, and if his family can't see him, that leaves me."

"You need to warn him about the pebble," Peter said, giving Felicia a sort of sneery look. He didn't mean it, I could tell. In fact, Peter was envious that my little sister could create something so dangerous.

"Eli needs to know Brightwood is dead," Felix said. "And he needs to know exactly why he's in jail."

Peter blanched.

"Peter, you got to carry the weight on this," I said. "It's you who put Eli in jail, though you didn't mean to. I know you were trying to protect your sisters. And it's your responsibility that Felix had to use his magic to kill Dima."

"Zaitsev's dead?" Peter looked even whiter than before.

"Yep. I was set to do it, but Felix got in there ahead of me. Your sister had to come with us to point Dima out."

"You let my sister go with you?"

That was what outraged Peter, that Lucy had been with us—not that he had himself brought about the need for the man to die.

"How else were we to know who to kill?" Felix was exasperated.

"I should have killed him!" Peter said, all excited. "You should have left it up to me!"

None of us said anything . . . because Peter had had enough time to work out what had to be done, and he hadn't taken action.

"You got to grow up," said my sister.

I think the fact that Felicia, younger and a girl, was telling Peter this just made Peter crazy. Because she was right. He struggled for something to say and then turned away to face the wall. I suspected he was crying, and that wasn't a bad reaction, as long as he also learned something. It was time to change the subject.

"Eli also needs to know the tsarina is working on getting him out," I said. "At least, she says so, sort of. I wish I could talk to the tsar."

They all looked at me as if I'd said I wanted to talk to a baboon.

"That's not going to happen," Felix said, giving me the narrow-eyed look he'd give a lunatic. "Alexei makes social appearances like Caroline does, but he seldom leaves the palace unless it's a state parade or he's greeting a dignitary from another country, or some such occasion. For one thing, he has bleeds, and then he has to have a transfusion, and healing spells."

"I don't understand his illness." I waited for Felix to explain.

"If he falls down and gets a bruise, it swells up because there is a lot of blood in the hurt area," Felicia said. "All the fluid puts too much pressure on his organs and joints. This causes great pain. If Alexei has a large cut, like the time he slipped on the dock, the bleeding is much worse than on a normal person, and it's very difficult to stanch the flow."

We all looked at her.

"I've witnessed some of this," Felicia said. "Alexei had fallen down one step, one! And he had a huge bruise on his knee, which was swollen like . . ." She held her hands apart and curved to indicate a globe about the size of a basketball. Felicia seemed more amazed than sympathetic.

"That was when they used your blood for the transfusion?" I said.

Felicia nodded. "And it worked," she said, not without pride. "With my blood and the healing spells, he was able to sleep without pain, and the next day he could walk."

"I hope he thanked you," I said, and Felicia looked at me funny.

"It is my job," she answered. "It's why I get free schooling and free board."

"Sure." I nodded. But I wasn't happy. I took a deep breath. "I hope the transfusion didn't hurt much."

"I got a drink afterward that helped ease the ache," my sister said. Her little face shut tight, like she'd pulled the curtains. "It wasn't bad." I wondered if that was really true, because her bony hands were clenched. "Lizbeth, it's worth it."

Guess I had been all clenched up, too, because after she said that, I could feel myself relaxing. I recalled how we'd gotten on this topic. "So who tells the tsar what he should do?" I said.

"He tells himself." Peter was stunned by my ignorance. "He is the ruler, and he decides what is right and what is not."

That sounded like a real burden.

"So if getting next to him is close to impossible, Felicia, what are your chances of seeing Grand Duke Alexander?" Felix was putting it on the table.

In turns, my sister looked surprised, pleased, and cunning.

"We are scheduled to sing for the men of the court in two days," Felicia said. "The grand duke is almost always at court occasions, so he can see the tsar and judge how he is doing."

"You can tell?" I couldn't believe the grand duke was that obvious.

"He's real polite to the tsar, but he doesn't talk to him that much," she said. "Alexander's got eyes on Alexei the whole time, and we think he's bribed one of the grigoris who helps with Alexei's health. Or Alexei's aide. Or both of them."

"I can't believe you know all this," I said. The kids at the grigori school knew more than the adults at the court, or at least it seemed that was true to me.

"We talk, we watch, we listen," Felicia said. "Grigoris work for the regime in power."

I'd never looked at it that way. "No grigoris go into private practice?"

Peter, Felix, and Felicia all shook their heads. "Grigoris registered with the school are bound to serve in various ways," Peter said.

"Are there loose ones?" Felicia's father—my father—had been such a loose one, in every sense of the word.

"There are," Felix said. "But in the normal course of things, they don't last long."

I wanted to go home. For a terrible moment, I wanted to ask Felix to take me to the train station. I would board a train to anyplace that wasn't San Diego. Anyplace out of the Holy Russian Empire.

But not without freeing Eli.

"So give Grand Duke Alexander a note, Felicia," I said, thinking as I spoke. "Tell him you were asked by a lady to deliver it to his hand."

"He won't open it himself, he's too suspicious," Felix said.

"Of course he won't," I said. "Unless he gets someone to check it for magic first. Right?"

Peter nodded.

"Who's his favorite grigori?" I looked from Felix to Peter, but it was Felicia who answered.

"Theodore Bronsky," she said without hesitation. "He's a fire wizard. He and Alexander are related somehow."

"So what can you do to make this Bronsky misfire?" I looked directly to Felix, because I wanted him to be challenged.

Felix had opened his mouth to tell me my idea was no good, but he shut it and looked thoughtful. "I could . . . make him love Felicia, so he would trust anything she handed him. I could make him sick, so Alexander would ask some other grigori to touch the letter. Alexander might open it himself if Bronsky was not on hand . . . though he hasn't lived as long as he has by being incautious. Neither has Bronsky."

"What if Bronsky was dead?" Peter asked.

"You've sure gotten bloodthirsty." I couldn't help but remark on that.

"I want my brother safe. Alexander might send Bronsky in there to execute all of the jailed grigoris. Since they are in cells and can't practice their magic, they are ducks in a barrel."

Bronsky would have to make sure he went down there alone. No null with him. "Wait . . . are the grigoris in jail all supporters of the tsar?"

"No, but they're all enemies of Alexander. Except Brightwood."

My idea underwent some rapid changes.

"Felix, have I ever told you about when the grigoris in Mexico sent someone who looked like Peter to Eli's room, so he'd hesitate to kill him?"

Looked like Peter didn't know about that, either, from the horror on his face.

"What happened instead?" Peter stood.

"Instead, I pulled your brother away just as the man tried to strangle him, and I got strangled instead." That had been very painful; not my favorite memory. "It was someone who had been spelled to look like you to all of us. Paulina killed him with a candlestick, and your brother threw up."

Peter seemed more impressed by this than anything I'd said. "Eli was that upset?"

"Yes, he was that upset. My point being, some grigori cast that spell on a man . . . we never did find out who the man was or why they picked him. Anyway, maybe Felix can do the same thing to me, and I can be the jailer they send down to the grigoris. The null."

Felix was staring at me. "*My* point being that the person who was spelled did not live."

"Only because Paulina killed him."

"And you think none of the grigoris in jail will kill you? They won't know who you are for critical moments."

"I think I can live through a critical moment." If I sounded snappish, I was.

Felix scowled at me. "Jane Parvin and Svetlana Ustinova are not followers of Alexander, so maybe you can tell them who you are in time to live. But I warn you, they are very capable."

I wasn't going to lose my temper, though it would have been a relief to let go of it. Felix wasn't fond of ideas that weren't his. Or maybe it was just my ideas that set him on edge?

"The question is, can you?" I said, staying on track. "Can you make me into Louise Hubble, the jailer?"

Peter looked from one of us to the other, like he was watching us play catch.

Felix huffed out a sigh. "I'll go lay eyes on her," he said. "You won't sound like her, you know. I can only reproduce the body."

The replica of Peter hadn't spoken, I remembered. In fact, he'd looked unconscious.

I nodded. "I can make it work," I said.

I had to. I'd had it with this city.

CHAPTER EIGHTEEN

After that, Felix was in such a rotten mood that Peter called a cab to take us all back to the Rasputin School, where he and Felicia would go to their dormitories. Like a few local students, Peter split his time between the dormitory and his home, but with his family under such scrutiny and the police in and out, the dormitory was better for him. The lower he lay, the better.

"Else I might end up with Eli," Peter said, kind of drawing himself up. "Hey, we missed dinner at the school. Can we stop off and eat somewhere?"

I thought I had enough money on me. Peter asked the cab to let us out three blocks north of the school, at a run-down diner he said served great food. He was wrong, but it was plentiful, cheap, and hot, and I was hungry, so I didn't mind.

Peter ate like a wolf, while Felicia ate in a dainty but efficient way. You thought she was just picking at her food, but then it was gone.

"Why is Felix always so angry with you?" Peter asked. He was mopping the plate with his bread.

"Felix loves Eli," I said, tired of pussyfooting around that prickly issue.

"Oh." Peter stopped moving for a moment. He put his bread down. "Oh. Okay. But why does that make him angry with you?"

He resumed his plate-cleaning project. After a moment, he said, very quietly, "So Eli loves you."

There was a long moment of silence as my sister and I dodged each other's eyes.

"We're together when we can be," I said carefully. "I don't expect . . ." But there I had to stop, because I didn't know how to finish the sentence.

Peter sat up straight. For a moment, he looked like a man. "I should have realized you were together," he said.

I had no idea what to say. Nothing would be best.

"Do you want some pie?" Felicia said, as if no one had spoken for ten minutes.

"No, thanks." Peter wiped his mouth and put his napkin beside his plate with the air of someone finishing a routine, no thought involved. He stared blankly across the table at her.

"I'm full," I said. "What about you, Felicia?"

"I could not eat another bite," Felicia said.

It had quit raining, and it was dark. The air felt chilly and raw. We walked the three blocks to the school in silence. The front door was locked; we had to ring a doorbell. Tom O'Day answered the door, and I went in and signed Felicia back into the school. Peter was old enough to sign for himself.

"I'm on my way back to the Balboa Palace, then. Be on your watch." I hugged my sister, quick and hard.

They both nodded, Peter without meeting my eyes. "Thanks for the dinner," he said, his voice even and calm. His hands were clenched into fists.

"Sure," I said, and turned to leave. I could not let him see I was sorry for him.

"Sister, see you soon," Felicia said softly, and I nodded without turning back. I was anxious to be alone.

As I made my way back to the hotel, looking around me at every corner, I wondered if the constant humming of my nerves was because of all the grigoris who lived here. San Diego was probably home to the highest population of grigoris ever in one city. The bit of grigori blood in me was responding to that, maybe.

No wonder I wanted to get out of here. It puzzled me that I'd been with Eli for days without having a problem. So it must be volume, quantity, that made me jangle inside.

Or maybe someone was trying to spell me.

I got to my room as quickly as I could. Once there, I took off every stitch I had on. I went over each item of clothing, from boots to jacket, looking at the seams and the pockets and the folds. Nothing. Spells could be cast without a physical object being transferred to the victim, for sure, but I didn't feel anything but jittery. I looked like myself in the mirror. I took a bath and washed my hair and every other bit of me.

And still the hum got under my skin. I'd gotten into poison ivy once on one of our trips to New America. It was like the itching from the ivy had gotten inside me.

Soon. I had to do something soon.

Felix was in the hotel restaurant the next morning, sitting by the big window where I liked to sit. I didn't know if I was glad to see him or really fed up with him, or both.

"I can do the spell," he said, before I'd had time to pick up my coffee cup.

I held up my hand. "Just hush for a little," I said. I'd tossed and turned most of the night, plagued by repeated dreams of the jail blowing up with everyone inside it dead. I was furious with Felicia and her pebble and my own gullibility in passing it to Eli, by the time I staggered down the stairs.

I'd never had a dream come true, and I didn't want to start now.

When I'd ordered food and poured more coffee, I nodded to Felix. His rough dark hair was even more tousled than usual, and his dark eyes were red. He hadn't gotten much sleep, either. I was even higher on his list of least-favorite people, and that was saying a lot.

"I have done research on the spell," he said, real low. "I think I can do it."

I glared right back at him. I couldn't think of anything to say besides "Thinking isn't good enough."

"It's very difficult. I don't know who laid the spell on the man who looked like Peter. That's unfortunate, because I would be glad to talk to him. Or her. How long did the spell last?"

"Until a little bit after he died. Say about five minutes after we found him."

"Tell me the whole story."

"It's not one of my favorite memories," I said.

"Do you want Eli free or not?"

So I relived the night in the hotel in Paloma again. I could feel the pain in my neck, the certainty that I was about to die. The crunch sound when Paulina brought down the candlestick on the phantom's head.

"It was someone who knows Peter well," Felix muttered, after I'd finished. "Had to be, to create such a good likeness."

"Probably a teacher at the school, then," I said. Seemed reasonable to me.

Felix sort of jumped, and glared at me even harder. "Why do you say that?"

"Because it makes sense," I said. "Of all the grigoris Peter knows, those are the ones who see him most often."

Felix gave me silence for a few more moments. He was still glaring, but kind of over my shoulder. Not at me, but at his own thoughts.

"So what do you have to do?" I said, finally.

"I'll wait for you in the lobby."

Couldn't seem to stand my company anymore, which was mutual.

I was glad to get my oatmeal and fruit. As I ate, I watched the people out on the street, which was about my favorite thing to do in San Diego. Until I saw Lucy Savarov. It was lucky I'd already paid my bill, because I was on my feet in a flash, in time to meet her coming into the lobby. She was standing just inside the doors, looking around her with some curiosity.

"Lucy," I said, slowing down to a walk.

Lucy looked very young that morning, because she was excited at her own daring. "I took the streetcar and found you," she said, very whispery, because it had been such a bold thing to do. For her.

"What are you doing here by yourself?" Felix snapped, popping up like a jack-in-the-box.

Lucy jumped. "Oh, Felix, you scared me!" she said, slapping at his arm. Like a playful child.

To my surprise, Felix's face softened into a smile. "The last thing I wanted to do," he said. "But I'm startled at seeing you alone." And displeased.

"She managed to get here just fine," I said. "Lucy, let's go sit over here, and you can tell us why you've come. I was just about to have a conference with Felix about Eli's situation."

There was a tight cluster of three chairs in one corner of the lobby, a fair distance from the others, and we settled there.

"How are things at your house?" Felix asked.

That wouldn't have been my lead question, but I waited for the answer.

"The police have absolved us of any wrongdoing," Lucy said. "And they seem to believe that Natalya and that disgusting man did kill each other." She reached over to pat my hand, very gently, as if killing the two had put me in need of consolation.

"That's good," I said, trying not to sound like I was agitating to move on.

"I wish I had been there to kill them for you," Felix said.

Now was when he'd picked to woo Lucy? *Now?*

"Because they deserved it," Felix added. He looked savage enough to do it on the spot.

If only I hadn't done it first. Ohhh. Felix had more than one reason to put me in the coal bin.

"Thank you, Felix," Lucy said with some dignity. "You're a true friend to our family."

"That is my deepest hope," Felix said.

I had a hard time keeping my face still, but I managed. We needed to get to the important stuff.

"Peter came to the house early this morning," Lucy said, and alarms went off in my head. "He mentioned a plan you have for getting Eli out of jail. Are you so convinced that the tsar will do nothing?"

If I could have caught hold of Peter at that moment, I would have shaken him like a dog shakes small prey. Felix's expression told me he felt the same.

"We just don't know," I said. And I leaned in closer and spoke very quietly. "What we do know is that the great-uncle"—I didn't want to say the name out loud—"is willing to kill your whole family, and if nothing is done soon, that may happen."

Lucy didn't look shocked by that. Russians! But she did look thoughtful. "Then I will kill him first," she said. "And my family will be safe. Peter says that is the best way, better than the other plan. Though he didn't explain it."

Felix was on his feet before her mouth had shut. He was about to burst into protests. I grabbed him and pulled him down to his chair. I looked around the lobby. The desk clerk, not my buddy but another one, was sorting the mail that had just come in. He was putting it all in the correct cubbyholes, and his back was to us. There was a lull in the lobby bustle. Most customers who were going out had gone. The maids were busy in the rooms, and the dining-room staff was cleaning up after breakfast.

"Lucy, that's a brave offer," I said, because it was. "Felix and Peter and I have talked about that. But we figure the killer can't walk out of that alive." I gave her a real straight look.

Lucy nodded. "I'm willing," she said simply.

I really admired her grit, while in no way thinking she could kill a flea.

"I will not let you," Felix said, his voice the more intense for being low.

"You don't have the say." Lucy gave him a very firm look.

"No, Felix, you don't," I said. "But the situation doesn't need to come to that."

"What do you mean?" Lucy had a little pucker between her fine eyebrows.

"We have another plan. Let us work that one out." Felix looked stern, but proud.

"I'm sure that as smart as Felix is, he can figure out a plan," I said with a straight face. "If all plans fail, I will take care of the grand duke. Eli will go free, with no charges hanging around his neck. If the tsar does what he ought, Eli can go back to taking care of him, and everything will be smooth."

"You would do that for him?" Lucy's eyes were wide.

"I would." Wasn't glad about it, but I would. I tried not to think about my mother's face. Or Jackson's. Or my sister's.

"We have to find out his schedule," Felix said.

So we were going with the kill-Alexander plan. Rather than the pretend-to-be-the-jail-guard plan. I was likely to die either way.

"Who would know that?" I was sure it wasn't published in the paper, but someone with the rank of a grand duke would have a full agenda. Someone had to keep track of it.

"His aide," Lucy said, as gently as if we had just gotten to school and I hadn't known what "red" meant.

"Who would that be?"

"I expect Captain McMurtry would know who Alexander's aide is," she said, still gently.

Felix and I didn't look at each other.

It really was best if you didn't have time to think about it.

CHAPTER NINETEEN

There were so many people in different uniforms in the imperial service I couldn't keep them all straight. Now I was wearing a uniform myself, for the first time in my life. It was a gray dress covered with a white apron, and on top of my head perched a white cap.

I looked awful in this getup, but I looked like I was part of the cleaning crew, which was the point. I was gathering garbage in the offices of the royal aides. It hadn't been easy getting here, and when I say "hadn't been easy," I mean "had been hell."

First of all, Ford McMurtry had been glad to get a phone call from Lucy. After Lucy had given me a laden look, I'd realized that McMurtry admired Veronika. (Now I wondered if the tsarina had sent him to their house in the aftermath of the Brightwood death, or if it had been the good captain's idea.) McMurtry was so pleased Lucy had called him for information that he didn't ask why she wanted the name of Alexander's aide. If he'd been Russian, he'd have been more suspicious. Or maybe he was suspicious but decided to pretend he wasn't. Couldn't tell with court people.

Grand Duke Alexander's aide was Captain Leonid Baranov, who preferred to be called Leo. Lucy told us it sounded like McMurtry didn't have a high opinion of his fellow captain. Baranov was older than all the other aides and had been on the boats with the grand duke.

Grand Duke Alexander, youngest brother of Tsar Nicholas, was now in his late fifties, and his aide was the same age.

Nina, the woman who usually wore this uniform, had been glad to be "kidnapped" for a day, for a good sum of money . . . which I supplied, since Felix said he had none, and of course Lucy did not have money, at least not the kind you carried around. I'd been careful with my cash since I'd gotten to the Holy Russian Empire, but each time I took money out of my hoard, I had a twinge of guilt. Who knew how much we'd have to spend to leave the country? Or rather, how much I'd need, since I was sure if we freed Eli, he'd stay here with his family. I steered myself away from this gloomy and familiar idea, in favor of recalling Felix's expression when Nina had shown up at his house in answer to a series of phone calls.

Nina had brought a stack of magazines to read. She was remarkably cheerful about the whole transaction, which made me wonder about a lot of things. Was being a maid on the royal island that difficult or boring? Were her working conditions terrible? Or did she simply want a little adventure that would not lead to any serious trouble for herself? Most likely, Felix had cast a little spell on Nina. He'd gotten her name from one of his guild members. I suspected she was a frequent source of information.

Nina had described her routine in detail.

I'd crossed on the ferry with all the other working people on the evening shift. I had Nina's identification card, and we didn't look real different, so . . . I felt nearly all right about it. Helped by a *don't notice me* spell—courtesy of Felix—the short trip had gone well. I'd only spoken to another woman who asked me for aspirin to relieve her hangover. I'd just had to shake my head.

Nina had described another maid who worked in the same building, Irina, who had a big birthmark on her cheek that made her easy to spot. I followed Irina to the palace annex where the aides had their offices . . . and their bedrooms, as it turned out, since the job entailed such long and irregular hours.

There wasn't a supervisor on-site, Nina had told us, though their work was checked after every shift. Nina was supposed to collect her supplies (I had a list in my head) from the janitorial closet (I had a floor plan in my head), and when she was ready with those, she would clean four offices and bedrooms on the western side of the corridor.

The ground-floor offices, totaling eight, were those of the aides to the top people: the tsar, the tsarina, Grand Duke Alexander, Grand Duchess Xenia Alexandrovna (who was the tsar's aunt, I discovered). When the baby prince was old enough to have social engagements, he would have an aide here, too. I didn't recognize the names of the other exalted people who'd been awarded aides. The title of the important person and the name of the aide were both on the nameplate affixed to each room door.

At this time of the evening, they were empty, which was a big plus as far as I was concerned. I went to the janitorial closet, tossed everything that I saw Irina take into my rolling cart, and went to my first cleaning task, the office and bedroom of the tsar's aide, Captain John Petrosky. It would have been easier if Captain John had been gone, but he was asleep in the small bedroom behind his office. Common sense told me not to wake him, so I eased the door shut on the dark room and began to straighten the office.

This was not a challenge. I could clean a room. Nina had told me that all the garbage got tossed into a large bag with a drawstring mouth, which I would turn in as I left the building. I dusted, straightened, put the used glasses and water jug outside the door of the room as I saw Irina doing. I emptied the wastepaper basket into my large bag. I was almost out the door when Petrosky stumbled out of his bedroom. "Oh, sorry!" he said, and half-turned as if to go back into his bedroom. "I didn't know it was maid service time." But he gave me a little special smile as he turned, and made sure I saw that his pajama pants were not buttoned all the way.

I nodded and headed for the door.

"Don't you want a tip?" he called.

I shook my head and shut the door behind me.

Irina, from the opposite doorway, gave me a wry sort of smile. And that was the most contact we had all shift. She never gave a signal that showed she knew I wasn't Nina, she never asked me where the real Nina was. After that one moment when she smiled, she pretended I wasn't there. I guess that was safest for her.

The next office was Captain McMurtry's, and I went through it with the force of a hurricane, I was so worried he'd come back. I figured *don't notice me* wouldn't work on the good captain. He knew me as a person, so he'd be far more likely to get in trouble if he didn't sound the alarm. His office and bedroom did not smell like cigarette smoke, as the previous suite had. That was a relief.

McMurtry's sheets were changed in five minutes. Bookcases, side tables, chair arms, straightened the desk, dusted. The trash emptied. Since he wasn't in the office, I was obliged to vacuum. I had never used a vacuum cleaner, though I'd seen one demonstrated in a store window. This machine was as heavy as a mule, and about as biddable. I steered it around the bedroom and office, and switched it off with a lot of relief.

I'd noticed McMurtry's desk was covered with press clippings about the attempt on the tsarina's life, and I was glad none of them contained any pictures of me.

My next office was the one I'd been aiming for. Captain Leonid Baranov and his wife had had three sons and a daughter, and all of them looked like Baranovs, which was . . . salt of the earth, my mother's term for people who were reliable and neighborly and charitable, but not gifted with good looks.

Baranov went home to his wife at night, so his bedroom only needed a quick dusting. He was a neat man. I was delighted to find he'd typed (well, somebody had typed) everything the grand duke was doing tomorrow and had the document centered on his desk blotter. Organized.

I couldn't write anything down. That would be impossible to explain if I were searched for any reason. Tomorrow the grand duke was attending a funeral at the Church of Christ Victorious. From there he would go to the home of the dead man, where the family would gather for a lunch. At four o'clock he was due at a ground-breaking for the Romanov Imperial Hospital. I got that impressed into my head pretty quickly, so I was collecting the trash when Captain Baranov came in.

He had to know someone was cleaning the offices, since it was done at the same time every day. Also, his office door was open, since the supervisor unlocked all the doors for the cleaners and then relocked them when they were done. But he made a lot out of being surprised I was there, gave me the slightest of nods, and then did his best to pretend I was invisible. He snatched up the very page I'd been studying, and he left with it, hardly disturbing the air with his brief entrance.

I took a few deep breaths after that.

Though my purpose was complete, I had to keep going with my work. One, Nina would need a job to come to tomorrow, and two, I had time to fill in before the ferry would take me back to the mainland.

Xenia Alexandrovna's aide, Vera something, was the only female on this side of the corridor. She made sure you knew it the minute you walked in.

Her suite looked more like a boudoir than an office. The bedroom had been converted into a dressing room, and the wardrobe was stocked with dresses and shoes and wraps and hats and so on. And a full-length mirror on the inside of the bedroom door. A dressing table had been crammed in, and the top of it was crowded with stuff. All of which I had to pick up to dust, and the mirror had to be cleaned, and there were clothes on the floor, too. It took me twice as long to straighten her suite as Captain McMurtry's, but at least she wasn't there to make an offer like Captain Petrosky, or to pretend I wasn't in the room like Captain Baranov.

Irina finished her tasks about the same time as I finished mine. It was hard to watch her every move without being obvious. In her footsteps, I carried all my cleaning things into the bathroom, leaving the vacuum cleaner in the hall. The larger bathroom was for men, the smaller was for women, and we cleaned them both. Bathrooms are all the same, and cleaning 'em is never fun. As we were finishing up, Irina said, "You're not Nina."

"I'm taking her place tonight," I said, in as empty a way as I could. I didn't want to be remembered, I didn't want to be remarked.

Irina nodded. We began putting our cleaning supplies away in the closet. I learned how to wind a vacuum-cleaner cord in a figure eight.

My duties weren't over yet. We had to take our large bags of trash to the incinerator, several buildings away. I was glad San Diego had such a mild climate.

To my surprise, Irina and I got into a long line behind the other cleaners. We all had the same burden, the garbage. Some unlucky cleaners had emptied whole offices full, from the way their bags bulged.

Once we got through the doors, the one line split into seven. I was careful to follow Irina into the farthest row. Once I was safe behind her, I had time to look ahead. The lines inched forward toward a row of seven men standing behind a long counter. Boys with wheelbarrows dashed back and forth behind the men, feeding open mouths filled with flame . . . the incinerators.

Nina had said nothing about this. I watched the routine, concentrating hard. By the time Irina carried her bag to the table, I understood that the men were searching the trash.

This was carrying security too far.

Irina's trash inspector, who had a giant mustache and looked as bored as a person can look, wore heavy gloves. He was running with sweat. The closer we got to the incinerators, the hotter it was. Mustache rummaged through the papers and cigarette butts and used tissues, finding nothing of interest until something metallic glinted under the big lights over the table. "Ha!" he said.

Irina flinched.

She relaxed when Mustache held up the glittery object. It was a woman's powder compact. Even I could tell it wasn't real gold, any more than the shiny things on top were real diamonds. The powder inside was cracked, and a lot of it had been used, anyway. Mustache told the boy behind him, "Put it in the keep-for-a-week bin." The boy put the cracked compact into a smaller numbered wooden box on the floor. The rest of the garbage was scraped into the boy's wheelbarrow, which he pushed to the incinerator to dump.

I didn't even have a shiny cheap compact to attract Mustache's interest.

After that was done, we were free to go back to the building we'd cleaned to get our coats and then return to the pier to wait for the ferry. The air was cold and crisp, having been washed off by the showers of the day before. I was so relieved to be through with my job, to be still free, that I had to keep telling myself I was still under observation, still was not back on the mainland.

Few of the workers seemed inclined to visit. Some women talked about a recipe they had tried, and two men discussed the chances of the new city baseball team, the Empire Sluggers.

The ferry lowered its gangplank, and we shuffled on board. Everyone else sat staring ahead of them into the night as we made the brief passage across the water.

I walked to Felix's, just in case anyone was watching. I was glad to take off the uniform and shoes that Nina had loaned me, and glad to watch her walk out of Felix's house and vanish into the night. I was even more glad to write down the grand duke's schedule. I was tired of chanting it over and over in my head.

"Do you think you can be ready for the funeral?" Felix asked. "Alexander will go to the church and the graveside. But the church is a surer thing."

"Where is this church?"

"I'll pick you up at the hotel. Bring your guns. In fact, better bring all your things." He called a cab to take me to the hotel, and I didn't object. I had finally had a few hours of working for my living, and it had worn me out.

I took a hot, hot bath and climbed into bed at the Balboa Palace, which was beginning to feel like home. I was tired, but I couldn't stop my head from churning. If I'd been caught on the island, I would never have gotten on the ferry again. No one would ever have known what happened to me. I would have been just . . . gone.

It wasn't like me to brood about what might have happened, or to worry about tomorrow. This place was giving me the creeps.

CHAPTER TWENTY

The Church of Christ Victorious was new. It didn't look like any church I'd ever seen. It had colored domes, three of them, all different colors, and they were all topped with a cross. There wasn't any yard; it was jammed against the sidewalk. In all fairness, it was a big church, very big to my eyes.

Christ Victorious was located in an area of San Diego where many Russians had bought or built homes over the past few years. In fact, it stood not too many blocks from the Savarov house. Maybe the Savarovs came here to the services.

The building opposite the church was an invalids' home, packed full of native Russians who'd been on the boats. Felix had told me that most of the "invalids" were aged aristocratic women with no family or aged retired military men, like the man whose funeral Grand Duke Alexander was attending. The church assisted with their fees for the home.

I was wearing Veronika's court clothes again. Though the look was a bit too fancy, I figured I could pass as a visiting relative. I'd checked out of the Balboa Palace, and Felix had all my stuff. I was carrying a cloth laundry bag from my hotel closet, and in it were my guns rolled in my jacket so they wouldn't click together. I was delivering clean clothes to my elderly grandfather-in-law, I decided.

In Veronika's purse I carried extra bullets. But I realized that if I had to reload, I was in serious trouble.

The invalid home wasn't as massive as the church opposite, but it was big enough. I went up the steps to the front door of the stucco home and walked in, smiling at the middle-aged woman on reception duty. She was wearing a white nurse's uniform—of course she wore a uniform—and she was busy arranging a sheaf of flowers in a huge vase. She paid me very little attention. I walked by her at a steady pace, as if I knew exactly where I was going, as if I were in and out every day.

As I started up the broad, carpeted stairs, I was thinking about how much I wanted my Winchester. I could make a distance shot with the rifle much more accurately than with the handguns. But this country was one where carrying rifles openly was guaranteed to draw the attention of almost everyone. At least in San Diego.

I wasn't challenged until the third floor, when the broad stairs ran out and the small bare stairs started in another corner. As I put my foot on the first one, an Asian man in an orderly's uniform said, "Ma'am, there's nothing up those stairs but the roof." He was the only person in sight. Good.

"My grandfather wants me to tell him if I can see the royal island from here," I said, smiling. I figured you couldn't disappoint a grandfather.

"Save yourself the trouble, ma'am. You can't," the orderly said, not smiling back so much.

"Don't tell me I have to disappoint him," I said. I was not smiling at all now. Someone else would come out of one of the rooms any second.

The orderly saved his life by remembering that he wasn't being paid to argue with relatives of patients. He looked doubtful, but he nodded and went into the nearest room. I heard him say, "Good morning, General."

If the orderly ever mentioned he'd seen a young woman going to the roof, I never heard about it. I bet he kept silent.

The steps were almost as steep as a ladder. I unlocked the door and stepped out.

The roof was peaked in the middle, but at least there was a parapet all around it, and a flagpole. It was a windy, clear day, and the HRE flag danced around in flashes of color. It was white, blue, and red with a walking bear in the middle. Felix had told me (though I hadn't been asking) that the three colors were from the original Russian flag and the bear was from the flag of California.

All I cared about was that passersby were used to seeing movement up here, and might not notice there was a person on the roof.

I looked down at the church. It had a porch covered by a roof, so I'd have to get him on the steps up to that porch. I was thankful there were a lot of them. I cast my senses around, estimating distance, wind interference, angle. I took out one of the Colts, and it felt good in my hand. It helped me concentrate, holding it.

This was what I did. I wasn't a damn courtier, or knife fighter, or maid, or tourist, or even a very good sister. I was a gunnie.

We'd cut the time close to reduce my exposure on the roof. But still I waited at least ten minutes before I could tell people were gathering.

There was almost no room for parking on the street. People were walking to the church from this building, crossing the street on foot. They were on the sidewalks, coming from either end of the short street. A few cars paused at the steps to let passengers climb out, and then pulled away to find parking. Then two large cars, black Kodiak limousines from Canada, pulled up.

I went on high alert. Where was my damn rifle when I needed it? I wasn't up to the task of this shot. I would miss.

Where had that come from?

I closed my eyes briefly and got myself back in the right mind. Just in time.

A man in a chauffeur's uniform had jumped out of the driver's seat. He was hurrying around to open the rear passenger door. I recognized the man who got out first; I'd seen him the night before. Captain Leonid Baranov stood aside, practically at attention, as his boss emerged. Grand Duke Alexander was of medium height, his beard and hair were white and thick, and his back was as straight as a ramrod. Somehow I'd thought he'd be wearing a military uniform—wasn't everyone wearing a uniform? But not Alexander.

He was wearing a black suit and a white shirt with a dark purple tie. I didn't know if he just liked purple, or if that was a royal thing. His son Vasily, the one Felicia had pointed out to me at court, climbed out of the car behind him. The younger man was the spitting image of his dad, though his hair was heavily graying. He also looked hale and strong. Kingly, if you will. Like his father.

I took a deep breath, looked hard, raised my gun. I told myself that this was the man who wanted to kill Eli.

Alexander turned his face to say something to his son. He looked like an old hawk.

I took my shot, the hardest shot I'd ever made. I felt the touch of something sublime as I aimed. I was hardly conscious of pulling the trigger.

A red mist haloed Alexander's head. Then he collapsed in the boneless, careless way of the dead.

I took a deep breath and let it out. It had been Before. Now it was After. I had to think other thoughts.

I crouched behind the parapet and duckwalked to the door, sliding my Colt back into the bag as I moved. I had to vanish before anyone started to think.

I opened the door from my crouch and scrambled inside. As the door swung to behind me, I relocked it and started down the narrow, steep stairs. I was quiet, so quiet.

No one was on the landing. I'd been afraid the orderly would have emerged, because now there was screaming outside, but he didn't. Without running, I went down the stairs to the second floor. I could hear doors opening in the building as people began to react to the shouting outside. Looking over the banister, I could see the receptionist open the front door to find out what was going on.

I turned to the nearest room and put my hand on the knob as if I'd just shut the door behind me.

When I turned away from it, three doors were opening. Residents and orderlies and a visitor or two came out, hesitant and puzzled. "What's happened, sir?" I asked the nearest visitor, a heavy man in his forties.

"I'm sure I don't have any idea, young lady," he said. "Something upsetting, sounds like."

Now there were more screams. The people in the church must have come out to find out what the ruckus was.

I moved toward the stairs and went down to the ground level at a quick but steady pace, just another curious and alarmed citizen.

Since no one was particularly looking at me, instead of walking out the front doors, I turned left and walked down the corridor to the back door, which led into the visitors' parking lot. I turned right to cross the street and go directly into the side entrance of the drugstore opposite. I looked at hair combs for a few moments, picked one at random, and went to the cashier.

"Wonder what's happening over there?" she said, nodding her head toward all the sound in the street in front of the church.

I shrugged. "Someone's doing a whole lot of yelling."

She laughed. "You got that right." She dropped the comb into a little bag.

"Do you mind putting it in a bigger one? I'm trying to carry everything in one hand." I looked embarrassed at asking.

She kept hold of her smile, got out a much larger bag, and transferred the comb. I put my cloth bag inside it, too. "Thanks," I said, and I meant it.

As I left by the side door, I saw a familiar car idling at the curb. I was smiling, had been ever since I'd gotten out of the invalids' home. I couldn't stop.

"You look like the Cheshire cat," Felix said.

I didn't know what that was, but I knew I had reason to smile. I'd made the shot, and it was over.

"He's dead," I said.

"Do you want to wait till things quiet down?"

We'd decided on combining ideas last night before I'd left for my hotel. This morning, we'd driven around this area twice, figuring out the possibilities and the fallback positions.

"No, I want to go get Eli out now. If we wait, there's no predicting what will happen." Vasily, the son who'd been with him, could take up Alexander's reins and attack the tsar, or the government could shut down the streets, or . . . anything.

I wanted to get the hell out of this country.

We drove directly to the jail. There were motorcycle police pulling in and out and sirens, and lots of activity in general. Felix and I went to the window. I'd left my handbag and the paper bag in the car. If I was caught with a gun, it would be all over.

The same police officer was on duty, but today his phone was ringing and he was shouting out from the back of his small room, and everything was chaos. He didn't have time for us, and he tried to send us back to the car.

"I'm sorry, I can tell you're very busy here," Felix said, as pleasantly as he was able—which wasn't very—"But Mrs. Savarov has important news for her husband, and she must speak to him now."

I scrabbled around for a reason to be smiling so big. "I'm going to have a baby," I said. "He must know."

That did soften the officer down to the point where he yelled, "Hubble! Up front!"

After a few minutes, Hubble came lumbering up, her face flushed and excited. "It's the grand duke, Bill! He's been shot outside a church!"

"Well, that's really a shock," Bill said, and he meant it. "What them Russkies going to do now? That tsar's going to die any minute, they say. Ain't no one else strong enough to hold the throne. We'll all go down the drain."

Hubble shook her blond head, worried but also excited.

"Why'd you call me?" she asked.

"These people need to visit downstairs." Bill inclined his head in our direction.

"This don't seem like a good time," Hubble said, with more brains than I'd believed she had.

Or maybe her animal side, the one that survived from instinct, was telling her we were wrong, somehow.

"Do your job, Hubble," Bill said. "They ain't going to call you to hunt down the killer."

She glared at him.

"Come on," Hubble said to us, resentment written all over her face. And we went through the same sloppy routine that I'd followed the last time I was there, which seemed like years ago. I could feel Felix fuming behind me as we descended the stairs. Hubble was ahead of me, key ring in her right hand.

The minute we came into view, the three remaining grigoris started pelting Hubble with questions. I was so anxious to see Eli I almost burst. Hubble was grouching and yelling back.

I'd had as much as I could stand. The door to John Brightwood's cell was open. Before I could think about it, I shoved Hubble into the empty cell, grabbing her keys from her hand as I did so. I pulled the door shut on her. And locked it. There. No magic necessary.

Hubble started screeching in a very irritating way.

"You'd better shut up now, or I'll turn the hose on you," I said. There was a hose coiled on the wall for use in cleaning out the cells.

Felix knocked her out with a spell. Hubble landed on the concrete floor with a thud.

There was a moment in which no one said anything. I swear they didn't breathe. The silence was beautiful.

Then Jane Parvin laughed, kind of tinkly, and Svetlana said, "Felix, young woman, you have my admiration." I unlocked Eli's door and took him into my arms. Felix took the keys to unlock the other cells.

"The grand duke is dead," I told Eli, after he'd kissed me and I'd gotten my breath back. "Your family is okay, but I had to kill John Brightwood and a couple of grigoris. And I'm not pregnant."

"That is a lot of news," Eli said cautiously. "Shouldn't we talk about it somewhere else?"

"Yes," Felix said very firmly. "Out of here, now. Police are everywhere, and they're all agitated. We must spell the officer at the reception booth. We can leave this woman down here."

"This is what she gets for being lousy at her job," I said. "Eli, you got the turquoise? We may need it. Felicia says throw it as hard as you can."

Eli nodded. He needed washing from his top to his toes, and his teeth needed brushing. I would have taken him on right there if no one had been around, though. My blood was up.

We swarmed up the stairs, Jane Parvin in the lead.

Bill heard the metal stairs clanging and half-turned while he said, "Hubble, you came up awful quick . . . ," when Jane was right in front of him, saying, "Ducks, look at me. Believe my words . . . ," and the rest of us glided by her, not running but not stopping to look at anything, either, and then we were in Felix's car somehow jammed in—good thing Brightwood wasn't there—and we began moving.

"Where are we going?" Felix asked. This was as far as our plan had taken us. We hadn't expected to survive this long.

I hadn't even had to look like Hubble.

"Good question," Svetlana said. She was in front with Felix, and I was between Jane and Eli. Closer to Eli. As close as I could get.

"I should tell my family that I'm free," Eli said, but I knew that wasn't his first thought. His hand gripped mine fiercely.

By now it was lunchtime, and people were streaming out of office buildings to eat lunch. Traffic going west, toward the Church of Christ Victorious, was at a standstill. There were ambulances and police sirens wailing in the distance there. I wondered if Nina and Irina would be going over to the island this evening. Alexander's aide would have to clean out his office soon. I was having a hard time paying attention to what was going on around me. Random thoughts were skittering through my head.

"So are you saying you want to go to your mother's home?" Felix said, impatience making his voice sharp.

"I don't know if that will be safe for your family," Svetlana said. "Do you need something from there?"

"A few things," Eli said. "Just a quick visit."

"Then let me off at the next corner," Svetlana said. "I'm going to say that an angel came down and opened the cell door. As far as I'm concerned, that's what happened. Somehow our grim Felix happened to be tagging along with the angel."

Felix kind of snorted, and I realized he was laughing. He pulled over. Svetlana got out. She strode away without looking back.

Jane asked to be dropped off close to the grigori school.

"Do you want me to tell your sister anything?" she asked me.

I was surprised Jane Parvin knew Felicia was my sister, and I was surprised she even knew Felicia. I'm sure that was written on my face. Jane smiled. She had a small face, and the smile looked very big. "My sister teaches at the school," she said. "She has a high opinion of Felicia."

"You'll be welcome there?"

"I'll be welcome with my sister," Jane said. "I don't know about the others. They'll have to be sure which way the wind is blowing."

"That seems crazy to me," I said. "You all are so powerful. You can do so much. You even keep the tsar alive. Why aren't you ruling them, instead of them ruling you?"

All three grigoris made little noises, gasps, or choky grunts. I couldn't interpret them. "What?" I said. "Surely that's crossed your minds?"

But neither Felix nor Jane nor Eli spoke. So . . . maybe it hadn't.

"Good-bye," Jane said. "You're an interesting person, Lizbeth. I hope we meet again."

And then she was gone, too.

Felix had to get to the Savarovs' street in a roundabout way because of the traffic congestion. He parked his car behind the house, and we hurried to the back door and knocked. Eli did not have his keys, naturally. In fact, he had nothing but the turquoise, which he'd been saving in his pocket.

Alice answered the door, opening it only a crack. Then she shrieked, "Mother! Lucy!"

She backed away to let us in, and we slipped into the kitchen. It wouldn't do to have a neighbor glimpse Eli and call the police.

It was really a nice reunion, all in all. Veronika, Lucy, and Alice could not hug Eli enough. Veronika called Peter, who said he was on his way over if he would be permitted to leave the school.

Felix and I came in for some hugs, too, after Eli explained that we had busted him out.

Then Veronika asked what the turmoil was in the city; friends had called her with garbled accounts of what was happening.

"The grand duke was assassinated," Felix said. "He was attending a funeral at Christ Victorious, and he was shot on his way in."

"Yes!" Lucy's voice was full of glee.

"Oh, my God! Who do you think shot him?" Veronika asked.

There was an awkward silence. Felix and I glanced at each other.

"I did," I said, not knowing if it was the right thing to do. But they were bound to find out sooner or later.

"You?" Alice's voice went squeaky, She stared at me, both in horror and admiration. "You did it?"

"I . . . have never been an assassin." I took a deep breath. "But it seemed like the only way for Eli to stay free."

Eli didn't know I'd shot the grand duke, since I just hadn't thought about telling him. I'd been so glad to see him—that had swamped everything else. I wasn't sure what he'd do.

It was strange to know someone so well in a few ways and not at all in others. Maybe he felt the same way. He bent to look in my face, and then he hugged me to himself fiercely. So we were okay, and that was all that mattered.

After burrowing into him for a moment, but not long enough, I became aware no one was speaking. I opened my eyes to see that everyone in the kitchen was staring at us with their mouths open, including Felix.

Above my head, Eli said, "Lizbeth and I are together."

And there was some more silence, until Alice shrieked, "You *got married*?"

"Not legally, though we have promised to each other," Eli said.

We had? Okay. I retrieved one of my arms, which had been clenched around his waist, and fished at my neck for the chain.

"Good, you have them." Eli sounded calm, which was not true. I could feel his heart hammer under my cheek.

With one hand, he worked the chain over my head and handed it to his mother. She looked down at the two rings, gave a little nod to herself, and unclasped the necklace to drop the rings onto her palm.

Eli took them both from her, and we stepped back a little from each other. As he'd done in Dixie, Eli slid the smaller ring onto my finger, and then he put on his own.

"In front of a priest?" Veronika asked in a small voice, so we could ignore this if we wanted to.

"No Russian priests in Dixie," Eli said. "But before a saint."

That was true. Before Saint Moses the Black.

I could feel my lips curving up.

Smiling at Eli was easy to do.

CHAPTER TWENTY-ONE

The moment couldn't last, but at least I had it. Then the kitchen door burst open, everyone jumped back in alarm, and Peter practically leaped inside, dragging my little sister behind him.

Peter saw Eli, and his face lit up. Whatever Peter's faults, he loved his big brother. "Guess what?" Peter said. "Bogdan has been arrested!"

It was a measure of Bogdan's character that everyone was pleased, especially Felix. From behind Peter, Felicia waved at me.

"How did you get out of the school? How did you get here so fast?" I said, when I could get close enough to speak to her without yelling over the hubbub.

"Peter kidnapped me," Felicia said, looking cheerful. "He told the headmistress that his family needed him at home and they had asked for me, too. She agreed only because the school is in a mess. No one knows what's happening, or if there's been a coup, or if the Americans are trying to take back California, or what. It's crazy! Peter had enough money for us to take a cab."

"We all have a lot to tell each other," I said. "Felicia, Eli has told his family that we are . . ."

"I knew it!" Felicia grinned like she really was eleven. "Wonderful!"

Peter was hopping around like popcorn on a hot skillet. He fired out bits of information, and no one was listening, because everyone else had something to say, too.

Veronika led us all to the family parlor, which was situated beside the kitchen at the back of the house. It wasn't as formal or depressing as the front parlor, where I'd talked to Veronika and the girls the first time I'd visited. Though we were only there because closing the curtains in the front might be strange and therefore suspicious in the early afternoon, I felt cozy and family-like.

Eli and I weren't looking at each other much, but we were holding hands pretty steady, so that was fine. Veronika, Lucy, and Alice were excited and all whichaways, because a lot of big family stuff had just been piled on top of 'em.

Felix was hard to read, as usual, and Peter was all over the place. We had to calm him down to start catching everyone up on the big day we'd already had.

Lucy went first, telling Peter to pay attention while she told him what had just happened. Peter knew that the grand duke had been shot, and he started to tell us how he'd learned, but Lucy shut his water off.

"It was our Lizbeth who did it," Lucy said proudly. I didn't feel like cringing this time. I would get used to what I'd done. Sooner or later. Eli's hand squeezed mine.

"Lizbeth!" Peter's face was full of hero worship. "Lizbeth, you are a great . . ."

"Bride to our brother," Lucy said steadily. "Eli and Lizbeth are married."

It was good Peter had been forewarned by our conversation the day before, because he took it pretty well for someone who'd had a crush on me.

"Congratulations, Eli," Peter said, with a lot of dignity. "It's wonderful to have Lizbeth join our family."

"Thank you, brother," Eli said, just as soberly. "I have finally done something intelligent, you think?"

Then Peter grinned and laughed, and we received congratulations all around. Even from Felix. Who'd had a crush on someone else.

Eventually, the whole story about getting Eli out of jail was told, even my substituting for the maid, Nina. That seemed more amazing to the Savarov women than my shooting Alexander.

"Oh! That's why!" Peter exclaimed. "Felix, did you tell Nina your name was Bogdan?"

"I might have," Felix said, looking down at his fingernails.

"And that Lizbeth's name was Yana?"

"That's Bogdan's wife," Eli whispered to me.

"I may have also said that," Felix admitted.

Nina had called me Yana, but I'd just figured it was some Russian form of address I didn't know yet.

Veronika looked down at her hands, clasped properly in her lap. She bit her lip. Then she laughed, a sound I'd never heard from her. "I'm sorry," she said, with a gasp. She didn't look a bit sorry. "That's just perfect. Sooner or later, he'll talk his way out of it, but I'm very all right with Bogdan having the scare of his life."

"After all the times he's scared you," Peter said.

"What?" Eli sat up straighter, let go of my hand, and became angry Prince Savarov, all in a second.

Veronika said, "Son, we didn't want to tell you this, but Bogdan and Dagmar came by several times recently, without calling ahead."

Dropping in was not a good thing in the Savarov household, I could tell.

"And what did they want?" Eli was leaning forward, his elbows on his knees.

"They wanted to threaten us," Lucy said, when her mother did not speak. "After the, the, incident at the library . . ."

"Ivan, a friend of Bogdan, made remarks to Alice," I said, to fill Eli in. "In front of Peter."

"Yes, I took care of it," Peter said. But not with pride. "I took care of it stupidly. That's why you were arrested."

"Wait. What?" Eli's brows drew together.

This family had had a *lot* of secrets. It was good we were clearing the decks. Letting all the horses out of the corral. However you wanted to put it. But that didn't mean it wasn't painful.

"Ivan was found dead," Lucy said. "Not that anyone told me until very recently. And he was killed by a technique that you, Eli, can use . . . that's what Felix tells me. But in this case, you didn't."

"Peter?" Eli said. "You did this?"

Peter, flushed, nodded.

"You extracted—?" Eli didn't want to finish the sentence, out of respect for the feelings of his mother and sisters.

"I did," Peter said.

"I'm impressed," Eli said, though there was no admiration in his voice. And left it at that.

"Once he knew this, Dima had to die," I said. "Ivan's friend, who'd also harassed your sisters. Dima Zaitsev."

"Thank you, Felix," Eli said.

"I helped," Lucy said proudly.

Eli, who'd been reaching over to shake Felix's hand, snatched his own back and glared at her. "You did *what?*"

Just one shock after another. Poor Eli.

Eli did not thank Felix when he found out that Lucy had identified Dima on the docks. He looked from me to Felix with narrowed eyes.

Then we had to tell him about John Brightwood. Who had been released after that, and probably in a direct reaction to the death of Dima.

Eli had to get up and walk around the room then, and the women were not able to hide how horrible it had been . . . and they should not have felt obliged to.

"I was not here to protect you," Eli said, his voice choked. "I was not here. There is so much blame here. You could blame me for getting arrested and not fulfilling my duty to you. You could blame Peter for killing the man who had insulted his sisters, though I don't. You could blame Felix for enlisting the aid of my little sister in identifying and killing the man who could connect Peter with the death of Ivan. But there's no blame attached to Lizbeth, who has done her best to set all of us straight, even when that caused her to have pain in her conscience."

"I did my share of bad things," I said. That was sure the truth.

"But you did it to protect me and my family," Eli said.

"No denying that, I guess." I smiled at him, with an effort. "Your mom and your sisters, they're made of strong stuff."

"You're right," Eli said. "I didn't know how strong." He turned to his mother. "Is there anything else you want to tell me? Have we gotten all our dirty linen out on the line yet?"

Felicia had not said anything in so long that I was worried about her. But she'd been soaking it all in. My sister, the sponge.

"I haven't killed anyone since Mexico," she said brightly.

"Good," Eli said, ruffling her hair.

"She's not a puppy," I said. Felix looked at me with a question on his face, but I said nothing more.

Startled, Eli turned to me. "Of course not," he said, with a little hesitation. "Excuse me, Felicia, if I've made you feel less than . . ." He didn't know how to finish his sentence.

"My sister's figured out I'm not eleven," Felicia said, still smiling.

"But in Mexico, you said . . ." Eli's voice trailed off as he tried to remember.

"Never said I was eleven."

"How old are you, then?" Veronika said.

She was real civil, considering we'd moved from major stuff in her family to minor stuff in mine.

"I'm almost fifteen," Felicia said, and the bottom of my stomach dropped out.

"When's your birthday?"

"February 8."

I hadn't even known her birthday. "Well, you don't know mine, either," I said, to comfort myself.

"It's in November, and you'll be twenty-one."

A curious look passed over Eli's face, but he said, "We'll celebrate, then."

I nodded. All of a sudden, I was numb. The day had been a hard one, a violent one, and full of suspense. I'd made the shot of my life. Eli was free. The Savarovs were facing all kinds of news about themselves. My sister could get pregnant; she was old enough for that. Eli had told everyone we were living like married people. No going back now. I sagged in my seat.

"Eli, your wife needs a nap," Veronika said.

"Yes," he said. Then he hesitated, looked at her with a question in his face.

"In the attic room," Veronika said. "You two can have it for tonight."

Lucy and Alice were shocked that their mother had given her consent. And they loved it. I could tell.

Eli only nodded and helped me up. I could not watch out for anyone else at the moment. They would all have to say what they would and be what they were while I took time away. We went up to the third floor. I held on to the banister and Eli, and he dragged my bag along with him.

Eli opened a door at the top of the stairs. We stumbled into a room about the size of mine at the hotel, a humble room with a double bed. "When we had a live-in maid, this was her room," he said, looking around. There was a sink in one corner, a toilet, a small bathtub, and an old wardrobe. Everything open to view. It was fine.

We got undressed and crawled into the bed. Looked like Eli'd decided he needed a nap, too.

"You smell," I said.

"Too bad to . . . ?"

I smiled. "Not that bad. But I can't stay awake long, so let's get cracking."

"You sweet-talker."

It wasn't what I had imagined, after our long separation, but then . . . I had been scared to imagine much of anything at all. I had Eli back, and Eli loved me, and at the moment we were safe.

Maybe.

I woke up to an empty room. Eli's prison clothes were in a heap on the floor, and he'd left the wardrobe door ajar to show me there was another dress inside. From the light, I could tell I'd slept through the night to the morning.

Great.

I took a quick bath and was happy to dig out my toothbrush. I felt fresher and refreshed when I pulled on the dress and went downstairs, carrying our previous day's clothes in my arms. I'd spotted the clothes washing machine on the back porch the night before. I dropped our things on top.

There were some strange rolls and some butter on the kitchen table, and I ate them like I'd never seen food before. I poured myself a cup of tea, because that was what was available. Felicia came through the dining-room door. She was still in her school uniform. "You're wanted in the front parlor," she said. "You'll never guess who's here." She was smiling.

I could see she wasn't going to tell me who was there, so I went to see for myself.

I was for sure surprised to find the aged Xenia Alexandrovna standing behind Tsarina Caroline, who was sitting on the couch next to a man somewhere in his thirties. He was pale, with dark blue eyes and dark brown hair. He was not wearing a military uniform but a good suit.

Damn, I thought, and did as good a curtsy as I could manage. If ever I was going to attempt it, the time was now. "Your Imperial Majesties," I said, and then didn't know what to do with myself.

"Lizbeth," said Eli, and once I located him I felt better.

"Please, sit with Ilya," Tsar Alexei said. I could tell that getting to sit in the presence of the tsar and his wife was a rare privilege, so I tried to appreciate it. I would have felt better if Xenia had been given leave to sit, too.

Veronika was also sitting, in a little armchair. Captain McMurtry was standing at the door. From his position, he could see both the front door and the people in the parlor. I was glad to see him, and I nodded when I caught his eye. He looked a little surprised, but he nodded back.

No Peter. No Lucy or Alice.

"I am glad to meet the woman who saved my wife's life," Alexei said.

"It was my honor." Figured that was safe.

"I understand you are an excellent shot."

"I am. That's my living."

The tsar's eyebrows drew together in a little pucker.

Okay, I must have said something odd there, and I'd only meant to be matter-of-fact.

"I wonder if you would like to be my wife's bodyguard," Alexei said.

This day was driving me to bad language, and I hadn't been up thirty minutes. "No, thank you, sir. I'm real pleased you think well enough of me for that, but I'm not a city woman, and I would go nuts here."

Clearly, Alexei was taken aback, but I saw that Eli was suppressing a smile. A very small one.

"I'm sorry you can't see your way clear to doing it," Alexei said courteously. "And I'm sure Caroline is disappointed."

Caroline did not look disappointed at all. She looked encouraging. There was something she wanted me to say. I just didn't know what it was. I did know what *I* wanted to say. "Your Imperial Highness," I began, thinking that starting polite was my best bet, "there are some things I'd like to draw to your attention, if you would not mind listening." I thought I'd put that real well, but a glance at Veronika told me that she was now sitting so straight she looked as if she'd sat on a poker, and her pleasant expression was frozen on her face.

Alexei seemed pretty surprised by my words. He glanced at his wife, and she nodded. Okay, I was going in the right direction. At least, Caroline thought so.

"It surprises me that you didn't know Eli was in jail. That someone who had served you well, someone you knew personally, was missing. How could that be?"

Alexei didn't look happy, but he didn't order Captain McMurtry to shoot me, either. "I understand your surprise," Alexei said. Then he seemed to be picking his words as carefully as I had. "I can only tell you that sometimes I am so ill I don't notice things I ought to be aware of. I realize that I have not been eager to ask questions. And I have had advisers who did not . . . draw the right things to my attention."

Had that been because Alexei didn't want to be angry with his uncle? Or because being sick made him wrapped up in his own problems? I was listening to him real intently, because I wanted to understand what he was saying . . . and what he was not saying.

"I have realized in the past few days that some people think I am not a strong ruler because I don't know everything that's going on in my empire. That I am ignorant of the problems of my people and the undercurrents at my own court."

I wanted to nod, but he'd just said he had learned all this stuff. So he didn't really need a gunnie like me to confirm it.

Eli had taken my hand. Maybe he did it from habit, a good habit, but also I thought he was telling me to be even more cautious.

The tsar waited to see if I was going to say something else. But I didn't.

"Caroline and I have been discussing this, once I heard that my uncle had spread a rumor that I was going to die any minute. We have decided I need to be among my people, both at court and in public, much more than I have been."

This time, he definitely waited for me to speak, so I said, "Yes, Your Imperial Highness?"

"You do not want to live in San Diego."

I nodded.

"Since Prince Ilya Savarov is free, and I will make it clear he should never have been imprisoned . . ."

I had no idea where the tsar was going with this long sentence. Eli did. "Your Imperial Highness, my wife and I will be leaving to visit her family in Texoma quite soon, after I have made sure my mother, my sisters, and my *younger* brother are all safe and secure here, and can continue their lives peacefully."

Throwing Bogdan and Dagmar to the wolves. Good.

"You can be assured of that. My wife's aide, Captain McMurtry, promises to keep watch over your family."

I looked at Ford McMurtry just at that moment and saw the way he was gazing at Veronika. Ha!

"And my sister, Felicia, Your Imperial Highness? She has already been trusted to help you when you needed her assistance." That was the fanciest I could say *When you were sick, she gave you her blood.*

"She will continue in the school as long as she likes," Alexei said. "And I am grateful for her assistance."

"Some of Rasputin's descendants have died suspiciously, I hear," I said. "I have no idea how true that may be. I would be very, very upset if anything happened to Felicia."

Now I'd pushed the conversation over a cliff, for sure. Alexei gave me a real cold look, and Eli squeezed my fingers too hard, and Veronika looked as though she were about to pass out.

Only Caroline remained cool. She said, "Any sister would feel the same concern, Lizbeth. We will be careful of your sister as we would be careful of any girl in our care."

I had to be content with that. "I'm very grateful," I said. "I thank you both."

"My husband's sons," Veronika said. "Your Imperial Highness has decided their disposition?" She didn't sound very concerned, but she was going through the moves.

Alexei looked over at his wife's aide. I wondered where his own aide was.

It was like Captain McMurtry had read my mind.

He said, "It's hard to imagine, but the tsar's own aide was colluding with Bogdan and Dagmar Savarov to make our emperor look frail and weak and to promote Grand Duke Alexander as his replacement."

"That's shocking," Veronika said, exactly as if she were hearing it for the first time.

"Now that Alexander is out of the picture, we have discovered documents that confirm he was lying when he swore to the tsar that he had no part in that plan," McMurtry continued. He might almost have been speaking from a piece of paper. I wondered if he'd written this out ahead of time. "Those traitors who were in Alexander's camp have been exposed, and they will stand trial. As for Bogdan, he had presented the tsar with assurances of his faithfulness, which makes his involvement all the more culpable."

I'd started thinking about something else, so I wasn't sure I was following all this. That was a lot of words. If Alexander was supposed to have been assassinated by Bogdan—and Bogdan had been arrested for that—how come the tsar was now sure that Bogdan (and his brother Dagmar) had been on Alexander's side all the time? I wanted to ask some questions, but everyone was looking so pleased I decided I better keep my mouth shut.

I could see past the tsar's head out the front window, where cars were clogging Hickory Street. There were soldiers in the front yard. Good. But as I watched, I noticed some of them were drifting off in the direction of the intersection to the east, and I heard some noise coming from there. No one else seemed to notice this, but McMurtry had a little frown on his face, and I caught his eye. I jerked my head. He went to the window.

"Your Imperial Highness, I must step out for a moment. Something is happening in the street. Please stay away from the windows, sir."

Caroline's eyes widened. For the first time, she looked directly at her husband. Alexei took her hand and said, "I'm sure everything is fine, my dearest."

Caroline tried to look calm, but as someone who'd recently been attacked, that wasn't easy for her. "At least the baby is safe," she said.

That remained to be seen. If the palace troops were loyal, and if the palace servants were loyal, both iffy, *then* Crown Prince Nicholas was safe. The Romanovs were going from the frying pan into the fire.

"Eli," I said, very quietly. He looked at me. "Where are your sisters?"

"They've gone to the corner grocery with Peter," Eli said. "They should be back by now."

"Excuse me, your highnesses," I said, remembering to bow before I ran up the stairs to retrieve my guns. I was back down the stairs before McMurtry returned.

"No vest," Eli said to me. I wondered where Eli's vest had ended up. I hoped not with anyone who knew how to use its contents.

The phone rang. Veronika hurried into the hall to answer it. She held it out to Eli.

"Yes," he said, and waited. His shoulders relaxed a little. "Felix," he told me.

Eli's face was wooden as he listened a bit. "Felix, thanks for the news. We have royal visitors. And my sisters are at the corner grocery with Peter. Yes, the one three blocks away. I have no idea if it's safer there or here." Eli listened again. "Good to know," he said finally, and put the telephone in its cradle.

"Your Imperial Highness," Eli began, and stopped, took a deep breath. "The followers of Grand Duke Alexander, led by his son Vasily, are attempting a coup. They know they won't be spared if they aren't successful."

Alexei's blue eyes were fixed on Eli. "Vasily is a base fellow," he said. "He will fight like a cornered rat."

I left them to their discussion. I went to the hall telephone.

I called the Rasputin School. I knew the voice that answered. "Tom O'Day," I said. "I'm Felicia's sister, Lizbeth Rose. Did you know that Alexander is dead and his son Vasily is attacking the emperor?"

"That's treason," O'Day said, after a pause.

"Then you come defend your tsar. We are at Eli's home on

Hickory Street. The tsar and tsarina are here. They are in danger. Are you loyal?"

"I'm loyal," O'Day said without hesitation.

"Then you come defend your tsar."

"I'll bring everyone who has power."

"Lilias Abramova should come," I said, remembering her promise. I described the situation to the grigori so he wouldn't be walking into more danger than he had to.

I returned to the front parlor. The royal couple was looking anxiously in my direction. They'd heard a bit of what I'd said. "Grigoris are coming," I said. "The school is behind you."

There was some shouting and screaming from behind the house.

Eli, stationed by the front window, said, "Mother, please go see what's happening out there. Don't show yourself."

Veronika hurried out of the room.

There was an explosion. It was strong enough to make the ground shake for a second. I could see smoke billowing across the clear blue sky. My guns were in my hands.

Sounded like it was coming from the east, where we'd seen the tsar's escort turning. I stood by the window, mostly hidden by the curtains, and looked out. I heard gunfire. Not far away. Not far enough.

"Crap," I said. When the tsar gave me a funny look, I figured he didn't hear that very often.

"Sir, you and the tsarina should go upstairs," Eli said. "As well as your aunt." He nodded at Xenia.

"My wife and Aunt Xenia should be safe upstairs. I will stay and defend this house," Alexei said, sounding quite calm. "You were loyal to me. I will be loyal to you."

Veronika went down on one knee to give Alexei a pistol. It was beautiful, but it was no time to inspect it. "This was my husband's," she said. "Now you can turn it to good use."

"Lizbeth," Eli said in a gentle voice.

I glared at him. I knew what was coming.

"Please. Guard the tsarina," he said.

"I stand by you," I said, feeling my lips pull back from my teeth. "Lizbeth."

"Eli. I just got you back."

I met his eyes, my whole face hard as iron.

"Lizbeth, please take my mother, the tsarina, and Xenia Alexandrovna. Upstairs."

He'd thrown his mom into the pot.

I gave up.

I jerked my head to the stairs. "Ladies, please go up." I could not be bothered to waste time with titles. Veronika sort of corralled the tsarina and the tsar's aunt with a sweeping hostess gesture, and without haste they went to the staircase.

"You better not die," I told Eli.

He smiled at me. "You know me better," he said. "I'm going to look in my room for my old vest. I think I left it here." He practically ran up the stairs to one of the bedrooms.

I said the worst words I could think of as I herded the three women up the stairs. But I said them in my head.

Xenia climbed the stairs heavily, her hand gripping the banister. Caroline kept looking back at her husband. I wondered what she was thinking. How brave Alexei was being? What would happen to her if he died? Was their son safe? Veronika looked determined.

Felicia's voice called out from the kitchen door, "Don't shoot! Felix is here!"

"Felicia! Up here with me!"

In a moment my sister was bounding up the stairs. "What are you doing?" she asked.

"I got the women to keep safe," I said, making it clear how I felt about that. "You better help."

Felicia nodded, her dark head with its neat braids bobbing up and down. "I will stand with you."

For a moment, I put one arm around her. "Thanks, sister," I said. "I'll bet you're loaded with surprises. Boom first, magic after, okay?"

"I understand." Felicia pulled her pocket open to show me it was full of pebbles. Explosive spells, made by a beginning grigori. I had to bite the inside of my mouth. We might as well be waving smoking sticks of dynamite.

"How come you didn't go to the store with the others?"

"Eh, I had a feeling I was needed more here," Felicia said.

"Felix didn't bring Peter and the girls?"

"He came in the back door pretty upset, but he didn't tell me why."

Eli ran up the stairs to the third floor. He was wearing a vest, yellow with age, but its pockets were bulgy. Good.

"What's he going to do?" Veronika said.

"I think he's going to defend the house from the roof. There's a way to get on it?"

"He could climb out the attic window," Veronika said doubt-fully.

I nodded. That's what he would do, then.

I couldn't do anything about the risk of this now. Time to make the second floor harder to breach.

"Let's block the stairs," I said, and Felicia and I threw chairs down. When Caroline and Veronika understood what we were doing, they joined in with vigor, while Xenia pointed out movable chairs. I glimpsed the tsar in the hall below, carrying the pistol that had belonged to Eli's dad. He looked like he knew what he was doing.

Captain McMurtry made a big entrance on his return. He flung open the front door and fell through it. Six men came in after him and pulled him to his feet to get him out of the way. They slammed the door behind them and locked it. As soon as the men (three very well dressed, three ordinary people) saw Alexei was present, they knelt.

"These are my neighbors," Veronika said, looking down the stairs into the hall and sounding surprised. "The captain has recruited help."

"Good idea," I said, hoping that all these men were really on the tsar's side, and hadn't just sneaked in under the cloak of loyalty.

Just as the thought crossed my mind, one of the men pulled a knife from under his coat and raised it, his body beginning to lunge toward Alexei.

I put a bullet through his head.

There was a long silence. All the men on the ground floor were staring from me to the man whose head had a big hole in it. The knife lay by his hand.

The tsar spoke first. "I'm obliged to you, Lizbeth Rose," he said, inclining his head as he turned to look up at me.

"Think nothing of it, sir," I told the tsar. I was keeping my eyes on the rest of the newcomers, in case some of them were likewise inclined. They didn't budge. And they didn't offer to shoot me back, though they all had firearms of one kind or another.

Behind me, Veronika said, "Ford is hurt." Her voice was as tense as a bowstring. While we were all looking at one another, Captain McMurtry was bleeding in the front hall. I took a moment to make sure his hands were moving. One of them was, anyway.

"If Eli has time, he'll work on him," I said. "Eli's pretty good at healing." It worried me that Eli had been out of sight for so long. Since he'd run back to talk to Felix, he hadn't returned.

"He is?" Veronika said.

"Yes, ma'am," I said. "He's been a big help to me."

"Because . . . you get hurt a lot?" Caroline asked.

"Bound to happen when people are shooting back at you." I kept my eyes on the men. The well-dressed one who'd brought in the traitor was blubbering and crying on his knees. The dead man had been his valet, he was saying. I didn't know what that was.

"Dead guy helped the weeping willow get dressed every day," Felicia said in Spanish. I didn't know if she'd read my mind or if she'd caught me looking puzzled. "Took care of his clothes."

"Really?" I could hardly believe anyone could make a living doing such a thing. Who needed help putting on his clothes? Only babies or the very old, and there were few of those in Texoma.

"Yep." Felicia nodded. "So, we dying here today?" She sounded bright and brave, but her hands were shaking.

"Nope. Not in the Holy Russian Empire."

"You thought if you shot Alexander this would all be done?"

"I did."

"I thought so, too," Felicia said very quietly. "But yesterday one of his cousins told me the oldest son, Vasily, was real good at maneuvering his father into doing things Alexander hadn't intended."

"So it would have been better if I'd gotten Vasily."

"Yeah, I think so."

I shrugged. "Didn't know."

This was always the hard part, waiting on the action to start. I wondered how many men were on this Vasily's side, how well they were armed. How loyal the tsar's men were.

I heard gunfire growing closer.

I wondered where Peter, Lucy, and Alice were. Their trip to the corner store . . . worst timing ever.

I wondered where Eli was and what he was doing.

I'd told my sister we weren't dying here. Maybe I'd been lying.

CHAPTER TWENTY-TWO

Captain McMurtry had quit swearing, so I guessed he was unconscious or dead. I checked my guns again. Missing two bullets, same as last time. I had some extra ammo in my bag upstairs, and I sent Felicia up for it. Replaced the bullets. Wished again for my Winchester. Listened to the tsarina, Xenia, and Veronika praying together.

"Felicia, you think there's anything suspicious about the girls and Peter deciding to get out of the house on the very day the house is attacked?" She hadn't spoken in several minutes, but I knew she was behind me.

Most girls her age would have exclaimed or been astounded. Not Felicia. "I'm not sure who would be the guilty one," she said. "Not all three of them. Peter really loves and admires Eli. I don't know Lucy and Alice. Felix talks about Lucy with respect. Alice is just a girl. I think when the tsar walked in, Veronika didn't have anything to offer him as refreshments, and she sent the kids to the store since there's no maid."

That "just a girl" was kind of funny, since Alice was about the same age as Felicia.

"You trust Felix?" I said, just to be talking.

"He's a great grigori, very dangerous. Trust? I don't know. He's clever."

"I've seen him in action. You're right about him being dangerous."

"I'm envious."

"Honey, you'll see Felix kill people if you know him any longer than this. They may not stay dead." I thought of the dead man I'd re-killed at the park. Ugh.

"I hope I have that much power," Felicia muttered.

When she grew up? I was scared to ask why. But then she told me.

"I want to stand on my own, so I don't ever have to do something I don't want to do," she said.

"I'm scared to ask."

"Not sex stuff," she said directly. "But our father made me the bait in some of his money-making schemes."

"Don't tell me now. Tell me tomorrow."

"What should I do, if you die?"

"Go back to the school. Eli will take care of you."

"What if he dies?"

Now she sounded every bit as young as I'd thought her.

"Felix will take an interest, and Peter. And the tsarina promised to watch out for you. Don't ask me what you'll do if they die, too. That's as far as I can go."

"I will watch out for you, Felicia," the tsarina said. I hadn't known she'd been listening.

"There you go, sister," I said, not turning my eyes. "The tsarina will be your sponsor."

"Thank you," Felicia said meekly. But her voice was empty.

Felicia and I both knew the person most likely to die this day was Caroline.

I closed my eyes, listening. The fighting was getting closer. No way of knowing if this was just a local melee, or citywide. No way of knowing if help was coming or not. They'd string me up, I figured, for Grand Duke Alexander. Not an easy death.

Oh, well. Eli was free. Again, I wondered why he wasn't at the door. The tsar was there. Then I heard footsteps overhead on the little-used third floor. Sounded like Eli. I smiled as I figured out what he was going to do.

"Felicia, get up there," I said.

"What?"

"Up on the third floor with Eli. You got things he needs. I guess he got on the roof from a window. He's defending from there."

Felicia had made a noise of protest, but when she understood me, she scrambled to her feet and ran to the staircase. I could hear her throwing open windows to find out how to climb up. Felicia would do it.

The noise of the fight was so close now I knew it was at the end of the Savarovs' driveway.

Deep steady breaths, now.

Yelling, and sounds of many feet on the gravel driveway. I set my attention on the front door, barricaded with the china cabinet from the dining room. Soon they would be on the other side of the door. Maybe they would set it afire.

I could hear Veronika taking ragged breaths behind me. "Steady, woman," said Xenia Alexandrovna, in the calmest voice I'd ever heard. "They are *dogs*. My brother deserved to die, and so does his son."

Then came the *boom* of an explosion.

I jumped as much as anyone else. "That was one of Felicia's bombs," I said, though I didn't know if the women behind me could hear me.

It was right noisy.

The men inside the house, ready to defend it, were as surprised as the men who'd been running to the front door to break it in. There were yells of surprise inside. And screaming, but that was from outside.

Despite another explosion, a panel of the front door splintered about four minutes later. The neighbors all stood back, which was wise. The tsar had taken up a brave stance, and once again I felt a bit of surprise that he seemed to know what he was doing. I let Alexei shoot the first man.

After that, I started in.

If the numbers weren't high, we could defend the house . . . if they kept targeting the front door. But sooner or later, we all would run out of ammunition, or they'd smash all the windows, or they'd come through the back door, or they'd set the house on fire. Only fools would keep trying the front door.

They were foolish for longer than I'd counted on.

When the shooting had slowed down, I heard Veronika right behind me. She said, "Eli called down. Enemies coming in the back."

"Thanks." I heard another *boom*, this time from the rear. There'd been two more at the front. Getting up on the roof had been a very good idea.

I didn't want to think about what the front yard would look like now.

So that our stair-blocking barrier would stay in place, I swung a leg over the banister and gripped it, letting myself down, guns in my pockets. I landed in a crouch and drew, surprised the grigori coming in the door. Didn't kill him, what with the crouch and the hasty draw from a pocket, but he was down for a while, and I wasn't going to spend another bullet on him. If Eli hadn't told Veronika to warn me, I would have hesitated, thinking he was a friend. Where was Tom O'Day?

Now there was an opening running the length of the house, front door to back, the smell of guns and death washed in and out. I had my back to the front door, but I heard the shots slowing down. Either the men were being more careful with their shooting, or their ammo was about out. I was the only one watching the rear, but the hall wasn't that wide, so I didn't ask for help.

A man in a strange uniform appeared in the kitchen doorway next, and him I shot dead, but I felt his bullet go past me. It was that close. And shooters from this direction might hit my allies in the front. I shouted out to warn them.

I heard a scream from the roof, and I was sure the voice was Felicia's. In that moment, a woman leaped into the house, a grigori, and my shot went over her head. She threw a spell at me, and it hit me full force. My body flew backward, and I landed on my rear on the polished floor, right next to the first intruder.

I did my best to look dead so she'd advance. She did. She didn't know I had some resistance to magic because of my grigori father. I shot her as she stepped over me. She collapsed to the floor like her strings had been cut.

But I couldn't manage to get up.

My head hurt pretty bad. I'd slammed it against the wood when I'd hit the floor. It was a huge effort to keep my hand up, my gun straight. It was so heavy. Maybe if I laid it down for a minute, I could recover some strength. I struggled with that feeling. I made myself keep looking at the opening through to the kitchen and the sky outside.

I could see Caroline and Veronika looking over the banister at me, and Caroline had something in her hands. "Now!" Veronika yelled, and just as a dark shape came between me and the sky, Caroline dropped something. The shape wavered and vanished, and then—to my surprise—I did, too.

CHAPTER TWENTY-THREE

My eyes were open, and I was looking up at Veronika's face. "Lizbeth!" she said, and she sounded like she truly wanted my attention.

"Yes," I said, but it didn't come out very strong. More like I was croaking.

Veronika said a lot of stuff in Russian. She was crying a little bit. I couldn't figure that out.

"Where is Felicia?" I said. Maybe she could explain.

"She is still on roof, keeping watch," Veronika said, and for the first time her Russian accent was heavy. "She is very excited," Veronika added.

"Her first big fight." I could understand that. "Any word from your girls and Peter?"

"No. I'm worried."

"I don't hear gunfire," I said.

"I think fighting here may be over," she said. "Caroline and I have come down to see if we can help the wounded. But we're ready to run back up and barricade the stairs behind us, if we need to." She attempted a smile.

"You do that, if you hear a single shot," I said. "Help me up. I got to reload."

She slid her arm under my shoulders. I was sitting up after a few bad seconds. I patted my pockets. I had a few bullets left. Very slowly and carefully, I reloaded the cartridge and popped it back into one gun, then put the remaining bullets in the second. I was as ready as I could be.

"How are the rest?" I said. I didn't know anyone's name besides McMurtry and the tsar.

"The tsar has not been wounded, thanks be to God," Veronika said. "The captain is in a grave situation." Her face went all tight to contain her worry.

"Where is Eli?" I asked, which was the question I'd wanted to ask all along.

"He's with a grigori named Tom O'Day. They're trying to keep the captain from bleeding to death."

The captain. Oh, McMurtry.

"He okay? Eli?" I said.

"He isn't wounded."

Finally, she'd told me what I wanted to know. "Okay, I need to stand now." With a lot of help from Eli's mom, I was on my own two feet in a minute or two. Everything stayed still. I didn't throw up.

"All right," I said, to encourage myself. "I'm going to go looking for Peter and the girls. Felicia!"

Felicia appeared above us on the landing. She looked like a different girl. Her hair was coming out of its braid, her school uniform was streaked with this and that—but not blood—and most of all, her face was alive with excitement. And she looked every minute of her true age. "Hey, did you hear my bombs?" she said, beaming.

"They saved us," I said. "Give me a hand so Veronika can go to the captain."

"Oh, sure! How are you?" Felicia's face went concerned as she really looked at me, and then she ran down the stairs. Her skinny arm went around me. I nodded to Veronika, who gave Felicia a look I couldn't interpret. Then she took herself off for the front parlor.

"No bullet holes, still alive and walking," I told my sister, but it came out in a croak. "What's the street like?"

"Quiet."

After a tense moment, I got myself moving.

"Back door," I said. Felicia steered me down the hall and into the kitchen. After a few steps, I managed on my own, more or less.

"Aren't you going to find Eli?"

"If I do, I might . . . give in." I didn't need to explain, not to Felicia. "It would be more use if I found his brother and sisters."

I shivered. Cool air was streaming through the door, which was hanging by a hinge. Something would have to be done about that.

But not by me. I felt like my bones were tired.

Felicia and I surveyed the former gravel drive leading to the garage, and what had been a nice plot of grass back when this area had been the backyard.

It was scattered with craters and dead men.

When I felt Felicia stiffen beside me, I knew that she understood she had done this. This understanding was part of fighting, too.

I remembered walking around the big truck with my first crew when I was sixteen. I had counted the dead who had attacked us to steal our cargo. I had shot them. I had seen them fall. But after all that was over, I'd had to know they'd never get up . . . and that was because of me.

When Felicia made a snuffly sound, I asked her to get a jacket for me, and she hurried back into the house. I took a slow, unsteady stroll among the dead. There were more grigoris back here than there had been in the front. I recognized the girl who'd followed Felicia and me back from our first excursion together, the girl Felicia had said such bad things about. She was missing her left leg. She'd bled out. Felicia didn't need to see that.

I pulled the vest off the closest grigori and put it over her face. Just in time. Felicia had brought me a jacket I didn't recognize, but it was warm and about the right size. I buttoned it up while she held my pistols. One of the dead men had dropped a rifle, and I picked it up.

"What is it?" Felicia was looking at the rifle with some doubt.

"It's an old-country Russian rifle," I said, turning it from side to side. "A veteran at home came back with one of these. I think it's a Mosin-Nagant." I worked the bolt. "It's loaded. I'd get five shots with this. Can you see . . . No, never mind."

A Russian rifle was better than no rifle. It had been lying by the hand of a fellow with a salt-and-pepper beard. He, too, had been badly damaged in the legs by one of Eli's and Felicia's magic bombs. But if he had more bullets, I wanted them.

I went down on a knee, not a good moment. But at least I discovered Old Man had brought along a box of bullets. "Put these in a pocket," I said, handing them to Felicia.

My sister didn't say anything, which was a nice change.

She helped me stand, and I looked through the sights. "This rifle is not good, but any rifle is better than no rifle," I said. "Let's go."

"Look," Felicia said. She pointed.

I followed her finger. There was a woman sticking her head out of the second-story window of the house next door, the one with the fountain.

"Is everyone all right in the house?" she called.

"Does it look like everyone's all right?" Felicia called back, with some justice.

"Well . . . no. Is Veronika unhurt?"

I figured I better answer this time. "Veronika is well, but others are wounded, and some help would be appreciated," I said.

Felicia opened her mouth, and I just knew she was going to tell the woman the tsar was in the Savarovs' house. "No," I said quietly. "Don't tell."

"I'll be over in a few minutes," the woman called. Her blond hair was carefully pulled into a roll on the back of her head, and her makeup was flawless. Considering the chaos in the house next door, I wondered how she'd managed this. She pulled her head in and shut her window. I wondered if she would really come.

"I'm going with you to the grocery," Felicia said.

"Go back inside and watch from the roof."

"No, I'm going with you. I don't want you to collapse halfway there."

I couldn't summon the strength to argue.

Felicia and I cut through the yard of the house behind the Savarovs' and moved carefully toward the grocery on a street parallel to Hickory. It was about three o'clock, I figured. There was a lot of activity in the neighborhood, which wasn't surprising. Friends were running from house to house now that the bullets had stopped flying. No one spoke to us, and they circled wide to avoid us.

"What I don't see is traffic," I said. "That worries me."

"What do you mean?"

A couple of kids started to come toward us, probably wanting to find out what we knew, but when they saw the Colts and the rifle, they backed off. Smart.

"Where is aid? The tsar is in a private home, with very little protection. Where is the army? The guard? Tom O'Day came, and he was bringing grigoris from the school, last I heard."

"I saw a few of them," Felicia said. "They're good, but there aren't a lot of them. I think . . . I think some of them were with the attackers."

Felicia had recognized some of the grigoris, then.

After a moment to get her mental balance back, Felicia said, "If some of the guilds had responded . . . that would have been better. More grigoris, more experienced." We reached the corner of the third block, and we turned right.

There was a traffic jam around the corner store. Vehicles were parked crazy, completely blocking Hickory Street.

Felicia said something in Spanish that just about blistered my ears.

We ducked into the alley behind the store. The smell of garbage was strong. I had to tell my stomach to behave. It didn't seem to bother my sister.

"What do you think?" she whispered.

"Put on this jacket to cover your uniform," I said, struggling out of it. "Go into the store by this back door. See if you can find out what's happening inside." Not for the first time, I wondered where Felix was. What had he done after he'd failed to get the kids out the first time?

Felicia smoothed her hair, pulled on my borrowed jacket, and started crying as if someone had just shot her favorite cat. She opened the store's back door, fumbling as if she could barely see, and stumbled into the store. There was a bell attached to the door, and I heard it tinkle. She wasn't going to enter unnoticed.

She was a piece of work, my sister.

I waited what seemed like a long time, leaning against the wall. Finally, I heard the bell again. I straightened and aimed. The first one out was Alice, who was scared out of her wits. She shrieked when she saw me, and then clapped a hand over her mouth as if she could recall the noise. Behind her was Lucy, who was angry. Then Peter, even angrier, and with the beginnings of a black eye. Maybe a broken nose. They clustered around me, asking a million questions at one time.

"Shut up and listen," I said.

They did.

"We held 'em off at the house," I said. "The tsar is there. He's okay. Your mom and Eli are not hurt. Where is Felicia?"

"Felicia told them Felix is her brother, and that she'd been looking everywhere for him," Lucy said. She seemed peeved about that. "So they let her stay with him."

"Why does Felix need someone to stay with him?" This was too slow.

"Because he's unconscious."

"Why is he unconscious?"

I must have sounded a little shirty, because all three of the kids stood straight and talked faster.

"He came into the store with his hands out," Peter said. "We'd seen him pass by before, but he didn't come in, because there were so many people inside, I think . . ."

But of course Felix had returned to try again, because this was something he was doing for Eli. And perhaps Lucy, too.

"But there was a grigori in there who recognized him . . ." Alice began.

"And that bitch knocked him down before he could say anything," Lucy ended. No mistaking how she felt about that. Steam was just about coming out of her ears.

"Lucy!" Alice said, shocked.

"So we pretended not to know him," Peter said, sounding ashamed. "Because we didn't know what would happen if we said he was our friend."

"That was the smart thing to do. But what did Felicia . . . ?" I'd figured I could rely on Little Miss Survivor to read the situation correctly.

"The same woman spotted the school uniform," Peter said. "Though Felicia was wearing a jacket over it," he added, as if he had to be fair.

Clearly, this clever grigori was the cause of a lot of trouble.

"Felicia. Is she tied up?" I said.

"No!" Peter smiled. "She began wailing and carrying on and told the grigoris and the followers of Alexander that Felix was her brother, and she hadn't seen him in two years, and what could she do to help him?"

"So?" I wanted the summary.

"So, Alexander's people—I guess now they're his son's people—are using this grocery as their rendezvous point," Lucy said.

God bless her. "And what is their plan?"

"They are waiting for reinforcements. The store is getting so crowded that they let us leave, when we said we wanted to get home to our mother and our sick old grandfather," Peter said proudly.

I took a deep breath. "Here's what you must do. You need to find a telephone. I'm not sure if the telephone at your mom's is still working. Peter, do you have the phone number of the dormitory for the Air Guild?"

"Yes, all the guilds share the dormitory," he said.

"Good, then call 'em and tell 'em we need 'em, or else. There aren't enough of us to hold off another attack. I don't think there's many of Alexander's folks . . . but there are fewer of us on the scene. We need magic and guns."

"What will you do?" Alice said. "Won't you be with us?"

Alice was clearly about to lose her head, but I had other things that were higher priority. "I need to get Felicia and Felix out of the store before the counterattack comes. You may get to the house first." They would, for sure. We might not make it out. "What's it like in front of the store?"

Peter said, "There are about twenty people standing on the sidewalk out front, waiting for their own reinforcements to arrive. More milling about in the street."

"How many inside?"

"Maybe four of them, plus Mother Heedles, who owns the grocery, and her brother, Dexter."

"Where are the Heedleses standing?"

Peter was fidgety and clearly ready to get going, but Alice and Lucy told me what to expect. I nodded.

"What's the grigori wearing, the one who took out Felix?"

"She's wearing a red dress and a black jacket," Lucy said. "She's about thirty, with short brown hair. Last time I saw her, she was standing at the left front window."

"Okay, scoot," I said. "Go as fast as you can."

Peter nodded and led the girls away, talking all the time. At least they were out of the way. Peter had left the door just a little open, and I swung it wide enough to step in. I was in a storeroom stacked high with cartons of this and that. There were some hams hanging, too, and the smell of them made my stomach jump around a little. I got to the next door, the door to the store proper, and found Peter had left it a bit open, too.

There weren't too many ways to handle this. The girls had told me Felix was lying on the floor close to the front door, and Felicia was with him. So there was a strong likelihood my sister was kneeling on the floor. I had to fire high.

I also didn't want to kill Mother Heedles or her brother, if I could help it. *Definitely* wanted to kill the grigori in the red dress, because she sounded most dangerous.

I pushed the door a little wider. My Colts would have been better, maybe, but I had the rifle up and ready. It was unreliable, strange. I would rather use it for far shooting. I pushed the door a little wider with the barrel.

The movement of the door only caught the eye of the store owner, Mother Heedles, easy to mark because she was wearing an apron and had silver hair. I feared she'd call out, but she didn't. Her brother was a strapping man, and she took hold of his arm, her whole face telling him to shut up.

I took another step into the store, which was dim because of all the people outside the windows and the gray skies. The grigori in her red dress, the biggest threat, had moved to the front door and was reaching toward it.

I shot her dead. The bullet passed through her and through the front door, shattering the glass. It was a much showier entrance than I'd planned on making. My judgment was . . . maybe I didn't have any.

Shadowy figures to my left on the floor had to be Felicia and Felix, and now that I'd located the two Heedleses, everyone else was fair game. This rifle had more recoil than I was used to. I missed the second grigori, but I got him with the third shot. I wounded a soldier with the fourth.

There was chaos outside, because no one had expected to be fired upon from inside the store.

"Get these two and get out!" I snapped, and Mother Heedles and her brother jumped to lift up Felix, who wasn't completely conscious. I caught a glimpse of Felicia's face. She was furious, she didn't know who at. She made as if to stand by me.

I said, "If you got another of your bombs, throw it out the front door and then get out of here!"

Giving her that one thing to do was smart. Quick as a wink, my sister pulled something from her pocket and pitched it through the hole in the glass. Then she ran out of the way, not giving me a look.

I was ready to shoot anyone who went after them. I started counting to three, when I planned to get the hell out of the store.

Felicia's little bomb went off as I said, "One."

There was a lot of screaming, which was good, but there was also flying metal, wood, and glass.

In the moment before the piece of glass caught me on the cheek, I felt sorry for the Heedleses. The store was badly damaged.

I felt the blood and then the pain. I've never thought of myself as vain, but the fact that the cut was on my face made me feel queasy. Damn, it hurt. And my own blood dripping. Ugh.

There was no way to stop it. Needed both hands for the rifle. I moved as fast as I could out the back, through the storeroom, out into the alley. The others hadn't waited, but they'd gotten only a block.

I caught up with them, though it wasn't easy to walk in a straight line. Felicia glanced back at me and shrieked, and the others just about stopped to look, but I yelled, "Keep on going! Go!" They had stampeded out of the grocery at a good clip, but having to keep Felix up had slowed 'em down almost from the get-go.

Felix was trying to make his legs move, but he wasn't having much luck. Peter and Lucy had turned back to help. They were dragging him along between them.

I flipped the rifle to my left hand and drew a Colt. The blood was really getting to me now, but I had to be ready to defend this group. The Colt was easier, more familiar.

The Heedleses had vanished.

"Where's the storekeeper?" I asked, as I caught up with the little group.

"They turned the other way to go home!" Lucy said, panting. Only Alice was managing to run. She was close to home already.

Lucy and Peter managed to keep up a stumbling trot, even with Felix to manage. Felicia, beside me, showed me she had one more pebble in her hand. She didn't say anything, which was kind of a miracle, but she glanced at me in a worried way.

It seemed to take twice as long to return to the Savarov house as it had to come to the grocery.

I expected an attack from behind, but no one followed us. Thanks to Felicia, we'd killed the people who would have tried to catch us. The only cost had been the Heedleses' big windows and my face.

CHAPTER TWENTY-FOUR

We went in through the kitchen door on the run. Felix was dragged along by Peter and Lucy, and when they'd gotten into the hall, they all collapsed. Alice went looking for her mother, tears all over her face, and I decided the place beside Peter looked good. I was feeling a little woozy by then. Shock and blood loss. Felicia looked down at me and went away. Figured she was going to find Eli.

Peter said, "I'm going to look for a telephone, like you said," and he got up and went back out. Good.

I closed my eyes, feeling the blood trickling on my cheek. I shuddered all over. Today had been full of nerves and uncertainty and loud noises.

"Over there," Felicia said clearly.

Eli was on his knees beside me, I knew his smell and his breathing and everything about him. "Lizbeth," he said. His voice was all ragged.

"I'm okay," I said, with a big effort.

"The hell you are," Felicia said. "You are *not* okay."

"The bomb worked," I said. "You did great today." I wanted to be sure I said that.

"Thanks." I could hear the pride in my sister's voice. "But all my explosives were on . . . speculation. I wasn't sure they'd all work, and I wasn't sure I'd ever need them."

"Yes, and yes," I said. I felt my voice trail off.

"Well, they didn't *all* work," Eli said, kind of absentmindedly, while he turned my head this way and that. "Mother, bring a bowl of water and a rag, please!"

While we waited, Eli asked Lucy what had happened to Felix. She told him, clearly trying not to sound as worried as she was.

"If she spelled him to stun him, he'll wake up. The fact that he was able to even move his legs to get back here is a sure sign," Eli told her. "It will just take a while. Why he decided to try again to get you, on his own, it's beyond me. Peter, where've you been?"

"I found a telephone, as Lizbeth asked. I called the dormitory. Finally, a fire grigori answered, said everyone was out in the streets looking for the tsar to protect him. I hope he was telling the truth, because I told him where the tsar is."

That was all he could do, and Eli told him so. Veronika had gotten back with the bowl and the clean rag, and Eli began working on my face. I could feel tears run down my cheeks.

"I should start carrying bombs, too," Peter said. He sounded bitter. "I had no vest, no nothing to protect our sisters. I should have been better prepared."

"We were just going to the grocery store," Alice said. She was doing the calm *Hush, now* voice a lot of women learn to use when dealing with men who are upset. She'd learned it young.

"And they would have shot you dead if you'd had on a vest," Lucy added, with some truth.

"Girls, Peter, would you go ask our guests what you can do for them?" Veronika said. "I need to get back to the captain." In a minute, we were the only people in the kitchen.

"What news?" I asked Eli. I tried to sound strong. I didn't.

"Captain McMurtry will live with good nursing. The tsar is unhurt, proud of himself, and finally got in touch with the palace due to one of his guards who escaped to get back to the island, and also a neighbor who had a working telephone. A guard regiment is on the way. Peter says the faithful grigoris are coming. If all of this falls into place . . ."

That was a big if.

"The tsar plans to drive back to the palace in an open car with the regiment around him, so the people can see he is alive and well."

Might be more to the point to mount the body of Alexander's son Vasily on the hood of the car, but I didn't say it. "The grand duke's family all rounded up? Including the other sons?"

"As far as I know. Sophia, the mother of his three bastards, has shown up here to plead for her life."

"Don't trust her," Felicia and I said together.

"She crawled up the driveway on her knees," Eli said. He'd been impressed, I could tell. I thought of the neighbor who'd entered camouflaged by good intentions.

"Don't leave her alone with the tsar!" I said.

Eli was on his feet in a second and dashed to the parlor just as a scream tore the air—a scream of rage, cut off in the middle. Eli's hands were up and remained steady as he called, "Tsar Alexei, Tsarina, are you unharmed?"

Eli returned shortly. "Sophie had a knife, but I killed her in time," he said.

I managed to nod. But my sister said sourly, "Crawling doesn't make you honest."

There was a lot more to-do after that. Russians.

"Like crawling made you honest," Felicia muttered in my ear.

"Can you get me a bandage?" I said. I was tired of the blood, and I felt weak. I imagined lying on the bed upstairs, the room quiet, me clean and bandaged. It was a beautiful picture. I opened my eyes just a flicker, saw that I'd bled on the kitchen floor.

"If you get me a bucket of cold water, I'll get it up," I told Veronika, who looked at me with wide eyes. I didn't know when she had come back.

"She's hallucinating," Veronika told someone over my head.

"No, she's apologizing because she bled on the floor," Eli answered.

"Don't worry about it, Lizbeth," Veronika said, bending close to me.

It wasn't a question of worrying, but somehow I couldn't open my mouth and say that. It was time to sleep. I'd clean up the blood when I woke. No, it would have set by then . . .

Too late.

I woke up a little in the dark of night. Eli was in a chair by the bed, but I knew someone was in the bed with me. I turned my head very slowly. In the moonlight, I could see Felix was beside me, sound asleep.

"Do you need to get up?" Eli whispered.

"Yeah, if I can." I thought my bladder would burst.

Eli's arm behind me helped me sit, and I swung my legs over the side of the bed. My head hurt like something big had gotten in my skull and started making horseshoes. *Pound, pound, pound.* But I went to the toilet and used it, and wiped myself, and then Eli helped me stand to wash my hands and dab water on the unbandaged part of my face. I noticed I had on a nightgown, and I was very relieved.

"Shouldn't he have woken up by now?" I said, as I lay back in bed. "You could put him in the chair and get in bed with me."

"You're not in any shape to—"

"I know. I'd just rather it be you beside me." And then I was out again.

Next time I woke, it was morning. Felix was gone, and Eli was brushing his teeth at the sink. He wore nothing, I was happy to see. Eli rinsed and spat and turned to look at me. He grinned when he saw I was awake.

"My sweetheart," he said.

I figured he was poking fun, so I didn't say anything.

"What? No 'my dear husband' for me?"

He sure seemed in high spirits. "How's my . . . how's the wound?" I asked. I hated to seem vain.

"Why, it's healed. I said a spell or two over you, and when Felix woke up, so did he. After he got through telling me how astonished and displeased he was to be in bed with you."

"Don't ever do that again."

"If every bed in the house had not been taken up with wounded or displaced, it would not have happened last night."

"Oh." I finally reached up to touch my cheeks and forehead. No bandage any longer. I felt a slight ridge on my forehead. I got up and went to the mirror, walking carefully. Eli stood aside for me. I couldn't read the expression on his face. There was a thin white scar across my forehead. It was at an angle.

"Makes me look kind of dangerous, doesn't it?" I said, relieved.

Eli's smile burst out again. "So dangerous," he agreed. "Makes me terrified to take you to bed."

"Oh, that's too bad. Because I was thinking that might be a good thing."

"Maybe I could overcome my fear, somehow."

I took him in hand and made him welcome. "Maybe you could."

He overcame his fear just fine.

An hour later, I had a hot bath, which did me even more good.

It was still early when I went downstairs. I could hear voices, but muffled. I was more interested in eating than talking, so I went into the kitchen. It was empty. Nothing was brewing or cooking. I started the coffee and some tea, and I rooted around until I found all the things I needed to make pancakes. And there was bacon. That smell would wake up anyone in the world. If there's such a thing as heaven, I bet it smells like bacon.

Alice wandered in. She'd dressed, but her hair was every whicha-ways. "I'm sorry," she said. "You shouldn't be doing this."

"I do it at home," I said, flipping three pancakes. "Why not here?"

"Because you are a guest," she said seriously.

I did not ask her if she knew how to make and cook pancakes. I was pretty sure I already knew the answer. "How many people in the house, you think?"

Alice said, "His Imperial Majesty and Her Imperial Majesty returned to the palace. Our neighbors went home. There were six of them. I have written all their names down."

"So you'll remember?" I was kind of at a loss here.

"Yes, in case anyone forgets who was loyal and who was not. They are the ones who came to the aid of His Imperial Majesty."

Alice seemed to be drawn a little tight this morning.

I could only nod, and found a plate to put the pancakes on. Bacon was about done.

"Sometimes one is conflicted," Alice said.

"How so?" I glanced out the empty doorway and saw Felix and Eli dragging a piece of wood toward the house.

"I would rather be called Alyona Ivanova Savarov than Alice Savarov, but that is the way of this country."

"You want me to call you Alyona?" It was my best offer. I had no idea what was eating at the girl.

"No, Alice will do. I'll set the table in the dining room."

"Great," I said. It was a relief to hear something that made sense.

Felicia straggled in, wearing what she'd worn yesterday. Her hair was braided neatly, but the clothes needed a wash, for sure. "I shared Lucy's bed," she said. "Lucy's on her way down soon."

"Is Captain McMurtry doing okay?"

"Dunno. He slept in Mrs. Savarov's bed while she slept on the chaise. She made a big point of spelling that out."

We gave each other a quick smile.

"You look a lot better," Felicia said frankly. "No blood, clean clothes, and a little skinny scar."

I nodded. "Eli did a great job. Felix is out there with him. He seems to be alert today."

Felicia went to the window to look out at them. "Good, they've found something to serve as a door," she said.

Alice came into the kitchen. The dining-room door swung shut behind her. I remembered pushing it open a few nights ago, killing the man and woman who'd been tormenting Eli's family. I felt good about that until I realized Alice was crying. I was no good with crying people. And I was holding a big platter of pancakes.

Felicia, reading the situation more quickly than I thought I would, was out the back door calling to Eli and Felix before I could put down the pancakes, which I didn't want to do.

Veronika came into the kitchen from the hall. She froze when she saw Alice's state, which was clearly way beyond being distressed. "Alyona," she said, very gently.

"I don't want to stay here," the girl said. "Our table is scratched. Everyone knows what that man made us do. I can't live with it."

Felix came in, Eli right behind him. Eli could see just fine over Felix's head. I could see a bit of Felicia behind them, though I didn't move my whole body, just turned my head a little. I didn't want to trigger whatever state Alice was plunging into.

Alice hadn't moved, but she was all tensed up. "You'll tell," she said to me. "Because you're brave and you killed them."

"Of course I won't tell," I said. "He was an asshole, and he deserved to die. Why would I ever talk about him?"

"You're not going to tell?"

"God, no." That was the last thing on my mind.

"All right, then," Alice said.

"Good, we can eat," I said, trying to sound brisk and not as relieved as I felt. "I fixed all these pancakes and bacon. Let's have breakfast. Veronika, can you get the butter and syrup if we have that? Alice has set the table, so if everyone serves their plates from the stove, we can all sit down together."

Alice lifted plates out of a china cabinet, just like nothing had happened. Veronika, white as a sheet, said, "Thanks, Alyona," and found the butter. There was honey, too. She served herself with trembling hands. Alyona herself went next, and then Felix and Eli, and then me and Felicia, who gave each other wide eyes when Alyona had left the kitchen. Lucy came in just then, and she was absolutely normal since she hadn't been present at the awful little scene. That helped.

We finished breakfast without any further displays. Lucy kept looking from one of us to the other, since it didn't take a lot of brains to understand that something had happened.

Veronika took some food upstairs for the captain. He was doing better, she told us. She said brightly, "Eli, can you come up to have a look at him in a few minutes?"

Eli nodded with his own smile. "Alice and Lucy, can you take care of the dishes since Lizbeth did the cooking? Felicia, maybe you could help?"

Clearly, Veronika needed to talk to Eli about what had happened, and Felicia needed to keep an eye on Alice, and I needed to be out of sight in case Alice got upset again.

I'd known people on the strange side before: Stella Collins, who'd decided her husband had been possessed by a devil and tried to cut it out of him. Juanito Hernández, who'd had to wash his hands seventy times a day. Gerald Harkness, who had never spoken, though he understood what was being said to him. Gerald was twenty now. All he did was sit and rock.

I tried to imagine what it was like to be Alice. I'm not too good at that, and it was a strain to picture myself as a gently-brought-up aristocrat who had endured the unwanted attentions of a thug, only to find herself humiliated and brutalized by John Brightwood, and soon thereafter exposed to a great deal of blood and violence. To say nothing of losing her father and then witnessing her brother's arrest.

While I tried to imagine this, I was upstairs making our bed and straightening our room. After that, for lack of anything better to do,

I searched for my own jacket and went outside to do my share of the cleanup.

I found the heaviest job had begun the day before, while I was out of it. The bodies had all been carried to the curb. Surely this neighborhood had never seen the like.

There were things left to do, though. I found a wheelbarrow and gardening gloves in the garage. I rolled it to the front. I began to toss in the odds and ends left on the lawn: rags of clothing and fragments of weapons, mostly, but also fragments of people—teeth, a finger or two, some bits of skin.

I was making progress when a flatbed truck marked CITY OF SAN DIEGO stopped at the end of the driveway. A pickup truck pulled in behind it. Men climbed out and began to load the bodies onto the truck. They didn't call to me or bid me good morning—maybe that would have been out of place, come to think of it. But they didn't even look at me.

That was the first odd thing.

Next, no one came to look and remark at this unusual occurrence.

At home, this would have drawn a crowd. Not here, not in this nice neighborhood.

The grim job didn't take long with four men working. They drove away as quietly as they'd come. I went back to my task.

After another half hour, everything that could be picked up with fingers had been retrieved. Then I didn't know what to do with my awful wheelbarrow full of people bits.

There was a bench in the backyard. I sat down and stared at the bushes, which had been pruned back. Eli came out to sit beside me.

"Veronika and Lucy are so strong," I said. "Did you know Alice was . . . not that way?"

"I absolutely did not. Since I'm so much older, I wasn't around for a large part of Alice's childhood. Not all of us are able to handle troubles equally."

"Peter know?"

"Mother and Peter and Lucy had seen signs that Alice needed a lot of protection. Which they did not see fit to share with me."

"That explains a lot about Peter," I said. "Those two men accosting your sisters on their trip to the library, I don't know if Peter told you, but the treatment of Alice was especially rude. No wonder his reaction was drastic."

Eli was scowling. "I don't think so. If I'd been there, I'd have killed them on the spot."

"Lucky you weren't, then." I mulled this over. "The past few days were hard on a tough person, much less a frail one. If Alice gets some peace and calm, this may not happen again. Is there any magic thing you can do to help her?"

"We heal bodies pretty well. Minds, no."

"She needs time, and someone to talk to who won't tell her to snap out of it." Which had been my first instinct. "She might talk to Felix," I said.

Eli stared at me with disbelief. "Why would she? He's the least sympathetic person I know."

"Because Alice knows Felix wants to marry Lucy, so he's safe. And he's older than you and Peter, so he's less likely to go off like a firecracker. And he won't be impatient with her, like your mom and Lucy might be."

Eli seemed doubtful. "Why would my mother be impatient with Alice?"

I couldn't even think of a way to say what I wanted to tell him. "Please take it from me that it might happen, okay?"

"I will, but I don't understand."

"I'm not sure I do, but I know it's true."

I still didn't want to go in. When Eli decided to go talk to Felix and his mother, I sat on the back steps to read the newspaper, which had been delivered as though there weren't dead men piled up at the curb.

All the stories on the front page were about the events of the day before. Since I'd been on hand for most of them, it was interesting reading.

I figured someone at the palace had gone over these accounts before they'd gone to press. The shot that had killed Alexander was "evil and dastardly," Alexander had been "a hero of the Holy Russian Empire and devoted uncle of the tsar." His death had emboldened a certain faction to attack the tsar, since Alexander had been such a strong protector of his nephew.

I shook my head. If the tsar wanted to stay in power, he could not be seen to need a strong protector. That just made sense.

The battle on this street was described as a neighborhood skirmish by partisans of both sides, and that was it. No mention of the tsar being present, no mention of grigori bombs, no mention of Captain McMurtry being wounded. This was all good, I figured. Less attention on Eli's family.

There was one surprise: a really good picture of the tsar, the tsarina, and the tsarevitch. Caroline looked polished, attractive, and motherly, in a suit and good jewelry. Her hair was done, her makeup was light, and she was holding a toddler in a cute outfit on her knee. The little fellow was smiling at the camera, with a toy in his hand. The tsar looked serious and protective in a military uniform, his arm around his wife and his gaze on his son.

"That's doing it right," I said out loud. I didn't know whose idea the picture had been, but it was everything people wanted to see in their leader.

I made myself go into the house, where I found Peter and Felicia reading schoolbooks.

"You're going back to school?" I said.

"When it reopens. In the meantime, we found Eli's old books, and we're trying to learn something. When are you going to Segundo Mexia?" Felicia said.

Not soon enough. "I guess whenever Eli thinks his family is fixed up for the future," I said. "I guess he will come with me." I was feeling pretty irritable.

"Of course he will," Felicia said. "Not only has he told everyone you've lived as man and wife, but the tsar kind of told him to get out of town. Where else would he go?"

I didn't want Eli to come with me because he didn't have anywhere better to be.

I looked down at my boots. I was so dumb. A few days ago, I'd been content to find Eli alive. Then I'd only wanted him out of jail and free to make a choice for himself. Then I'd wanted him to get out from under the cloud of Alexander, so his family wouldn't be oppressed. Now I wanted him to have the pick of his future.

Everything had happened, though not as I'd wanted it to, and I was still bitching at fate. I had better whip up some gratitude, and fast. "I don't like to take it for granted," I said finally. "Do you think you might come visit me when you all get a break? I don't know your school terms."

"We get a month off in the summer," she said. "If we can get the money for the ticket, I'll come."

"I live real humble. It won't be like here."

"You're forgetting where I came from," Felicia said. She looked away. "How do you think your mother will take me showing up?"

"She'll be a little down for a day or two, because her memory of our father is bad. But you're not him. Mom is fair and smart. She'll be okay." But that triggered a whole other train of thought. My worry right to hand was about Eli coming back to Segundo Mexia with me, and it was practical: the size of my cabin. I'd have to add on a room. If Eli really intended to stay with me, we needed a proper bedroom, especially if Felicia was going to visit.

I didn't fully believe any of this would happen. But I felt a little trickle of excitement.

The telephone rang.

"They fixed the line!" Peter said, and jumped up to answer it.

Peter came back looking happy. "The tsar's new aide called to say that they are sending over workers from the island to repair the lawn and driveway."

So the repairs would be free. That would be a relief to any home-owner. It was only right of the tsar to take care of the damage to the Savarov property, but assuming royalty knew the right thing to do and actually getting royalty to act on the knowledge . . . even I knew that was two different things.

I had noted the sound of cars slowing down to have a good look at the house and the lawn, so the stories were spreading. No surprise there.

There was a knock at the front door. Peter went to answer it. The short man standing on the doorstep had a high collar, a monocle, and a mustache waxed out to the tips. It was a sight. A car was pulling around to the back of the house, and a cab was coming up the driveway.

"I am Dr. Josef Bartofsky," said the man.

"Hello, Doctor," Peter said, sounding cautious. "I'm Peter Savarov, son of this house." Peter waited. The visitor clearly hadn't expected this, began getting indignant that Peter wasn't moving. Peter was right.

"Why have you come to call, Dr. Bartofsky?" I asked.

"Princess Savarov asked a neighbor to call me to request my attendance."

"How do I know that's true?"

The little doctor gave me a look that said *How dare you?* without actually speaking the words. "You may go upstairs and ask her if you doubt my word," he said, with the utmost offense. "She asked me to examine the wounds of Captain McMurtry, and to examine her daughter Alyona."

Bartofsky made a mistake. He tried to push past me.

Next moment he was up against the wall with a knife to his throat. He could have fought more if he'd been willing to drop his doctor bag, but he kept hold of it like it was a grigori vest.

That made me wonder what was in it.

"What is this?" Eli said from the stairs. He sounded mighty displeased.

The doctor made garbled noises.

"What are you doing, Lizbeth?" Eli asked me in a sharp voice. "This is the doctor recommended to Mother."

"Can you ask, after yesterday?" That was dumb. Obviously, he could. "Look in his bag. If the right stuff is in it, I'll let him go."

I could feel Eli's unhappiness pushing at me. But he did look. "The usual things," he said. His face was stiff and cold.

I'd embarrassed Eli in front of someone he knew.

But I was right, dammit.

"Ease up," Eli said, impatience snapping in his voice. He was as on edge as I was. Because of Alice? Or something else?

Be it on his head. I stepped back, giving him a very unfriendly look.

At that moment, I didn't feel at all like building another room onto my cabin.

CHAPTER TWENTY-FIVE

While Eli made polite with Dr. Bartofsky and gave me the cold shoulder, I flew up the stairs to "our" room. I did not slam the door. Felix came in without knocking. I glared at him.

"I think Bartofsky's an ass, too," Felix said. He sat in the chair Eli had occupied the night before, while I slumped on the bed. "And it was reasonable to want to search his bag since you didn't know him. Bartofsky doesn't like grigoris, and he doesn't want to believe there are people who haven't heard of him."

"How come Veronika thinks McMurtry needs a physician when he's got you all to heal him?"

"The doctor is Alexei's show physician," Felix explained. "Alexei doesn't want to admit he has to have the help of grigoris to live, though everyone knows it. His bleeding disease is feared and not understood by most Russians. Or most born Americans, for that matter."

I sure didn't understand it, so that made sense. "But Bartofsky is such a dick," I said. Then flushed. That was something I'd never said out loud before. My sister was a bad influence.

"I've heard worse," Felix said. "I will never understand you, Lizbeth."

"Likewise."

He laughed, a sort of bark. Felix didn't do laughing very well. "So why is Eli angry?" he asked.

Felix was focused on Eli, as usual. "I wouldn't let Bartofsky in unless someone verified he was who he said he was. Bartofsky tried to get past me, and I didn't let him. I guess that's it."

"Did you hurt the doctor badly?"

"Hardly at all. But Eli got on his high horse. He was all, 'This is what my family does, how dare you be rude to this court-sent doctor.'"

"Your Russian accent is terrible. The man is the real Bartofsky, I know him," Felix said.

"I just wanted to check what was in the bag," I said. "That's what I'm supposed to do."

"Bartofsky carries the bag everywhere. Most medical doctors do," Felix said, with the air of someone trying to be fair. "I have never seen inside one, myself."

"Did you get to have a talk with Alice?"

"What?"

"I suggested to Eli that Alice might talk to you."

Felix looked at me with some surprise. "Why?"

"Familiar but disinterested," I said. "Alice had a different reaction from her mom and Lucy about the incident with Brightwood."

Felix's black brows drew together. "That would be a terrible ordeal for any woman."

"It triggered something in Alice that it didn't in the other two."

"If you think confiding in me would help her, I would be glad to listen to her."

I liked Felix a lot better when he said that. "I think she might tell you what her fears are. And if she does, she might get better." I shrugged.

"You know, Eli was scared and embarrassed." Felix offered me this like he was repaying me for my confidence in him.

I got angry all over again. "It's *embarrassing* to have a little sister who breaks down in tears? He's not scared when I go to rescue his sisters and brother from an armed force, but he's scared when a girl can't stop crying?"

"Yes. Eli loves you," Felix said.

Flattest voice I'd ever heard.

"He loves me some of the time," I said. "Other times, he's a little scared of me."

"That, too."

"Some days he's my friend and companion and his name is Eli," I said. "Sometimes he's Prince Ilya and I'm the lowly peasant hanging on his coattails."

"I don't think he's ever imagined you hanging on to him. More likely, he's imagined you walking away."

I could and I would, if Eli put his foot wrong. And maybe that was what Felix saw when he looked at me.

"I'm going to talk to Alice," Felix said abruptly, shoving himself up and out of the chair. "You should be proud. You've done what you set out to do, Lizbeth. You've freed Eli from his captivity, you've reinstated his family's status with the tsar—at least to some extent—and in the process you've saved his mother and sisters and brother from terrible fates. You're a hero. If you just hold on a little longer, everything will work out."

He shut the door quietly behind him as he left.

After a few minutes, I heard Alice crying. But it was normal, not the awful silence of her earlier fit. I did not move. Felix could handle it.

I looked at the clock on the wall to find out it was noon. I should assemble lunch, but I wasn't their damn cook.

But who else would do it? Who else *could* do it?

There was a radio in the kitchen, so I switched it on to listen to the news. There wasn't any. It was all music and weather reports. That seemed real fishy. I began trying to fix a lunch because I was bored and I was hungry. There was a ham in the refrigerator, and for the first time I realized how lucky we were that the electricity was still working. There was a slightly stale loaf of bread, so I sliced it and toasted it. I found some pickles and some mayonnaise in the refrigerator that seemed good. It was store-bought. Wouldn't be as good as my mother's.

There were potatoes, too. I peeled and cut them up and fried them. Veronika came in, looked shocked to see me in the kitchen again. Who did she think would show up to cook? I'd killed the maid.

"I am a terrible hostess," she said.

Even grumpy as I was, that struck me as funny. "Yeah, all the explosions and gunfire. I'll never come back," I said.

She smiled back, and I felt more comfortable.

"The tsar's yard people are coming," I said.

"Peter mentioned they'd called. Thank you, Lizbeth. And thanks for breakfast and lunch. You are keeping us going. My ad was in today's paper, but I can't imagine anyone will be eager to work here."

"You need to get groceries," I said, trying to sound like it was just a suggestion. "Not from Heedles, because it's wrecked."

"Of course." I was relieved when Veronika opened the pantry door, looked over the shelves, and began to make a list. I made her a sandwich, too, and put it on the kitchen table. I ate my own, and watched her sit to devour everything on her plate.

"Thanks," she said, dabbing at her lips with a napkin. "That was really good."

It took no great skill to make a ham sandwich and fries.

Eli came in, looked around him absently. I got up and made another toasted ham sandwich. There were some fries left. I put the plate on the table, he thanked me, and he sat to tuck in to the food. After a couple of mouthfuls, Eli said, "I saw Dr. Bartofsky out. I stayed with Ford while Bartofsky looked him over and said that he would be fine, in time. I listened in for a few minutes while Felix talked to Alice. He is doing a good job. And I made our plans to leave town."

I looked up at him, my mouth open. This, after he had been such an ass about the doctor?

"Really?" I said, and I may have sounded a little edgy. "Now we're leaving town together? Then I believe we need to have us a talk."

Eli glared at me. "I have been *having* a talk. To the priest at Holy Savior."

"What?"

Eli jerked his head at his mother.

"I want a proper marriage ceremony," Veronika said serenely.

For a second, I thought Veronika had decided to marry Captain McMurtry. But I caught on in time to save myself from that blunder.

I decided the best thing I could do was sit there without saying a word. I turned to Eli, who still looked grim in a very un-groom-like way. I raised my eyebrows. His turn.

He nodded. "If you will have me."

I stared up at him. And I knew his anger was directed at his mother, for insisting on something he was not sure I would want to do. And maybe he was not sure he would have chosen to get married in such a rush. But he wanted me.

I felt my face turn hot, and I knew I was flushing. He knew what I could do, what I would do. He knew so much about me. And he wanted to marry me.

"I will," I said. "Providing you know that you have the right to get mad at me, and you have the right to think I'm wrong. But you don't have the right to treat me like you did today." I gave him a very level look.

Eli blinked. Then he looked relieved. "Good," he said. "I agree. I was an ass."

"What's going to happen?"

"The priest is coming over. While he's here, he can bless the house to cleanse it of violence and ill will. That will make our family happier," Veronika said very firmly.

"So I'm guessing you and your mom have been talking about this all morning," I said, while Veronika went back to work on her grocery list.

"Since after breakfast," he said gloomily. "With breaks to worry about Alice. This is very important to Mother. I'm sorry if it . . . offends you."

"It does not," I said. "I would just as soon start out a life together with your mom happy, thanks very much."

Eli took my hand and squeezed it, and we had a happy moment.

It was good we shared that.

Without looking up from her list, Veronika said, "Would you like to call your mother and stepfather, Lizbeth?"

That seemed silly, since of course they couldn't be here. But she wouldn't have brought it up if she hadn't thought it was important.

"I guess I could call the hotel," I said. "I might catch Jackson there."

"Then please, feel free."

I knew it was expensive, calling long-distance. Eli had to walk me through it. Far, far away, on the counter of the Antelope in Segundo Mexia, I heard the telephone ring.

"The Antelope, Jackson Skidder speaking."

I was so grateful he had answered.

"Hey, it's Lizbeth," I said.

"Girl, are you all right?" he said. You would have thought he was about to scold me for something. That was just Jackson's way.

"I got him out," I said. "There's been a lot of trouble, but today we're getting married, looks like."

There was such a long silence I said his name.

"Yeah, I'm here," Jackson said, sounding even more gruff. "Well, all right, then."

"His mom wants their priest," I said. "And we got to leave town pretty quick."

"I understand. He better treat you right. You coming back here?"

"As fast as we can get there." And to my own surprise, I said, "I miss you bad."

"Then we'll see you in a few days," Jackson said. "I'll tell your mother. We miss you, too."

Another surprise.

"Okay. See you soon." And we both hung up, kind of overwhelmed.

I sat for a moment, looking at the telephone. "That was real strange," I told Eli.

"You two really wallow in the emotion," Eli said, his voice dry. "Let me get a handkerchief."

I grinned at him. "That's me and Jackson."

"If you want to fancy up, this is the time," Eli said. "My mother is looking through the clothes I have left here for something suitable. And she's found things for you."

The front doorbell rang. Again. This time it was the priest. He was a short, heavy man with a thick beard, and he was wearing a black cassock like the Catholic priests in Segundo Mexia. But this priest's was bigger, and he wore a strange black hat. He looked pretty grim.

"Eli, Lizbeth, this is Father Kirill. Eli, I need to borrow Lizbeth. You talk to our priest."

My mother-in-law-to-be took my hand to drag me up the stairs. If she hadn't been Eli's mom, I would have pulled away. I know when I'm being railroaded.

Veronika towed me to her room. It was as clean and neat as if there hadn't been a war at her house the day before, with the exception of Captain McMurtry in her bed. He was bandaged and sleeping and needed a shave. McMurtry's eyes opened a slit when we burst into the room.

"Ford," Veronika said, "I have to get Lizbeth changed into something more appropriate. You just go back to sleep."

Captain McMurtry muttered something that might have been "Okay."

"More appropriate?" I said, and even to my own ears I sounded stupid.

Veronika was delving into the huge wardrobe. It only held women's clothing; she'd gotten rid of her husband's things. She made a triumphant sound and pulled out a clothing bag. "Here we are!" she said.

"Where are we?"

"Did you bathe this morning?"

"Yes."

"But you worked out in the yard, I saw you. Jump into the tub and scrub off," Veronika commanded. She handed me a dressing gown. I went out into the hall and found the bathroom empty. I washed my hair, and I was clean in no time. I carried my clothes under my arm as I retreated to her room, the dressing gown clutched around me.

While I'd been out, Veronika had removed the dress from the bag and had hung it on the wardrobe door.

It was a wedding dress. She had hauled her wedding dress with her all the way from Russia.

The dress was white and silky and tight across the shoulders, though it fit right everywhere else. The veil was the silliest thing I ever saw. I could have started down the stairs, and by the time I got to the landing, it would still be up on the top step. I drew the line there. No veil.

Veronika's wedding shoes had not survived the years of wandering the ocean, so she loaned me a pair that wouldn't show up too bad. The dress pretty much covered the shoes, anyway.

Veronika stuck her head out the door to call her daughters and Felicia. I was a little uneasy about Alice, but the girl seemed just fine, even cheerful. Lucy offered to help with my hair, and as she tried to bring order to the curls, a tear trickled down her cheek. I froze.

"You look so pretty, and I'll have another sister!" Lucy said, blotting her face. She bent to give me a quick hug.

I hugged her back and muttered something. She made my hair look orderly with a couple of pearl combs holding it back.

"Is this like weddings in Texoma?" Alice asked. She'd left while my hair was being arranged and returned all dressed up, to huddle on a love seat by the closet. She did not look anything but happy, but I was keeping a sharp eye on her.

Felicia said, "Here's Eli's ring." She made to hand it to me.

"No, you carry it down," I said. "You be my bridesmaid."

"Oh, all right." Felicia made a show of being bored, but then she grinned. "I am really, really happy and amazed you are in a real wedding dress."

I wanted to tell her to shut the hell up, but that didn't seem right on my wedding day. "I'm fairly surprised by that myself," I said. "I guess Eli has my ring?"

"His mom took it down."

Lucy, who had ducked out, came back in, all gussied up. Felicia was wearing a dress I assumed was Alice's, since she was the only one near Felicia's size. It was a dusty sort of rose color. She looked real pretty.

I wondered what Eli was doing. I'd heard him going up and down the stairs, and I'd heard Felix exclaim about something, and I'd heard people coming in the front door. I had no idea what was happening.

I tried to rouse myself from the numb feeling, but the last few days had been a lot of rousing and not enough rest. I couldn't shake it off.

So I stood in the middle of the large bedroom, being combed and cinched and polished. I had on makeup. Perfume, too. I would have thought Veronika would have realized her son wouldn't want his wife to smell like his mom, but she dabbed on her own scent behind my ears after she'd changed into her best dress.

Mostly, Captain McMurtry slept, but sometimes he stared at me with narrowed eyes, puzzled. He was trying to figure out who the stranger was, the woman all in white.

Finally, Veronika stepped out of her room onto the gallery and called down, "Are you ready?"

Felix called up, "Ready and waiting."

"Peter's acting as best man," Lucy said, patting my hand. "Felix is giving you away. Come on, Alice, let's get down there."

Eli's sisters left the room, smiling. Veronika said, "I wish you much happiness with my son." She hesitated, and then she said, "Eli tells me I should say I'm sorry for pushing you two into this." She waved her hand at the dress I wore.

"I was willing to be pushed," I told her.

"I'm going downstairs to wait in the parlor," she said. "After I get down the stairs, you come down with your sister. Felix is waiting."

"Poor Felix," I said, and I meant it . . . but I had not thought before I spoke.

Veronika gave me a blank look, and then she understood. "Then how could he ask to marry Lucy?" she whispered.

Then Veronika gave a kind of huff, as if she was blowing that problem away for right now, and she nodded at me, and she left. She did not close the door behind her. I heard the buzz of voices from down below.

"Captain's awake," Felicia said.

I glanced at the bed. His eyes were fully open.

"You been playing possum?" I said.

"Do you want to marry Eli?"

"I'm already married to Eli."

"But not in their eyes. To them, you have to have the priest."

Most of the Catholics in Segundo Mexia believed that, too.

"So if you pop the question to Veronika, you have to go through this yourself."

"If I ever get the courage," the captain said.

"You idiot. Ask her while you're here."

His eyes came open then, for sure. "You think she's going to say yes?"

"I do, especially if you tell her you stand ready to defend Lucy and Alice."

"I do plan to do that. What you were saying to Veronika, about Felix? What did that mean?"

"Don't know what you're talking about," I said. "Good luck with the proposal." And I stepped out onto the landing and started down the stairs, Felicia on my heels.

CHAPTER TWENTY-SIX

I'd only had time pass by in such a slip-sliding way when I'd been badly injured. I came down the stairs slowly and carefully, with the clingy slithery dress holding on to my legs as though it wanted to trip me.

Felix was waiting for me, his hair smooth and combed. That was what dressing up meant to Felix, that he brushed his hair. He looked real odd.

Without looking at me directly, Felix took my hand and wrapped it around his arm.

"What are you doing?" I whispered.

"I'm giving you away," he said, with no meaning in his voice.

I had never been Felix's to give, but like everything else about this day, I seemed to be going along with it. This morning, picking up bits of bone and teeth in the yard. This afternoon, getting married.

The priest was in the parlor, and there was a reading stand in front of him with a book on it. The priest looked less angry than before. When he saw me, he looked almost friendly—or maybe he felt sorry for me. It was a lot of dress.

I'd seen everyone else prettied up. But they were nothing compared to Eli. I stopped dead when I saw him.

His hair was all slicked back somehow and braided very neatly into a long plait. He had shaved. He wore a real suit. It was dark blue. That was all I could remember, later.

I couldn't read Eli's face or posture; he seemed frozen after he saw me coming into the room with Felix. Felix led me up to Eli; we were both looking up at Eli as though we'd never seen him before. Then Felix let go, assumed a position by Lucy, and took her hand as though that were his regular habit.

Eli's eyes were wide and green and bright, and they were all I saw during the priest's reading.

Which took forever, let me say. In fact, the service took so long that I had time for my mind to wander, to realize there were people there I didn't know, and a few I did. There were a couple of grigoris standing as far away as they could and be in the same room. They listened to the priest with polite interest. There was the blond woman from next door and her husband. (I later learned they were longtime friends of Veronika's.) There were a couple of men in uniform, who'd come to take Captain McMurtry back to the base hospital, under the mistaken impression he was a burden on the Savarov household.

I thought, suddenly and sharply, *My own mother should be at my wedding. And Jackson. And* . . . I came up with a few other people I would've liked to have seen in the little knot of witnesses. I regretted letting them know by a phone call. Not having them here. But there was no way around it: if we had to leave town to satisfy the tsar, and we had to be married Russian Orthodox, then we had to do it now. I couldn't imagine trying to find a Russian priest anywhere in Texoma.

Though the priest's voice hadn't changed, Eli's hand tightened on my arm, and I looked up. "Your mother," he mouthed, and all of a sudden I felt fine. He had thought of her, too. We would be okay. This wedding wasn't the seal of doom. It was something we had to do to make Veronika happy. And making my husband's mother happy was a good thing.

Eli looked surprised when I smiled at him, but when he saw I meant it, he smiled back.

After that, everything was okay.

Normally, there would be a wedding lunch or dinner, Veronika explained later. But under the circumstances—blood and craters on the lawn, no cook, and no food—that couldn't happen. However, we'd been married, it had been witnessed, and it was done. And now we ought to leave.

Veronika didn't exactly say that, but I understood: The tsar had asked that we leave, and then Eli's name would be cleared. Therefore, the Savarov family would be back in favor. And Eli and I would be correctly hitched.

Eli had to hurry back to his rooms in the grigori dormitory to get all the things he'd left when he'd been arrested. Felix took him.

I had a talk with my sister, up in the room Eli and I had shared. Veronika insisted I take some of her clothes, though I had no idea where I'd wear them. I had the pants outfit and the jacket I'd bought, too. But as soon as I'd taken off the wedding dress and hung it up, I put on my jeans and my boots and my heavy shirt. I would put on my guns as soon as we were out of the Holy Russian Empire. And I was wearing my wedding ring on my finger, for the first time in months.

I didn't need to talk to Felicia about sex, because her father and her uncle had brought women back to the hovel in Ciudad Juárez, and Felicia was well aware of what happened, she had given me to understand.

"What's your goal?" I asked her, when I couldn't see anything else that should go in my leather bag.

"It's enough to be safe, fed, and dressed," Felicia said. "All I have to do is learn and be ready to give blood, otherwise."

She was sitting on the bed, so I took the chair. "I don't believe you," I said. "You got a plan, I know it."

Felicia grinned at me. "Maybe I do. Maybe I wanted to look younger for a while so I could get the lay of the land here. Maybe I know a lot of magic my teachers don't. It's the kind they despise, low-level stuff, but I'm really good at it. Our father's gift came to me strong."

"So you want to learn more and more?"

"I want to be a great grigori. I don't want to be a blood donor forever. I want to think of a way the tsar can maintain his health and strength without having to rely on descendants of Rasputin."

"I knew the 'safe, fed, and dressed' was only smoke," I said. "You got eyes for Peter or Felix? Or anyone else?"

"Felix would never care for any woman the way he cares for Eli. Besides, he's got his eyes fixed on Lucy. And Peter?" She looked thoughtful. "He's too impulsive. I don't really see Peter having a very long life unless he learns to think before he acts . . . and speaks."

"Have you been reading my mind?"

"Nope, we both have common sense," Felicia said. The smile flashed again.

"I meant it about you coming to stay. I warn you, the way I live is closer to Ciudad Juárez than to this." I waved a hand around me at the big house.

"I'm not worried about it."

But I thought she was, a little bit.

Eli returned an hour later with two crammed bags. Veronika

had consulted a train schedule. We had just enough time to catch the last train out for the night. We'd have to piece our route back to Sweetwater, the nearest train station to Segundo Mexia. She had made a reservation for us for the night train.

The Savarov women and my sister cried a little when the cab came, and even Peter's eyes looked red, so we left pretty quick. (Felix had already said a really brief, hard "Good travels," and taken himself away, to my relief.)

And then we were in the cab alone.

It felt strange to be going somewhere with Eli without a mission, without anyone trying to kill us or steal from us. I had nothing to guard, other than him and our luggage. We did not speak on the drive.

At the train station, the one from which I'd walked into San Diego exhausted and terrified days before, Eli and I went to the ticket counter.

"We have a reservation for a sleeping compartment," Eli said. This was news to me.

"Yes, sir!" The old man cackled and started to say something, but after a look at Eli's face, he canceled that and simply took Eli's money and gave us our tickets.

I must have made some kind of noise—it was a lot of money. But Eli said, "We didn't have a big wedding. We can at least have this," which was the right thing to say, not boastful or wasteful. And he took my hand.

We boarded immediately. Got shown to our compartment, which was really nice, two double seats facing each other. "How do we sleep?" I whispered to Eli, after we stowed our luggage and took one of the seats.

"The porter will turn these seats into a bed at night," he said. "There'll be another one over our head."

The people across from us, I assumed, were a mother and her girl, who seemed to me to be about ten.

The mom nodded at us. "We'll try not to snore, won't we, Pamela?" she said.

Pamela looked anxious. Maybe her first train trip. "I don't even know what that is," the girl said.

We all laughed politely, and then the mother fell to telling Pamela about what they would see out the window tomorrow, and I leaned against Eli, unable to count the things that had happened that day. It was a big runny blur in my head. The train got under way. As soon as we could, we made our way to the dining car. I didn't think I'd gotten anything to eat since the ham sandwich, and that felt awful long ago. Maybe it wasn't newlywed-like to be hungry, but Eli and I plowed through our food like horses after a long day's work.

Some time later we were at the border. As they had when I'd come into the Holy Russian Empire, the police had us all get out and checked our identification.

The man who took our passports, a naturalized American with a Russian accent, looked down at Eli's identification and said, "Prince Savarov!"

Everyone within hearing froze and gave us a big stare. I could have smacked the guard.

"Eli Savarov is fine," my husband said calmly.

But the damage had been done.

"And you are?" the guard said, turning to me.

"This is the new Princess Savarov," Eli said.

"Ah, that explained the name," the guard said, beaming at me. "Well, young sir and madam, I knew the prince's father, and he was a fine man."

Could *not* have been worse. I felt Eli freeze beside me as the man got all talky about Eli's father and how wonderful he'd been.

"But I am chatting too much," the guard said, way too late. "You must be tired. Have a good evening, you two!" He beamed at us, which made it even worse.

We got back on the train to find the beds had been made up. I would have liked to watch the process out of curiosity, but any interest I had was quenched now by the way the other passengers were looking at us. I had to ask Eli how we got into the bed, and he gave me my bag and told me to go down the car to the bathroom and change in there.

"I don't have a robe or nightgown," I whispered.

"I'll bet you money my mother put those in your bag," he said, smiling.

And he was right. I had a pink nightgown and robe folded neatly on top of my clothes. I cleaned my teeth and face and took care of the bathroom situation before I went back to him. It felt real strange to get into our bed, especially since I had to take one of my guns in with me. I wasn't about to sleep without a weapon when we were so accessible. The curtain across the bed kept anyone from seeing us, but that was the limit of our privacy.

The mother and Pamela had already climbed up into their bed above us, and I didn't even get to see how they did it. I wondered how they'd get down in the night if they had to go to the bathroom. I was grateful that wasn't my problem. Though it might be, if their feet landed in our faces.

Eli parted the curtains and slid in beside me. The fit was snug. I was glad we were both slim. There were plenty of people still moving around, and the perpetual sound of the train, but Eli still whispered when he said, "Our first night as newlyweds, Lizbeth."

"Our first night as Russian Orthodox newlyweds," I said, and even my whisper sounded tart. "To me, we been married since Dixie, at least mostly."

He chuckled right in my ear, slow and low, and then we were both asleep.

CHAPTER TWENTY-SEVEN

Pamela's mom was raising her to be frank and open, so after the girl would stare at us a while, she'd pop out with "Why do you have scars?" (That was directed at me.) Or "Why is your hair long like a girl's?" (To Eli.) Her mom kept saying she was embarrassed, but she didn't do anything about it. Pamela's manners had not gotten any better by the time we parted ways the next day.

I didn't mind a question or two. But one question led to another, every single time, and I never knew when Pamela's brain would start firing. It was hard to read a magazine or talk or think with the girl around. We got off the train in Albuquerque around noon the next day. Went right to the ticket window and found out our best route was a train leaving for San Angelo in Texoma, but we'd have to spend the night in Albuquerque to catch that one the next morning.

We found a hotel close to the station, got a room, celebrated being married (finally), and then cleaned up and walked around the town. We ate enchiladas and beans and rice in a little restaurant where my Spanish came in handy. We had on the heaviest clothes we had. Albuquerque was real cold.

Next morning, we had breakfast at the hotel and trudged back to the station with all our stuff. While we waited inside the little station for our train, I saw something go by the window. "No," I said, real soft. "It can't be."

"What?" Eli was all alarmed.

"Look," I said, very quietly, so I wouldn't interrupt it.

"At what?"

I pointed at the window.

It was snowing.

He looked at me like I was trying to play a joke on him.

"Have you never seen snow before?" Eli asked.

"I never have." I went out on the platform. He followed me out and put his arm around me. We watched in silence for a few minutes.

"I arranged this just for you," Eli said.

"Generous of you."

"Anything for my *solnyshko*."

"You've called me that before. What does it mean?" I was ready for it to mean something sly, like rabbit or something.

"It means sun," Eli said.

Took my breath away, so I didn't say anything.

"And you would call me what?" he asked, after a moment.

I could tell from his voice that he expected me to make the joke, call him my eagle or my big gun, something silly.

"My moon," I said. "You're my moon."

We watched the snow until our train came in.

The leg of our journey from Albuquerque to San Angelo was horrible. No sleeping car, so we sat up all night. This train was old and worn, and nothing was as comfortable. At least Pamela wasn't there. I fell asleep against Eli's shoulder, which was bony and hard and not a good pillow . . . but it was Eli's shoulder. When I woke and shifted, he slept on me for a while.

I was able to send my mother a telegram about when we'd arrive in Sweetwater, though I had no certainty she'd get it before we reached Segundo Mexia.

But when we stumbled off the train at the Sweetwater station, there was my family.

"Mother, Jackson," I said, hugging them with a lot of love. "You remember Eli, I know. Look!" I held up my hand with the ring on it.

My mother fixed Eli with a look that would have killed a lesser man, but Eli was up to it. "We are married very thoroughly now," Eli said, with a lot of charm. "Lizbeth told me we were married—*pretty much* was the phrase she used—here in Texoma. But my mother wanted to be sure Lizbeth couldn't get rid of me."

My mother smiled, because she couldn't help it. "Then I am glad to welcome you into our family," she said. She gave Jackson a real heavy look.

"Me too," Jackson said, just a little late. "You be good to Lizbeth, or I'll kill you. If she doesn't first."

I had to laugh. He absolutely meant it.

Eli said, "If I mistreated Lizbeth, I would deserve it."

I smiled down at my feet.

Jackson had recently bought a car he kept at the stable and often rented out. (If he wasn't using it, someone else might as well, he figured.) He'd driven it to the train, and we were able to stow our bags in the trunk and fit comfortably in the back.

The drive from Sweetwater to Segundo Mexia wasn't a long one, but we both fell asleep.

"We're home," Jackson said, and I opened my eyes. We were at the base of the hill behind Segundo Mexia. My house was close to the top.

Eli and I shouldered our bags. I hugged Jackson and my mother, told them I'd see them later. Eli said, "We'll talk soon," and that seemed to satisfy my mom and stepdad.

"You got him out of jail," Jackson said. "I'm proud of you, Liz-beth."

"I got a lot of your money left," I said.

Jackson just laughed and put the car in gear.

Up the hill we started. It was the middle of the afternoon. Chrissie was hanging out her wash, which was a never-ending task with her husband, the two boys, and the baby girl. She paused when she saw me, and she smiled, a breeze fluttering her blond hair across her face.

"Ray said he heard on the radio that some big Russian royalty got shot," Chrissie said. "I figured that was you. Glad you got away with it!"

"Glad to be home," I said. "Chrissie, this is Eli. We're married now."

Chrissie clapped her hands. "That is wonderful news! He's the right one, aren't you, Mr. Eli?"

"I am definitely the right one," Eli agreed, while I went up the last few feet to my front door and unlocked it. Everything was fine, which I had figured, since Chrissie—and everyone else on the hill—kept watch while I was gone.

I hadn't known how long I'd be gone, so my refrigerator was empty, and I had nothing to eat.

"After I have a nap, I'll get groceries," I said. "And I reckon we need to get a new bed pretty soon." We'd slept on my bed before, but we'd known it was temporary. It was a real basic bed, and not nearly wide enough.

"We will do all this together," Eli said.

"Okay. Yes." The cabin felt cold, so I started up a fire in the stove, moving stiffly. I had an indoor bathroom, and it worked well now that the water system had new pipes. I had a hot bath and put on my pink nightgown again. Pink. Well, it had probably suited Veronika.

I dimly heard Eli splashing around in the bathroom, and then he was in bed with me. I was on my side so I could put my arm over him, and he wiggled his back to me. I kissed his back. I didn't know how we could make this work, but we were both going to try.

We'd be okay if the tsar kept his word to us.

And if no one else—besides the people of Segundo Mexia—figured out it was me who'd shot the grand duke.

And if Felix didn't go nuts with jealousy.

"I think we got as good a chance as anyone, Moon," I said.

"I think so, too, Sun."

And we slept.